"You do have qualities in which I am interested," Marcus said.

"There is a man in London on whom I wish, very badly, to be revenged. He has several weaknesses, and I intend to attack accordingly. Firstly he is a gambler, who cannot resist a challenge when the stakes are high. And secondly he has a marked liking for pretty women who are skilled at card play."

"So I'm ruled out for certain, surely, if you are looking for someone pretty? Since you make it quite clear that I am nothing of the kind!"

She saw a half-smile flicker across his strong mouth—a dangerous, all-male smile. "Those weren't my precise words, minx," he said softly.

* * *

The Major and the Pickpocket
Harlequin® Historical #325—February 2012

The Major and the Pickpocket

LUCY ASHFORD

TORONTO NEW YORK LONDON
AMSTERDAM PARIS SYDNEY HAMBURG
STOCKHOLM ATHENS TOKYO MILAN MADRID
PRAGUE WARSAW BUDAPEST AUCKLAND

Recycling programs
for this product may
not exist in your area.

ISBN-13: 978-0-373-30634-3

THE MAJOR AND THE PICKPOCKET

Copyright © 2010 by Lucy Ashford

First North American Publication 2012

This edition published by arrangement with Harlequin Books S.A.

For questions and comments about the quality of this book please contact us at Customer_eCare@Harlequin.ca.

www.Harlequin.com

Printed in U.S.A.

Author Note

I've always adored historical romances. I grew up daydreaming about King Arthur's knights, Rosemary Sutcliff's Roman heroes, the Scarlet Pimpernel and, of course, Georgette Heyer's Regency rakes.

So you can imagine that, although I'd had some success writing historical thrillers, I was really longing to create a romance set in a bygone age. And who else to approach but Harlequin Books?

After a lot of fun dreaming up my plot and characters, and with a great deal of help from skilled and sympathetic editors, I finally became a Harlequin author with *The Major and the Pickpocket*. The story is set in 1780, at a time when gambling fever was really starting to take the nation in its grip. Great lords and ladies would lose and win mighty fortunes in all-night sittings. My feisty heroine, Tassie, is as skilled as any of them at tricking her way out of trouble at the turn of a card—that is, until the wounded war hero Major Marcus Forrester calls her bluff!

So here it is—my first Harlequin® Historical romance. I do hope you enjoy the story of how the major and the mischievous pickpocket Tassie discover true love together.

LUCY ASHFORD,

an English Studies lecturer, has always loved literature and history, and from childhood one of her favorite occupations has been to immerse herself in historical romances. She studied English with history at Nottingham University, and the Regency is her favorite period.

Lucy has written several historical novels, but this is her first for Harlequin Books. She lives with her husband in an old stone cottage in the Peak District, near to beautiful Chatsworth House and Haddon Hall, all of which give her a taste of the magic of life in a bygone age. Her garden enjoys spectacular views over the Derbyshire hills, where she loves to roam and let her imagination go to work on her latest story.

Chapter One

London—February 1780

Heavy rain that night meant the streets were almost deserted, and so it was even more startling for the few pedestrians in the vicinity of Pall Mall to see a big chestnut mare being pulled up in a frenzy of sparking hooves outside the porticoed entrance of one of London's most discerning clubs. The mare had been ridden hard. Its glossy flanks were heaving, and its eyes rolled whitely in the gleam of the yellow lamplight. Swiftly the horse's rider dismounted, thrusting the reins and a few coins towards a hovering groom before swinging round to face a footman who watched him uncertainly from the shelter of the imposing doorway. At this time of night, and in this sort of foul February weather, club members usually arrived by carriage or sedan, not like some whirlwind from hell on horseback.

But before the footman could issue a challenge, the dark-haired rider, his mouth set in a grim line, was already striding up the wide steps. It was noticeable now that he had a slight limp, but it didn't seem to slow him in the least. His long riding coat, glistening with rain, whirled out behind him as he crashed open the door, and his whip was still clutched in his hand. As the gust of cold air he'd let in billowed through the lofty reception hall, all the candles were set a-flicker, and a number of disdainful faces turned to stare. A plump butler started busily towards the intruder, but found himself brushed aside, like a moth.

'I'm looking for Sebastian Corbridge,' announced the man. 'Lord Sebastian Corbridge.' His voice was calm, but the menacing gleam in his eyes was like sparks struck from flint.

He looked as if he had been riding hard all day, to judge by the mud on his boots, and the way his dark, unpowdered hair fell in disordered waves to his collar. He was not old, perhaps no more than twenty-five or twenty-six, but the taut lines of fatigue that ran from his nose to his strong jaw made him look older. The butler backed away warily, because he could see that this tall stranger with the limp wore a sword beneath his loose riding coat. And unlike most of the primped, scented men of leisure who frequented this club, he looked as if he would know how to use it.

By now the man's abrupt intrusion had registered even in the furthest recesses of the reception hall. Murmured conversations died away; startled faces, adorned in many cases with powder and patches, turned one after the other towards the doorway. Even the sombre portraits hanging from the oak-panelled walls seemed to gaze disapprovingly at the abrasive stranger whose clothing continued to drip water on the fine parquet floor, creating little puddles around his leather riding boots.

'Lord Sebastian Corbridge. I want him,' the intruder repeated softly, his hand flicking his whip against his booted leg in unspoken warning.

Someone rose languidly from a deep leather chair in a shadowed alcove. He was about the same age as the intruder, but his appearance could not have been more different, for his elegantly curled cadogan wig was immaculately powdered; his blue satin frock coat, with its discreet ruffles of lace at cuff and throat, was quite exquisitely fitted to his slender body. And his haughty, finely bred face expressed utter scorn as he gazed at the man who spoke his name.

'So, Marcus,' he drawled, taking a lazy pinch of snuff from a filigree box. 'You're back. As usual, dear fellow, you seem to be in the wrong place at the wrong time. The army hasn't done much for your manners, has it? Members only allowed in here, I'm afraid—'

Sebastian Corbridge broke off, as the dark-haired man threw his whip aside, then covered the ground between them to grasp his blue satin lapels with both hands. 'My God, Corbridge,' the man grated out, 'but you've got some explaining to do. Let me tell you that I've just returned from Lornings, and I didn't like what I found there. You'd better start talking. You'd better think up some excuses, and quickly.'

Corbridge looked down with pointed disdain at the hands that gripped his exquisite lapels. 'So you've ridden all the way from Gloucestershire,' he sneered, the slight tremor of fear disguised by heavy scorn. 'Dear me. And there was I thinking you might have come straight from some modish salon—after all, I suppose it's just about possible that clothing such as yours is permitted at fashionable gatherings now that there are so many unemployed ex-army officers around town...'

The taller man's powerful shoulder muscles bunched dangerously beneath his greatcoat, and Corbridge was lifted from the ground.

'Do put me down, Marcus!' breathed Lord Sebastian Corbridge. 'You smell of horse, man. Wet horses. All in all, you're rather overdoing it—betraying your origins, you know?'

All around the room their audience watched the scene in breath-holding fascination. A young footman, who'd just come through from the inner salon bearing a brandy decanter on a silver tray, froze into immobility at the sight, his mouth agape, and the candlelight danced on the golden-amber liquid as it shivered behind the cut glass. Slowly, the dark-haired man called Marcus let go of his victim. His steel-grey eyes were still burning with intensity, and the skin around his grim mouth was white. He drew a ragged breath. 'At least, cousin Sebastian, I don't stink of trickery and theft.'

Nearby an older man whose face was red with indignation jumped to his feet. 'Enough, man,' he rasped at the intruder. 'Guard your tongue, or we'll have you thrown out bodily!'

Corbridge shook his head quickly, smoothing down his satin lapels. 'No need for that, eh, Marcus? Firstly, I'd like to hear you explain yourself. And, secondly, I'd much, much rather you didn't address me as cousin.'

'I'd rather not have to address you as anything,' said Marcus. He was more in control of himself now. 'But the fact remains that we are, unfortunately, related. And you ask me to explain myself; but first I'll ask you this. How do you justify the fact that you've managed to rob my elderly godfather of everything: every acre of land, every penny of savings, and above all the home he loves so dearly?'

Lord Corbridge arched his pale eyebrows, just a little. 'Facts, dear Marcus, let us look at the facts! Though facts, I remember, were never your strong point. Always emotional, weren't you? Must be your unstable heritage showing through...'

Marcus's face darkened and his fists clenched dangerously at his sides. Corbridge, after taking a hasty step back from him, went on hurriedly, 'I've robbed Sir Roderick Delancey of absolutely nothing, I assure you! In fact, I tried to help him, tried to dissuade him from plunging into yet greater debts… Gambling is *such* a sad sickness, especially at his age.' He shrugged, an expression of concern creasing his smooth features. 'But in spite of my every endeavour, Marcus, the foolish Sir Roderick continued to plunge yet deeper into the mire. I extricated him from the likelihood of a debtors' prison at vast personal expense. In return, he agreed to offer me as security the great hall at Lornings and the land that goes with it.'

'If he loses Lornings, he'll be a penniless bankrupt!'

'Wrong again, Marcus.' Corbridge gave a thin-lipped smile, drawing confidence from those who'd gathered around him. 'Your godfather will always have a roof over his head— the Dower House, to be precise—and some income from the home farm. Though it's more than the pitiful old fool deserves. Gambling is a quite fatal disease, I fear.'

'And one that he was never infected with, until you decided to poison him!'

Corbridge shook his head. 'You've been away for two years, Marcus. What's the matter? Didn't find fame and fortune soldiering in the Americas? Managed to get yourself a lame leg instead? Hoped to come back and live off weak-witted old Sir Roderick's fat purse—only to find the purse no longer so fat? What a shame.' He turned with mock concern to his rapt audience. 'Something should be done about our returned war heroes. They should be awarded a better pension, perhaps. We heard about your promotion, Marcus—pity it wasn't with a decent regiment, though. Perhaps the beautiful Miss Philippa Fawcett would have revived her interest in you if you'd had a little more to offer her on your return.'

The other man's eyes blazed. 'You know damn well why I didn't get in with a fancier regiment, Corbridge. It was because I didn't care to go around oiling palms with false compliments and fistfuls of money that would have kept some of our badly paid foot soldiers in luxury for the rest of their lives.'

'How noble,' breathed Lord Sebastian Corbridge. 'How infinitely noble of you, Marcus. Of course, your particular family circumstances don't exactly endear you to your superiors, do they?'

Someone in the audience laughed jeeringly. 'Have the man thrown out, Corbridge. Unstable streak in the whole family, if you ask me. Isn't he the fellow whose mother went mad? Mad as a hatter, they say. She actually ran off with one of his father's grooms...'

Marcus turned. In the blinking of an eye, so fast that no one there had time to register it, he had whipped out his sword and held it so that its point just nicked the lace ruffles at the throat of the man who had spoken. The man's eyes were suddenly round with fear; his plump face had gone as white as a sheet. After a second's paralysing silence, Marcus let his sword fall. He turned back to Sebastian, slamming the long blade back into its sheath.

'This quarrel is becoming too public for my liking,' he said flatly. 'I don't care to discuss my private affairs, or my family, in front of specimens like these. Let us arrange a duel.'

The flash of fear that crossed Lord Sebastian's face was quickly concealed. 'A duel? With an injured man?' he queried, looking pointedly at Marcus's leg. 'My dear cousin, what must you think of me?'

Marcus lifted his dark, expressive eyebrows. 'Do you really want me to explain exactly what I think of you? In words of one syllable, so everyone here understands?'

But Lord Sebastian Corbridge did not reply. Instead he was looking furtively over Marcus's shoulder; and Marcus, seeing that look, swung round, his sword once more at the ready, to face several burly-looking footmen who were advancing rapidly towards him with their fists clenched.

Then, suddenly, another figure moved swiftly out from the shadows, knocking Marcus's weapon aside with a deft blow of his arm. A voice—cheerful, almost laughing—called out, 'Now, Marcus! Time for the *disengage*, dear boy! Live to fight another day, eh?'

And Marcus found himself being hustled, almost pushed, towards the big outer doors, which were kicked open with a crash by his companion as he hurried Marcus down the wide steps into the chilly street.

Once on the pavement Major Marcus Forrester shook himself free and reluctantly sheathed his sword. 'Hal,' he said with a sigh. 'You're a good friend, but you should have let me hit him, at least.'

Hal Beauchamp, whose compact, expensively dressed frame nevertheless hid considerable physical expertise, relaxed into a smile and handed Marcus the riding whip he'd tossed aside earlier. 'What, and give those beefy minions who were creeping up behind you the chance to beat you black and blue?' he objected. 'Not the best of ideas, Marcus! A strategic retreat is definitely in order, I think, before those painted fops in there combine their scanty brain power and come after us!'

Marcus grinned back at his friend. 'A pursuit? And you reputedly the best swordsman in the regiment? Hardly likely, I think, Hal.'

'No. Hardly likely.' Hal held out his hand warmly for the other to shake. 'Good to see you back in London, Marcus. Really good. Now, I assume from your attire that you arrived here on horseback?'

'A hired horse, yes—I paid a groom to see to it.'

'Very well, then, dear fellow; so now I insist you come and share a bottle of claret with me, somewhere more congenial than that hole, and tell me—' Hal's brown eyes gleamed '—absolutely everything.'

* * *

Inside the hallowed portals of the club, Lord Sebastian Corbridge, smoothing down his satin frockcoat like a bird preening its badly ruffled feathers, returned to his table and affected nonchalant disdain. But his hands were still trembling, and he was aware that his acquaintances had rather enjoyed the spectacle they had just witnessed. Corbridge was not a popular man in London.

'Is he really your cousin, Corbridge?' grinned the portly Viscount Lindsay, generally known as Piggy. 'You kept quiet about *that* side of the family, dear boy.'

Lord Corbridge paled slightly beneath his fashionably applied powder and patches. 'I have numerous distant cousins,' he replied disdainfully. 'My great-grandfather, you will recall, was the Earl of Stansfield—'

'Oh, we remember all right,' replied Viscount Lindsay, sharing a covert sneer with the others seated at their table. 'You remind us of it nightly, dear fellow.'

'The Earl,' continued Corbridge stiffly, 'had a variety of offspring. Major Marcus Forrester, whose mother was the only child of the Earl's disreputable youngest son, is one of the least significant of them all.'

'Fellow didn't look insignificant to me,' drawled Viscount Lindsay, raising his eyebrows. 'Fellow looked damned frightening to me, Corbridge, when he had you dangling there like a gasping fish.'

The others joined in the laughter, and Corbridge paled again. 'The army's all he's fit for,' he muttered in a low, angry voice. 'There's bad blood on that side of the family. He was scarcely out of infancy when his mother fled to Europe with her lover, some lowly serving man. Since then, Marcus Forrester has shown a dangerous instability. I never thought to see him return alive from the war in America.'

'No,' put in Viscount Lindsay rather maliciously. 'I bet

you didn't, Corbridge. Seems as if young Marcus has found out, too, exactly what you've been up to while he's been away with his precious old godfather and that rather splendid estate at Lornings. All in all, it's rather damned bad luck for you that he's returned at all, isn't it? Alive and well and primed for action, it seems.'

Lord Sebastian Corbridge was silent. But his slender white hand, which glittered with jewelled rings, twisted in some agitation around the stem of his glass.

Outside the sepia clouds still surged menacingly overhead, and the pavements glinted with puddles in the yellow light of the street lamps as Hal and Marcus proceeded on foot towards the Strand. But at least the rain had ceased; and the citizens of London were heading out again for the gaming clubs of St James's, or the colourful taverns and theatres beyond Leicester Fields. Hal Beauchamp—as fair as Marcus was dark, with a slighter build, and an open, sunny countenance—was cheerfully extolling the merits of the dining parlour at the Bull's Head. 'They'll set us up with some excellent victuals, Marcus!' he promised. 'The claret's first rate as well, I assure you. And then we could go on somewhere for a decent game of hazard—'

'No! No gaming.' Marcus's vivid, handsome face, which had relaxed in the company of his friend, was suddenly serious once more. 'I don't think I'll ever cast the dice again, Hal.'

Hal Beauchamp pulled a droll expression. He was dressed as usual in the most expensive, if discreet of styles; his long greatcoat that swept almost to the ground was exquisitely tailored, and his beaver hat and shining top-boots bore evidence of the tender care of a skilful valet. 'Oh dear, oh dear me,' he sighed. 'It's the end of the world indeed if Major Marcus Forrester renounces the fine art. What would your devoted soldiers say? Remember the game of hazard we had in camp, just before the raid on Wilmington last year? The enemy were all around, and you were saying, "One more throw, gentlemen. Just one more throw. I feel that my luck is in…"'

Marcus laughed, but his eyes were bleak. 'It hasn't been in lately, Hal.'

'No.' His friend's expression softened. 'I heard about your injury, at the siege of Savannah. Do you have somewhere to stay in London?'

Marcus shook his head. 'Not yet. The army pensions office offered me some tedious post in recruitment with lodgings all in, but I refused. And I haven't started looking for anywhere else yet. I just wanted to find Corbridge.'

'And kill him? So I must assume you were planning on sleeping in Newgate gaol tonight,' said Hal lightly as they jostled their way through the crowds that thronged Haymarket. 'I have a better suggestion. Come and stay with Caroline and me, in Portman Square. Far more comfortable than Newgate, I assure you.'

Marcus struggled, then smiled. It was very difficult *not* to smile when Hal was around. They'd been at Oxford together, then the army; they'd shared good times and bad. But now they were both out of the war; Hal because his only sister, who had been recently widowed, needed him at home; and Marcus because of a rebel's musketball through his thigh.

'You are more than kind,' said Marcus, turning to face his friend. 'But your sister—I would be imposing, surely?'

'Not at all, dear fellow. She always had a soft spot for you. And your injured leg will give her something to fuss over.' Hal hesitated. 'I heard, you know, about your godfather, Sir Roderick, and the business with Corbridge. It must have come as a blow to you. The loss of your inheritance, the decline in your prospects…'

Marcus said quietly, 'The worst of it, Hal, was seeing what it has done to my godfather. This business has all but finished him off.'

Hal nodded, frowning in sympathy. 'Then stay with us, while you see what can be done.'

'I have no wish whatsoever to be in anyone's debt.'

'My dear fellow,' responded Hal swiftly, 'let's have no talk of debt. Consider our house your home for as long as you wish.'

And to ensure there could be no further argument, Hal resumed his steady pace along the Strand, where the candlelit shop windows with their displays of millinery and trinkets glittered enticingly. Carriages clattered by, and sedan-bearers pushed through the crowds, their polite calls of *'By your leave, sir!'* swiftly changing to their usual ripe curses if people failed to move out of their way. Marcus hurried to keep up with his friend's loping, athletic stride, knowing he shouldn't have ridden so damned hard for the best part of two days—but what else could he have done other than resolve to take action, any kind of action, once he'd seen the state his gentle, kindly godfather was in?

Sir Roderick Delancey had been a friend and neighbour for as long as Marcus could remember to the Forrester family on their rather ramshackle Gloucestershire estate, and when Marcus's mother had run off, amidst such disgrace that her husband, a broken and impoverished man, died soon after, Roderick took responsibility for his godson Marcus without hesitation. Not possessing any children himself, Sir Roderick had paid for Marcus's schooling; and in the vacations Marcus spent long weeks at his godfather's beautiful country mansion, which he came to regard as his home, his own home having to be sold to cover his father's debts.

After Oxford, when Marcus set his heart on joining the army, Sir Roderick had offered to buy him a commission in one of the top cavalry units; but Marcus, who had his own kind of pride, refused, and became a captain in a line regiment. He was swiftly promoted, and when his regiment was sent to America to fight under Cornwallis, Sir Roderick continued to write regularly to his godson—but last autumn the letters had stopped.

And now Marcus knew why.

Some day, Marcus had resolved, he would return to active service. But not yet. He had another battle to fight first, on Sir Roderick Delancey's behalf.

At the corner of Half Moon Alley, a crowd had gathered around a couple of street entertainers who, using a stretch of low wall as their table, were tempting passers-by to bet on which of three upturned cups covered a coin. The first of the pair, a ragged-looking man with a wooden leg, was dextrously switching the cups to allow onlookers tantalising glimpses of the bright coin, while his accomplice, a slim youth wearing a long coat and a cap rather too big for him, was strolling around and drumming up trade in a light, cheerful voice. 'Roll up, roll up, ladies and gennelmen! Put your penny down, guess which cup hides the sixpence—it's easy, see?—and win it for yourself! Yes, win a whole, shiny sixpence! Roll up, roll up—'

Then the lively youth broke off, because his sharp eyes had observed what Marcus now saw—a fat member of the Watch huffing and panting towards the pair with his stick raised, and two of his companions coming up behind. 'Haul them two coves in!' the watchman roared. 'They're thieves and scoundrels, the pair of 'em!' The man with the peg-leg had his coin and his little cups thrust deep in his pockets in no time; tucking his wooden limb under his arm, he raced away on two exceedingly sound legs, while, doubtless by prior arrangement, his young companion took off in the opposite direction towards Hal and Marcus, twisting and turning nimbly through the crowds that thronged the pavement. Marcus watched, interested and impressed, as the lad, though caught briefly by the wrist by one of the Charleys, kicked his way free and ran on boldly, his ragged coat flying and his cap crammed low over his head. As he drew nearer, Marcus glimpsed emerald green eyes glinting above an uptilted nose, and a merry mouth curled in scorn—until the lad realised some more watchmen were hurrying up from the other end of the street, thus cutting off his escape.

Now, Marcus Forrester could never understand why a pair like this—up to no real harm, as far as he could see—should arouse the full ire of the law, when murder and mayhem went on without interruption in some of the hellish back streets where the Watch were afraid to even set foot. 'Let's even the odds,' he murmured to Hal. And just as the lad was hesitating, no escape in sight, Marcus reached out, grabbed him by the arm—'Let go of me, you dratted coneyjack!' was his only thanks—and thrust the slim fugitive, whose head barely came up to his shoulder, behind his back into a dark doorway. More colourful protests came flowing in abundance from that clear, expressive voice; but Marcus ordered through gritted teeth, 'I'm trying to help, you young fool. Stay there. And shut up.' Hal, brown eyes a-twinkling, completed their bodily barricade of the lad's hiding place; then the pair of them, arms folded, pretended to look on as if faintly bored, while the breathless old watchmen—the Charleys—elbowed their way through the swirling London crowd, up and down the street, looking in vain for their quarry. 'Where's that there lad?' one of them bellowed. 'Old Peg-leg's helper? Up to no good, 'im and all his kind, should be 'anged the lot of them—which way did 'e go?'

Marcus cast a swift glance back into the doorway, where the youth, having decided rather sensibly to co-operate, was now crouching silently behind him and Hal. Marcus saw again, with a kind of startlement, that pair of wide, incredibly green eyes taking everything in; and just at that moment the young fugitive, sensing his gaze, looked up at him and— grinned.

No fear. No fear at all, in that smooth young face... Marcus frowned, then quickly switched his attention back to the watchmen, who were shaking their heads, swearing volubly and stamping off down the Strand. Marcus looked back into the doorway and nodded. 'All clear now. Off you go.' The lad, emerging blithely from behind the long folds of Marcus's riding coat, whispered, 'My thanks', and quickly vanished into the crowds.

Hal lifted one querying, humorous eyebrow at his friend. 'Still on the side of the underdog, I see?'

'Most definitely,' declared Marcus. 'Why the hue and cry? They were only a couple of street entertainers.' But even as he dismissed them both, he was aware that the younger one had puzzled him considerably. *'My thanks...'* That voice, if you ignored the insults, had been expressive and clear. No hint of low-life in those parting words. He shook his head, swiftly banishing that bright, green-eyed gaze from his mind. 'On to business, Hal. Where are we heading after we've eaten?'

'I thought we'd go to a new place in Suffolk Street, called the Angel,' explained Hal. 'It's discreet, private, and has some of the best gaming in town. Oh, yes. I know—' he raised a finger to silence Marcus's protests '—*you're never going to gamble again.* But let me just say this. You want to get your revenge on the loathsome Corbridge, for ruining your godfather. Am I right?'

'You are,' replied Marcus, his mood grim once more.

'Then remember your army training, dear boy. Go to the kind of haunts your enemy would frequent. Probe his weaknesses. And Corbridge's are...?'

'You've got all night to listen? Well, apart from his general obnoxiousness, his weaknesses, from what I remember, are spending and gambling. And beautiful women, with rather doubtful reputations—'

'Especially young fillies with an eye for the gaming table,' broke in Hal. 'Lady Franklin, Cecilia Connolly, and that ravishing blonde known as La Fanciola from the Opera House—they are all exquisitely golden-haired, all greedy for money by fair means or foul, and he's dallied with them all! So listen, it's quite simple. What you must do is find another of the same kind—young, accomplished, preferably with guinea-gold curls—persuade her to entice him to the card tables at some private establishment—and use her to get back all your godfather's money off Corbridge!'

Marcus laughed, shaking his head. 'That's meant to be simple? I've got a better idea. Why don't I just run him through? It would be a damn sight easier.' His hand moved instinctively to his pocket, to check that he had enough money for the night ahead. And then he went very still. 'My wallet,' he breathed. 'It's gone.'

Hal's eyes widened. 'Are you sure? You might have left it somewhere, or dropped it in the street, perhaps...'

Oh, no. Marcus knew he hadn't dropped it. Suddenly he remembered the young fugitive with the mocking green eyes. He remembered, too late, the light hand that he felt brushing his coat as the lad departed. He turned to Hal and said flatly, 'If you're still set on a game tonight, you'll have to lend me the stake. Until I get to my bankers in the morning, I've not a penny to my name. That young wretch we helped back there has repaid me by picking my pocket.' And, Marcus vowed, if he ever caught the lad, he would give his backside a beating he'd never forget...

Hal frowned. 'The ungrateful rogue! Well, of course I'll

lend you something, Marcus. Who knows? Tonight at the Angel your luck might change for the better!'

'I certainly hope so,' replied Marcus with feeling. But his bleak eyes did not echo that smile. And Hal, who had been intending to ask Marcus if he had seen Philippa yet, decided that perhaps now was not the best time to broach that rather tricky subject.

Chapter Two

The street trickster whom Marcus was cursing so roundly was meanwhile twisting and turning knowingly through the assortment of narrow alleyways behind Maiden Lane before finally sidling into the shadows of an empty doorway and listening hard.

Nothing. No pursuers. No Charleys. With a sigh of relief the young thief sauntered off northwards whistling 'The Bold Ploughboy', cap pulled down low over forehead, hands thrust deep into shabby greatcoat; because, although it had stopped raining, the February night was still damp and cold. One hand encountered a leather wallet, and those bright green eyes were troubled, just for a moment, at the memory of its owner; then the youngster strolled onwards. Doubtless the dark-haired swell was rich enough not to miss it over-much.

Carefully avoiding the clusters of hard-drinking men who gathered around Bob Derry's Cider Cellar, the pickpocket, now munching on an apple filched earlier from a fruit stall, chose a secret way through the warren of courtyards that lay behind Drury Lane; then at last came to a halt, gazing up to where a flickering lantern illuminated a faded inn sign. This was the Blue Bell tavern: a pretty name for a low-life inn run by a steel-tongued landlady called Moll. Frowning briefly at the thought of Moll, the youth straightened his shabby coat and marched through the crowded, smoky taproom to push open a small side door into a private parlour, occupied only by a group of men clustered intently round a card game. The sudden draught from the door made the tallow candles flicker. Three of the players leapt to their feet, their hands clutching their cards. Then the fourth one, a gangly young fellow with rather startling tufts of red hair, grinned broadly. 'No cause for alarm, lads! It's just our Tassie, bin up to her usual tricks, no doubt.'

The men sat down again. Tassie closed the door with a deft kick, pulled off her cap and threw it defiantly on the table as her long golden hair tumbled around her shoulders. 'What do you mean, 'tis only me?' she challenged. 'Haven't you missed me, all of you?' No reply. Sighing a little, she let her keen eyes rove over the well-worn cards splayed out on the table. 'Fie, Georgie Jay, if 'tis whist you're playing, then I hope you remembered to keep the guard on your pictures, as I told you last night!'

Then the girl sat among the men, quite at ease, as the sturdily built, black-haired man in his thirties whom she'd addressed as Georgie Jay, looked frowning at his cards. 'God's blood, but you're right, Tassie,' he said.

'Course she's right,' said the red-haired lad, still gazing admiringly at the newcomer. 'There's no one to beat our Tassie at cards.'

'Or dice,' grinned Georgie Jay. He patted the girl's shoulder and turned back to the game.

The girl let her fair brow pucker a little. 'Weren't you— worried about me, Georgie?'

'Why, lass? Should we have been?'

She shrugged. 'Not really. I helped the cups-and-sixpence man up on the Strand.'

'Old Peg-leg? Did you make much?'

'Didn't get the chance. We were chased off by the Charleys.'

'Good job you can run fast, then.'

'Indeed.' Tassie stretched out her legs in their over-large boots and leaned back in her chair, her hands in her pockets, secretly a little upset that they weren't more troubled by her encounter with the Watch. She decided to say nothing about the dark-haired man and his wallet, though at one time she'd have told Georgie Jay everything, for he was the undisputed leader of this motley crew of travellers, and had been like a father to her ever since he'd found her eight years ago, alone on a country lane. 'We work when we can,' he'd told her, 'and when we can't—for times are hard for poor folks like us—why, then, we take a little from those who have enough and to spare!' Yes, Georgie Jay had been her saviour and protector, and she would always be grateful to him. But things had changed. Oh, how they had changed.

Moll, the buxom landlady, had just come into the room to see what was going on, Then she spotted Tassie, and scowled. 'Our Tassie's had a run-in with the Watch, Moll!' Georgie Jay told her.

'Lord's sake,' said Moll, 'what a fuss you all do make of that girl. 'Tain't natural, a grown lass like her trailing round with you all.'

Tassie met Moll's glare with stony dislike, and began to get to her feet, but Georgie reached out to forestall her. 'Tassie's one of us, Moll. Bring the girl some food, will you? You know she'll be ready for her supper.'

Tassie was; but she fought down the hunger pangs gnawing at her ribs. 'My thanks, but I'm not hungry.' Most certainly not for anything Moll dished out.

She picked up her cap, ready to leave; but just at that moment Georgie Jay exclaimed, 'Tassie! Now, what in the name of wonder is *that*?' He was pointing at the ugly bruising on her wrist, where the Watch man had grabbed her.

'It's nothing. Nothing at all.' She stepped quickly back, shaking down her sleeve.

'So you *were* in danger! Look, Tass, perhaps it really is time you stopped all your trickery out on the streets…'

'Oh, fiddlesticks, Georgie,' she said airily, 'you all have close shaves with the Watch every now and then, don't you? Tonight was no different!'

But Georgie Jay was sighing as he gazed at Tassie's defiant face beneath her tumbling curls that glowed a fierce gold in the flickering candlelight. 'You're a lass, Tassie,' he said regretfully. 'It's as simple as that. Things just can't go on the same. Why, you're nigh as tall as young Lem! How old are you now—fifteen, sixteen?'

Tassie shrugged her shoulders, guessing now was not the best of times to tell him she was seventeen. 'How should I know how old I am? Do you really think anyone used to celebrate my birthday?' No, indeed. Painful memories flashed through her mind. The big old house where she'd spent her early childhood. The long days spent locked in her room, learning her letters or struggling over hateful stitching with frozen fingers. The endless fear of punishment. She'd run because she felt that nothing, anywhere, could be worse.

She realised now that she'd been more than lucky to be found by good-hearted Georgie Jay, who still lived by the honourable code of the travelling folk, and insisted that his followers did the same. He'd stoutly declared that Tassie had a place with them for ever; but even he, it seemed, was now having his doubts. And so, perhaps, was she.

'All the same,' he was saying now, 'we need to have a talk, lass.'

Tassie gazed at him steadily. 'Are you trying to tell me that you don't want me with you any more?'

Georgie Jay looked unhappy. 'We've been doin' a bit of thinkin' and Moll's got a grand idea that might suit you just fine!'

Tassie's eyes flashed warningly as she looked at the older woman. 'Oh, *has* she now?'

'Moll's got a brother,' Georgie pressed on. 'He and his wife, they've got a small farm—Kent way, isn't it, Moll?— and they could do with some help around the place—'

Tassie turned on Moll incredulously. 'You think that I'd go as a *servant* to your brother? The one you were going on about the other night, saying he was a miserable skinflint and a tyrant?'

Moll coloured and looked angry. 'There's a good opportunity for you there, young madam, and don't you scoff at it!'

'I'll scoff at it all right,' Tassie breathed. 'You'd better think again, Moll, if you want to find your brother a—a *cheap skivvy.*' And, holding her head high, she marched to the door that led to the stairs, and closed it with a resounding bang behind her.

Once in the inner hallway, though, Tassie stopped, fighting to control the emotions that were now shaking her body. Despite her words of bold defiance, there was a huge lump in her throat, and her heart ached sorely. She'd known for some time that things couldn't go on as they were. But if Georgie Jay and his comrades didn't want her, she had no one. No one.

She heard them all getting up. One by one the others— Lemuel, Billy, and kind old Matt who played the fiddle at country fairs, who'd all been her friends for years—traipsed out through the other door to the taproom to have their meal, until only Moll and Georgie were left in there. Tassie bit her lip. Moll and Georgie. Usually Georgie Jay and his friends kept pretty much on the move, taking rooms at various inns or lodging houses depending on the work they found. But this winter they'd spent all of the last two months at the Blue Bell—because Georgie Jay had taken to sharing landlady Moll's room, and Moll's bed. And now Tassie could tell by the sound of clacking little heels on the flagstones that Moll had moved towards the jar of gin that she kept for herself on a high shelf near the door. Georgie Jay must have followed her; he was saying, in a low voice so that Tassie could only just hear, 'I did warn you she wouldn't like the idea, Moll.'

'Such a fuss about a silly girl,' Moll snapped back. Tassie heard the rattle of gin jar against beaker; and could just picture Moll drinking it down in one greedy swallow. 'All right, then. I'll not interfere! But you'll have to think of somethin' for her, Georgie Jay. Sakes alive, you must have seen the way men are starting to look at her! Lemuel worships the ground she walks on, and that big simpleton Billy watches her all the time. She's becomin' a real pretty piece, and there'll be trouble soon if you don't look out...'

Tassie could stand to hear no more. Horrified to find that her eyes were smarting with tears, she almost ran up the rickety staircase to her tiny attic room, where she was greeted by the loud squawking of a brightly coloured parrot gazing at her from its perch by the window. Georgie Jay had bought Edward for her seven years ago in Dorchester market, and now she angrily dashed away her tears with the back of her hand and stroked the bird's beautifully-crested head, whispering, 'How can Georgie Jay be so taken in by that—that *strumpet*, Edward? Moll's fat, and she paints her face, and she pickles herself in gin!'

Edward cocked his beady eye at her. *'Who's a pretty girl, then?'* Tassie almost smiled. But she couldn't ignore the fact that what Moll had said was right. Tassie couldn't go on pretending to be what she was not for much longer. 'If only I were a boy!' she went on in anguish, jumping up to pace the little room while at the same time trying to resist the temptation to chew her fingernails, something she always did when she was distressed. Edward just put his head on one side, his bright eyes blinking, and crunched steadily on the remains of a crust. Tassie drew a deep breath, then flung her big coat on the bed.

Soon after she had joined Georgie Jay's band, she'd taken to dressing like a lad because it was easier, and when her breasts had started to swell she'd worn loose shirts buttoned to the neck and hoped no one would notice. When her monthly courses began, a kindly serving girl at the farm where they were working came to her rescue and gave her some strips of linen to use, and into the bargain gave her an earthy lecture on how men were fiery creatures, and likely to be aroused beyond reason by the presence of a young, pretty maid. So Tassie tied up her bright golden hair with a piece of twine and pushed it under a cap; as she grew she continued to dress in loose breeches and boots and a rough cambric jacket several sizes too big for her that concealed her swelling curves; and season after season she tramped the dusty roads in the cheery company of Georgie Jay and his band, never complaining of weariness, always hoping that things would remain the same, because in truth she had no other life to turn to.

But she knew, in her heart of hearts, that things were changing fast. Moll had spotted the trouble with Billy already.

Billy was big and strong, but he was simple-minded. His family had been turned out of their cottage when the local landowner wanted to pull it down to make more space for sheep, and Billy had attached himself to the company like a faithful dog, invaluable if there was any kind of hard physical work. Tassie had always felt quite safe with him, as she did with all the others in their little band. But a couple of weeks ago, a little after midnight, Billy had knocked at the door of Tassie's bedroom. 'Tass,' he called out. 'Let me in, will you? I want ter tell you somethin'.'

She'd opened the door, and instantly smelled that he'd been drinking. Big Billy, with his thatch of wiry black hair, had always been a little over-fond of his ale. So she told him that she would talk to him in the morning; but he'd muttered something and a strange, hot look had spread across his face as he gazed at Tassie, with her hair loose past her shoulders, and dressed only in her thin cotton nightshirt.

He'd tried to kiss her then, grabbing her shoulders and pulling her close. Tassie struggled desperately to push him away, but Billy wrapped one arm around her waist, trapping her, while with the other hand he began to fumble at her breasts. She could feel the hardness of his arousal pressing against his breeches while his hot lips smothered her mouth; and Tassie, gasping, twisted violently and used her knee, very hard, in the place where she knew it would hurt him the most. Billy had whimpered with shock and gone limping off to his room. Tassie hoped fervently that the hateful episode had vanished into the shadows of Billy's slow mind; certainly he'd not troubled her again in that way, and she didn't think he would. But it had been an unpleasant reminder that Moll's warnings were only too true.

And now, they thought they could just pack her off to Moll's brother in the country! Oh, never. Suddenly she remembered the wallet she'd stolen from the gent in Half Moon Alley. Pulling herself up on the dingy little bed, she sat cross-legged in her boots and buckskin breeches and her man's shirt, and tossed back her long blonde curls from her face. Then she eased the slim leather wallet from her hip pocket; but her heart sank again, for there wasn't much in it. A few coins, amounting to little more than two guineas, and a pencilled note, folded up. The coins she put carefully into a little locked box hidden beneath her bed; the note she casually unfolded, preparing to crumple it and toss it aside. But then her eyes opened wide as a curling lock of chestnut hair tied up in a pretty blue ribbon fell on to the bed. Tassie read the note avidly. *For my darling Marcus. A little memento. All my love for ever, Philippa.*

Well! So her noble rescuer—Marcus—was in love! Tassie instantly held it closer. Philippa's handwriting was dainty, with lots of curly flourishes, quite the opposite of Tassie's bold, clear hand; Tassie would be prepared to wager that Philippa didn't chew her nails as she did, or fuzz the cards at whist, or swear like a trooper when the occasion arose. A prim parlour-miss indeed; the writing was a little faded, but the sheet was still scented with the remnants of some exotic and no doubt expensive floral perfume, which made both Tassie and Edward sneeze. Tassie went over to the window, preparing to hurl the lock of hair and the note out into the darkness. *All my love for ever.*

Just for a moment, she paused. Just for a moment she wondered what it must be like, to love a man like that; to be loved, in return. Then she pushed the window open and tossed out the lock of chestnut hair and the note into the courtyard, to join the heaps of stinking rubbish down there. 'Fancy carrying that around with him, Edward.' She shook her head. *Darling Marcus. A little memento...*

Edward squawked appreciatively and repeated, *'Darling Marcus! Darling Marcus!'* Tassie hesitated again; then she pressed her lips together and hurled the wallet through the window as well.

The noise of singing and laughter came up from the tavern below. She went to put more coals on the slumbering fire, and caught sight of her face in the cracked mirror over the hearth. A pale, haunted face, with shadowed green eyes, and clouds of golden curls tumbling to her shoulders. Tassie, the street thief. Tassie the trickster. Who was she really? *Why* was she all alone, forced to run long ago from a place of hateful cruelty?

She went slowly to count up the coins in her money box, and the old memories came crowding in. The great old house, miles from anywhere. Well-bred, hateful voices, snarling over her: *'This brat's trouble, William, I tell you! Nothing but trouble, and some day she's going to find out the truth...'*

Thoughtfully, Tassie put her money box away and picked up her much-worn pack of cards from beside Edward's perch. Outside she heard the nightwatchman call the hour, *'Ten o'clock and all's well...'*

No. No. All was most decidedly not well. Sitting cross-legged on her little bed, she began by the light of the flickering candle to practise one of the tricks she'd persuaded old Peg-leg to teach her in return for her help today. The time had come, as she'd always known it would, for her to make her own plans—before somebody else tried to make them for her.

She might, perhaps, have felt even more trepidation had she realised just how ardently Major Marcus Forrester was thinking thoughts of revenge against the ungrateful wretch who'd removed his wallet. He and Hal were at that moment dining at a fashionable chop-house just off the Piazza, where Hal, guessing that his friend's forlorn financial prospects must be lowering his spirits, talked to him encouragingly of the money that could be made by investing in cotton and shipping. Marcus listened, pretending to take an interest. Then Hal, taking the plunge, started to tell Marcus that his sister Caroline had recently met Miss Philippa Fawcett out walking in the park, and that she was looking unusually lovely, and was there any chance of Marcus calling on her;

at which Marcus shook his head swiftly and ordered, 'Talk of something else, Hal. *Anything* else.'

And as Hal recounted inconsequential gossip, Marcus's thoughts drifted far away to Lornings, the beautiful estate in the Gloucestershire countryside that belonged to his godfather, Sir Roderick Delancey. The place Marcus had always thought of as his home. As soon as Marcus, freshly returned to London just over a week ago after a storm-racked Atlantic voyage, had heard the news about Sir Roderick, he'd set out to see him. He'd found him, not at the great hall itself—which to Marcus's dismay looked totally abandoned—but in the much smaller Dower House, which lay close by.

'It's all my own fault,' Sir Roderick had replied simply. He seemed to have aged terribly in the two years of Marcus's absence. 'Dear boy, what a homecoming for you.'

Marcus had gone quickly over to his godfather and put his strong hand on his shoulder. 'It wasn't your fault. My cousin Corbridge is a lying, deceiving toad.'

'And I should have known it! But I'd got so badly in debt, you see, thanks to the company Sebastian led me into; and only Sebastian seemed to know the way out of it—'

'By taking you to one gaming house after another?'

'He assured me I could not help but win, Marcus! But I lost so heavily, night after night. Corbridge saved me—at least I *thought* he did—by promising he would see to my bills until September of this year. But in return—' and Sir Roderick sighed heavily '—I had to sign a letter promising him the entire Lornings estate as security.'

Marcus listened, tense-faced. 'But surely your debts, however great they are, aren't equivalent to the value of Lornings?'

Sir Roderick hung his head. 'Believe me, they're bad enough. If Sebastian hadn't taken on the bills, I would have had to put myself in the hands of moneylenders; and then, you know, what with the interest they demand, my debts would have doubled and trebled, until even the sale of the estate wouldn't have paid them off. I had no choice, Marcus. I'm so sorry. Lornings was supposed to be yours. I shall never forgive myself!'

Marcus shook his head vehemently. 'I don't give a fig for my inheritance. You've given me support and encouragement all my life—what more could I ask? But I can't forgive Corbridge for forcing you out of your rightful home. And I swear to God I'll make him pay.'

'Lornings is still mine for the moment,' Sir Roderick had said, with a gentleness that tore at Marcus's heart. 'Until the autumn, that is. But—I cannot afford to maintain the Hall now, so it seems best to live here, in the Dower House.'

Marcus was silent, thinking. Then he said suddenly, 'This last gaming house Corbridge took you to. Where you lost everything. Was it some backstreet den?'

'It was disreputable, certainly. But if you're thinking of contesting the letter that I signed, then don't trouble yourself, because Corbridge had it legally drawn up and witnessed.' He looked around him rather helplessly. 'I'm comfortable here, really I am. And I've still got some land and livestock—I've always fancied trying my hand properly at farming...'

At your age? thought Marcus sadly. His godfather, who was sixty-three, suffered from arthritis. He had two ageing retainers, husband and wife, who had stayed loyally with him for a pittance, and a capable man called Daniels who ran the small farm. Otherwise he was on his own, with hardly any resources now that his fortune was so badly compromised.

'I'll come and help you,' promised Marcus. 'We'll get the land to rights again, believe me. But first—' his steely eyes narrowed '—I've got Corbridge to deal with.'

Sir Roderick was watching him with loving but anxious

eyes. 'Please don't do anything foolish, my dear boy! I know how impetuous you can be!'

And Marcus had smiled grimly as he replied, 'Impetuous? Don't you worry. I shall consider every action—*extremely carefully.*'

But so far, concluded Marcus, so far his plans had not gone well. He'd confronted Corbridge earlier tonight in the white heat of his rage, and been forced, publicly, to retreat—then he'd had his wallet stolen. Not the best of starts.

Hal was calling for the bill. Marcus hated not being able to pay for himself, but Hal brushed his objections aside. 'If you're staying with us as you promised, then you'll have plenty of opportunities to repay me when you're ready. Caro will love having you, and we might even persuade her to host one or two small gatherings; you could invite *anyone you liked*—'

Marcus interrupted. 'If you're thinking of Philippa again, then I must tell you I don't think I'll be inviting her anywhere. You see, she knows that my inheritance has gone.'

'Marcus, I don't believe—'

Marcus topped up their glasses. 'Actually, I think she knew before I did.' His voice was lightly casual, but Hal saw that his friend's expression was bleak. 'No doubt her doting parents found out and told her. I called on her just before I set off to see Sir Roderick. Oh, it was all very civilised; Philippa talked of how we both needed some time to reconsider our rash youthful commitment, and her foolish mother hovered by her side all the time, looking terrified in case I should try to change Philippa's mind. I didn't, of course.'

Hal frowned as he absently counted out the coins for the bill. He knew that Philippa's parents, the businessman Sir John Fawcett and his wife, lived, when not in town, on a moderately prosperous estate in Gloucestershire that bordered Lornings to the south. Happily willing to overlook

Marcus's slightly dubious parentage in view of his being the great-grandson of the Earl of Stansfield and his expectation of Sir Roderick's substantial estate, the ambitious father and vain, silly mother had openly encouraged the friendship that had grown up between their daughter and Marcus. Even Marcus's long absence in the American wars had not dulled everyone's belief that the two of them would marry.

But Sir Roderick's catastrophic change of fortune had altered all that, and now Philippa was doing her Season in London, intent on wealthier prospects. Hal felt deeply angry for his friend, who had come back from two years of brave service to his country to be faced with calculated rejection. But of course Hal knew that Marcus didn't want his, or anybody's, sympathy.

Instead, Hal leaned forwards, and poured out the last of the wine. 'Time to re-plan tactics, dear boy,' he said briskly. 'Plenty more where she came from.'

Were there? Marcus had been remembering a summer's day, just before he had set sail for the American war two years ago. He and Philippa had ridden out along the Gloucestershire lanes, unchaperoned—Philippa had laughingly escaped from her groom—and on a grassy bank by a secluded stream Philippa had allowed Marcus to kiss her and promised him that she would wait for him for ever...

Hal was still talking. 'Capitalise your assets, Marcus,' he was pronouncing gleefully, 'and get your revenge on Corbridge. Remember gambling is his fatal flaw!'

'Revenge on Corbridge indeed.' Marcus echoed Hal's toast at last, and knocked back the last of the claret. 'Talking of gambling, Hal—didn't you mention a gaming house called the Angel?'

It was eleven o'clock, and the night was just beginning.

Chapter Three

'*G*ot it!' Tassie was still sitting cross-legged on her bed in the light of a tallow candle, so utterly absorbed in her task of getting all the hearts to the bottom of the pack that at first she didn't hear the quiet knock at her door. Then it came again, and she tensed, afraid that it might be Billy. But, no, it was Lemuel's voice that she heard, calling out quietly, 'Tassie. Tassie, are you in there? I was just wonderin' if Edward's all right, seeing as I was lookin' after him for you...'

Quickly Tassie scrambled off the bed, pushing her loose hair back from her face and tucking her big shirt into her slim buckskin breeches. Lemuel was a bit sweet on her, she knew, but she trusted him to keep his distance. She opened the door wide. 'Come in, Lemuel, do. Yes, Edward's fine. Moll hasn't poisoned him—yet. My thanks for keeping an eye on him.'

'*Darling Marcus! Darling Marcus!*' cackled Edward, pleased with his new-found phrase.

'Marcus?' Lemuel stood in the middle of the room, frowning in puzzlement.

Tassie laughed and coloured a little. 'Oh, it's just some

nonsense he's picked up.' She tapped Edward's perch lightly. 'Be quiet now, Edward, do.'

Lemuel nodded, his face expressing eager shyness. 'And you, Tass? Are you all right? After—after—'

She shrugged, thrusting her hands into the pockets of her breeches. 'After hearing that Moll wants to get rid of me, you mean? Aye, Lemuel, I'm all right. She'll not get the better of me, never fear.'

Lemuel grinned at her approvingly, then his eyes fell on the pack of cards. 'You been practising your tricks then, Tass? There's none of us can beat you at cards, is there?'

'No one,' said Tassie earnestly, because it was true. She could even beat Georgie Jay, without him realising exactly which trick she was up to—the Kingston Bridge cheat, or shaving the cards, or even the difficult *sauter la coupe.* She'd mastered them all...

And then, suddenly, she realised what she had to do next. It was so blindingly obvious that she almost laughed aloud. Her green eyes gleaming, she gestured Lemuel to the battered chair at the foot of the bed. 'Sit down, Lemuel,' she said encouragingly. 'I want to talk to you.'

'To me?' His freckled face lit up.

'Yes, Lemuel.' She perched on the edge of her bed again and gazed at him thoughtfully as he lowered his gangly frame into the chair facing her. 'Last night,' she went on, 'I heard you talking with the others about a private gaming parlour that's just opened up in town. You were saying that everyone of fashion—all the swells—are crowding into it. And I heard Georgie Jay tell how someone lost five hundred guineas at basset there—in just one evening.'

Lemuel's perplexed brow cleared a little. 'Oh, the Angel, you mean? Aye, Georgie Jay was talking of us dressin' in our smart togs and goin' along there some time. Though it's a bit risky, 'cos the place hasn't got a full gaming licence, you see. That means it could be raided by the Horneys, any time.'

Tassie nodded, her chin resting in her hand. Mmm. So it was an illegal gaming den, patronised by the fashionable and the rich... Already her pulse was speeding up in anticipation. 'I see. And what else do they play there, Lemuel, beside basset?'

'Oh, the usual. Faro, vingt-et-un, piquet—you know, Tass, all those fancy French games! Apparently it's full to busting every evening. Attracts everyone, from the highest blue-bloods to—well, to—'

'People like us?' slid in Tassie gently.

'Aye! Though I told Georgie Jay I thought we'd be a bit out of our depth, seein' as how the stakes are so high. And, like I said, it could be raided any time.'

'So all the more reason,' said Tassie thoughtfully, 'to go as soon as possible.' She smiled at him. 'Like—tonight.'

'Tonight?' Lemuel shook his head. 'Oh, no, Georgie Jay's far too busy. He's promised Moll he'll move her some barrels of ale up from the cellar.'

'I wasn't thinking of Georgie Jay,' whispered Tassie sweetly, leaning forwards from her perch at the edge of the bed. 'I was thinking about *you and me*, Lem dear.'

He gaped. 'We can't, Tassie! We'd never get in! And we've not the stakes—'

'I have,' she responded calmly. She patted the little money box at her side. 'And of course we'll get in. Ladies are admitted, aren't they?'

'Why, yes,' stuttered Lemuel. 'They say the ladies of quality think it fine sport to go along without their husbands knowin', and play in secret. But you're—'

'But I'm what, Lem?' Tassie stood up and gracefully pirouetted around his chair. 'I shall dress up like a fine lady, and you can be my escort. And I shall win more money than you've ever seen before, and I'll pay you your share, *if you do exactly as I say!*'

Lemuel was still open-mouthed. 'But, Tassie, we can't just walk into a place like that and start fleecing them high-up swells.'

She broke off her pirouetting to declare, 'You're just scared, Lemuel, that's your trouble.'

He jumped to his feet at that, burning with hurt pride. 'I ain't scared of nothing! But it's too risky for you, girl! There'll be all sorts lurking there amongst the gentry—cheats, rakes, whoremongers—bad company, Tass!'

She gazed at him, her hands on her slender hips, her green eyes gleaming. 'Then come with me to protect me. If you won't come—why, then, I'll just have to go on my own. Won't I?'

'Very well, then! I'll go with you! But if Georgie Jay finds out…'

'And why should he find out, unless you tell him?'

Lemuel let out a low moan of defeat.

Already Tassie had worked out that all she needed to do was 'borrow' one of Moll's gowns, and pile up her hair in the foolish way all the ladies of fashion did. 'Dear Lemuel,' she grinned, 'I knew you'd agree. Give me twenty minutes to prepare myself, would you? And you must put on your best brown suit, and polish your shoes. Not a word of this to anyone else, mind!' She held the door open for Lemuel and he stumbled out, looking rather stunned. She started humming 'The Bold Ploughboy', then broke off to call after him, 'No ale, now, to fuddle your wits. We're in for a lively night, you and I!'

It was an hour later. The Angel was crowded; and Marcus was uneasy, because it was becoming apparent to him that his good friend Hal was being systematically cheated. How, exactly, he could not say. Hal, playing piquet, had easily won the first game, and the second also. His female opponent appeared almost hesitant, pausing over her discards and frowning like a Johnny Raw.

But the third game she won in six quick hands, a look of unwavering concentration on her face.

From then on, the usually unflappable Hal began to look flustered. Marcus knew that his friend was no mean player, but his female opponent never seemed to put a foot wrong. Marcus himself had stopped playing at the faro table some while ago, because he was unwilling to risk any more of the stake that Hal had lent him; and now he drew closer to study the girl's face, because there was something about her that puzzled him. Of course there were plenty of women amongst the men up here in the candlelit, luxuriously furnished back room of the Angel. Some of them were ladies of high rank out for a secret adventure without their husbands, though others were scarcely better than women of the streets. Was this one a Cyprian?

Whatever part she was playing, she certainly played it demurely, keeping her head lowered and speaking at all times in a cool and alluring voice. When she looked up to smile at Hal, Marcus saw that her face was sweetly heart-shaped, and dominated by huge green eyes that drew his gaze time and time again. And her hair was glorious: a rich cluster of golden curls piled in artful disarray, with just a few stray locks trailing down around the slender column of her neck in a way guaranteed to make most men dream of kissing her there...

But she wore far too much rouge and lip paint, and as for her gown... Her gown was a hideous contraption, made of some reddish-brown fabric in the style of years ago; it was too large for her slender figure, and the shabby lace ruffles at her wrists were yellow with age. Who was she? Who had brought her here?

At that very moment, she looked up at Hal and said, in her gentle voice, ''Tis my game, sir, I believe. But no credit to me; I rather think fortune smiled on me.'

The somewhat bemused Hal put a brave face on it. 'Nonsense. You were by far the better player, ma'am!' Gallantly he pushed his guinea rouleaux across the table to her. 'Will you honour me with another game?'

The young woman hesitated before saying, 'Very well, then. Just one more.'

'One more is probably all I can afford,' said Hal ruefully, and his opponent laughed, a pleasing, merry sound that to Marcus was strangely familiar, though he was damned if he could place it. Surely he would remember a girl like that if he'd met her before! Her face was almost—*beautiful*, and yet her clothes, and her lip paint, were ridiculous... Marcus looked round. All in all there must be fifty or sixty people crowded in here, and every table had its punters and watchers, all eyeing every turn of the cards, every cut and deal. Hal's table was in a corner of the room, and quite a few of the usual gamesters had gathered round, their greedy eyes devouring the golden-haired girl as she began to deal.

Then Marcus saw that somebody else a few yards away was also watching her closely; a nervous long-limbed young fellow in a homespun suit too tight for him, with shockingly cut red hair. Here was her accomplice, thought Marcus scornfully, ready to safeguard the girl's winnings and perhaps sell her on for the night! He frowned. Yet her clothes, her entire manner, were just not right for a whore, though God knew she'd tried her best, with that face paint.

Marcus again found his memory stirring tantalisingly. Then he saw something. She was spreading her cards in her hand in an attempt to study them, her green eyes wide and her brows drawn together in apparent puzzlement. Her fingernails looked as if she made a habit of chewing them; her painted lips were moving in what appeared to be a naïve endeavour to calculate the value of her cards.

But there was nothing naïve about the way she reached to flick a loose fold of the tawdry lace at her wrist, while at the same time making another very quick, almost imperceptible movement. *She's drawn a card from her sleeve and interchanged it with one from her hand.* Marcus swore softly under his breath. Of course it was over in an instant, and Hal hadn't noticed a thing, because he was too busy frowning over his own cards. And now, Marcus saw, those thick eyelashes of hers were fluttering demurely as she displayed her cards to Hal and said, in her sweet voice, 'I think you will find that I've spoiled your *repique*, sir. The game is surely mine.'

Hal was soundly routed. His pleasant face twisted ruefully in acknowledgement of his fate as he pushed the last of his guinea rouleaux across the table. 'How clever of you to have kept the guard! Well done, ma'am, well done indeed; I wish I had half your skill at the game.'

The girl, smiling, was already gathering her winnings together. 'You must take consolation, sir, in the fact that most certainly I had the luck of the cards tonight.'

Luck? questioned Marcus grimly. *Luck?* He could see that her edgy red-haired companion was already sidling through the crowd towards her. No doubt they'd swiftly exchange for golden guineas the rouleaux she'd won and move on to some other backstreet gambling haunt, ready to fleece some other innocent—if he, Marcus, were to let them…

No time to explain to Hal. As Hal rose, Marcus was there in his place, saying quickly to the girl, 'Your pardon, ma'am, but I could not help noticing that you play an intriguing game. Would you care to indulge me before you go?'

She looked up swiftly, and just for a moment Marcus could have sworn that there was a flash of something—was it fear?—in her eyes. But then she said, with only a trace of hesitation, 'Why, with pleasure, sir.'

Hal, surprised, muttered to him, 'You'll find your match there, Marcus. She's good.'

'Perhaps that's the attraction,' said Marcus, gazing coldly at the girl, whose heart-shaped face still looked somewhat pale beneath her rouge. 'Shall we say ten shillings the point?'

The girl seemed to catch her breath, and then nodded. Marcus beckoned a groom-porter for a fresh pack, and put some card money on the tray. Looking up, he was in time to catch a scarcely perceptible glance between the girl and her red-headed companion, who had perched nervously on a chair nearby. Marcus smiled grimly to himself and handed the pack to the girl. She won the cut, and opted to discard five of her twelve cards. Once more her pretty face with its delicate tip-tilted nose was a mask of concentration.

For a while the play was even. Marcus went down on the first rubber, though not by much. But then, gradually, the girl began pulling away. He watched her fingers, so quick, so agile as they drew his tokens relentlessly towards her. His keen grey eyes, that on active service had been able to see the gleam of gunmetal in woodland over a mile away, strained to see more. This time she made no move towards her wrist-lace; in fact, she'd—deliberately?—pushed back her cuff to her elbow. He frowned as he noticed a faint ring of fresh finger-shaped bruises around her slender wrist; someone had been rough with her recently. But then he saw what he had been waiting for. *Yes.* She was marking the cards, indenting certain corners very, very lightly with the sharp little fingernail of her right hand, in a gesture as swift as the blinking of an eye! Marcus carried on playing and was aware of Hal's increasingly puzzled frown as his pile of rouleaux continued their journey to the girl's side of the table. The girl's companion was watching, too, his unease scarcely hidden.

There it was again. A tiny squeeze of his opponent's fingernail as she delicately indented yet another glossy card. Moments later she carefully spread out her winning hand, and her cheeks dimpled in a sweet smile. 'Four aces and three kings, sir! I think I have you, if you please!'

Marcus was very still for a moment. Then he deliberately leaned forwards, and picked up the girl's cards at one stroke, breaking all the rules of play. Hal, at his shoulder, gasped aloud. The girl's painted smile flickered, but her big green eyes were still wide and innocent. 'Is aught amiss, sir?'

'Indeed, there is a slight problem—ma'am,' Marcus replied, equally calmly. 'You see, I discover in myself an aversion to playing with out-and-out cheats.'

He was aware of Hal drawing closer, standing tensely at his side. Of the thin, anxious fellow in brown also edging nearer to the girl, his face tight with strain. The girl was better. In fact, she was amazing. She gazed across the table at Marcus, saying in that same sweet, polite voice, 'I'm afraid I don't quite follow your meaning, sir.'

'Ha! Don't you, by God!' Marcus was gathering up all the cards now, and throwing them on the table, picking up one picture card after another with his strong, lean hands and jabbing at the telltale indentations. 'You're trying to tell me you didn't do *this*?' he grated out. 'And this? And *this*?'

His raised voice was drawing onlookers now. And the girl's slender figure seemed frozen to her chair as she realised, at last, that her game was at an end. Marcus reached across the table scornfully for the winnings she'd garnered from himself and Hal. And then, suddenly, he heard shouting from the street outside, and the sound of feet clattering up the staircase, and the room was filled with cries of alarm.

'The Watch! The Watch are upon us!' Marcus was on his feet already, but not before the wretched girl had grabbed all the rouleaux back and was elbowing her way through the panic-stricken punters towards the back staircase. Marcus lunged after her, and just managed to catch hold of her arm. 'Not so fast. Not so fast, you bloody little cheat...'

She fought him quite ferociously, though no one noticed, because all around them people were pushing and jostling and calling out in panic. This was an illegal gaming parlour, after all, and none of them wanted to spend the night in a magistrate's cell. Chairs were being overturned, candles extinguished, cards sent flying to the floor as they all tried to get to the stairs that led to the back exit. The girl continued to struggle wildly, but he hung on all the tighter as they were swept towards the top of that staircase with the rest of the fleeing crowd. He must have hurt her; she let out a low cry; then suddenly her elbow in his diaphragm all but winded him, and she hissed, 'Take your hands off me, you *coneyjack*, you!'

Coneyjack. Thieftaker. Marcus almost dropped her in his surprise. 'It was *you*!' he exclaimed. 'You, running from the Watch earlier this evening in the Strand! I hid you from them, told them you'd gone the other way—and then—then, you ungrateful wretch, you damned well picked my pocket!'

The press was even tighter now because they were almost at the top of the darkened staircase. For a moment her huge green eyes glinted vividly in the shadows. With fear? Not for long. 'Maybe,' she breathed, 'that's 'cos all you overbearing, arrogant gents *deserve* to be robbed!' Then she twisted violently to get free of his grip and called out wildly, 'Lemuel, Lemuel, where are you? Come and help me, you great slow-witted fool!'

Marcus clung on grimly to his captive as the tide of people in full flight swept past them. 'Lemuel,' he growled. 'So that's your young friend's name, is it? I'll wager he's out on the streets by now, running full tilt for whatever hovel you call home—'

He got no further, because she brought her knee up and thudded it, hard, against his right thigh.

Marcus swore fluently and almost lost her. He snatched a swift look over his shoulder, but of Hal there was no sign, damn it. He tightened his grip on the wretched girl and dragged her with him—she was still kicking out—to the crush at the top of the stairs. He wasn't going to let her go, yet if the minx carried on fighting him like this, they'd end up tumbling down the steps, and being trampled underfoot in the stampede...

Nothing else for it. He picked the girl up and put her over his shoulder, then let himself be carried down the rickety staircase by the crowd of nervous punters hustling towards the back doorway, and the safety of the warren of dark alleyways that lay behind Great Suffolk Street. Within seconds the girl had started to pummel his back, but fortunately his coat was of good, thick broadcloth; his strongly muscled shoulders were as impervious to her clenched little fists as were his ears to her colourful threats. All the same, he was glad when at last they got outside and he was able to swing the jade down and set her on her feet. It was starting to rain again. Around them the crowd was melting swiftly away; the girl tried to hop off, too, but he gripped her and pulled her into a nearby doorway. There were no lamps here, and the shadows clustered like sepia pools, far away from the candle-lit windows further along the street. *'Let go of me!'* She was still struggling, like a wildcat; he almost shook her into submission and suddenly she went limp in his arms. Another trick? If he did let her go, would she fall—or run?

Somewhere in the darkness fiddle music was spilling out from a lively tavern. But out here, as the last of the

Angel's fleeing patrons vanished into the blackness, they were quite alone. The doorway gave them little shelter from the rain, which was landing on her cheeks, washing away her rouge and starring her thick lashes—or were they tears he saw? Her golden hair was tumbling from its pins and falling around her shoulders in damp disarray. What would she try next? He expected more insults, more oaths; but this time the cunning jade adopted a different tactic. In a voice that quivered slightly she begged, 'Please, please, sir, don't hand me in. I'm but a poor orphan; I do swear I meant no harm...'

Marcus had no difficulty hardening his heart against this plea. 'I'll let you go with the greatest of pleasure. But not before you've given me back my winnings, and also the wallet you stole from me earlier this evening.'

She caught her breath. 'Wallet? Fie, what wallet? I've not the faintest notion what you mean!' Marcus wanted to shake the girl; he found her cheek incredible; but before he could reply he heard the sound of clattering footsteps as some of the magistrate's men came rushing down the back staircase from the gaming hell and out into the alley, furious because so far they'd been deprived of their prey. Until now. Marcus cursed thoroughly under his breath. 'Leave this to me,' he hissed at the girl.

'Here's one of 'em, lads!' called a constable, jabbing his finger at Marcus. 'Now, *you* was up there, wasn't you, eh?' He jerked his head towards the deserted upper storey of the ill-fated gaming club. 'Reckon we need to ask you some questions, sir—you're coming along with us, *if* you please!'

Marcus had absolutely no intention of doing so. Swiftly he drew the rainsoaked girl into his arms and laughed. 'A gaming hell, constable? Not me. In fact, I've just been down to a little nunnery in Haymarket, where Mother Bentley—you know her?—rules the roost. And from there I picked out this charming maid for a night of pleasure. A whole guinea, I've paid, and we were just on our way back to my lodgings—now, do you think I'd have time to waste on cards, or dice?'

Even as he spoke he heard the girl's sharply indrawn breath as the damned little minx prepared to protest. The constables were muttering and scratching their heads, eyeing him dubiously. One word of denial from the girl, and he'd be finished.

Swiftly he pulled her hard against his body and bent his head to kiss her. He could taste the cool rain on her lips, could feel her heart thumping through the wet silk of her gown as she struggled like a trapped bird in his arms. He was surprised, because she smelled so clean, so fresh. Surprised, too, because, as he continued to kiss her for the benefit of those gawping officers of the law, she seemed to freeze in shock, as if she had never been kissed before...

But that was impossible! Inevitably, though, he felt the spearing of desire at his loins. Her mouth was strangely tempting—cool, tender, tantalising—and as he held her closer, just in case the jade once more tried to run, he felt her slender body tense against him, felt the thrust of her nipples pressing against his chest through her thin bodice in a way that made the blood pound in his veins. Aware of some sudden, unguessed-at danger, Marcus relaxed his grip on her and fought down his arousal. She sagged in his arms, just as if he'd drawn all the strength from her slender body. Marcus felt a pang of pity for her, then reminded himself grimly that she was a pickpocket, a cheat, and no doubt a whore. He tried not to wonder again whether it was rain or tears that had gathered on her thick lashes.

'You're an excellent actress, minx,' he muttered grimly in her ear. 'But you're not getting out of this one. Two guineas were in that wallet of mine, and two guineas' worth of a kiss I shall have, if only to save us both from a night in the magistrates' cells.' In a louder voice he called out to the watching men, 'Would you leave us in peace, gents? I told you, I paid dearly for this little lightskirt!'

'You made a mistake, then,' jeered one of the men. 'Pretty she may be, but she ain't got enough flesh on her to keep a man warm for a minute, let alone a night.'

'Oh, let 'im alone,' muttered another. 'The fool's probably lost all his money gambling. He'll be glad of any doxy he can get. Come on—I'm cold and wet. The pair of 'em ain't worth the blasted trouble.'

Marcus still held on tightly to the girl even though the officers of the watch were disappearing down the street; for he could hear fresh footsteps hurrying towards them from the opposite direction. But it was only Hal pounding up the alleyway, his boots splashing in the river of water that ran down the cobbled streets, his expensive wide-brimmed hat dripping with rain. 'Marcus, there you are!' he exclaimed. 'I went after the girl's accomplice, but he bolted like a ferret. See you've managed to hang on to the girl herself, though. By all that's holy, never seen such a neat gamester in my life!'

There was almost admiration in his voice. Marcus pulled the girl back into the shelter of the doorway, out of the rain. 'So you realised she was cheating you, did you? Just a little late, if I may say so. Any ideas what to do with her? I'm wondering if I should hand her over to the magistrates for her own good...'

That started her up. 'No! You can't prove a thing! You'll not send me to gaol, you'll not!' The girl was starting to struggle wildly again, her breasts rising and falling rapidly beneath her soaking gown.

Then Hal, scratching his elegant head in some bemusement, said, 'I agree with the girl; not sure, you know, that the magistrates are the answer, dear boy. But,' he added in his droll way, 'she certainly brings to mind what we were talking of earlier.'

'What the devil are you talking about?'

Hal shrugged defensively. 'Well, with that hair of hers, and her skill at cards, you could almost dress the girl up and use her to tempt your cousin Sebastian…'

'Corbridge!' Marcus's eyes opened wide as he stared at his captive. Her ravishing blonde hair had tumbled from its pins and was glittering in the rain: *guinea-gold curls.* 'Corbridge… Yes. *Yes.* The girl's an expert at trickery. Yet with that look of wide-eyed innocence, she had both of us fooled; Hal, my friend, you've maybe hit on the answer…'

Hal was staring at him. 'But, Marcus, I didn't really mean it. Only a joke. Look at her. She's dressed like a scarecrow, swears like a trooper…'

'She's also a fine little actress,' Marcus announced. 'It was she who stole my wallet earlier this evening.'

'No!' Drawing warily nearer, Hal regarded the girl with a kind of horrified fascination. 'By God, yes, I see it now— it's the fleet-footed lad you saved from pursuit! Not at all sure, you know, that Corbridge's fancy runs in that particular direction, dear boy. But then again, his taste for whores is said to range far and wide.'

Marcus felt the girl suddenly freeze into stillness. 'Are you calling me a whore?' she breathed.

Hal stammered, 'No! Not exactly, you know, I merely suggested…' But with a last desperate burst of strength the girl had broken free, and Marcus was lunging after her, catching her round her slender waist; which was just as well because Tassie, who had hardly consumed anything all day except for one over-rich glass of wine at the Angel, suddenly swayed on her feet.

Hal called out, 'Gently there, Marcus. Go easy with her, man!'

'Trickery,' said Marcus dismissively, 'all trickery.' But even as he spoke, he had to move quickly, and was just in time to catch her as she crumpled slowly into his arms.

Chapter Four

Tassie woke to find herself in a big four-poster bed curtained with damask drapes. Feeling suddenly as if she couldn't breathe, she pushed her way out to find that it was daytime, and she was in a vast room full of dark mahogany furniture with gloomy paintings on the walls. Fear dried her throat. There was no sound at all, except for the ticking of an ormolu clock on the marble mantelshelf above the fireplace. The fingers pointed to just past three o'clock. She must have slept all night—and half the day.

She flew to the door and tried the handle. It was locked. Her panic mounting, she hurried across to the big, velvet-draped window through which the low February sun was sending slanting rays of pale afternoon light. There was no escaping this way either, for from the window it was a straight drop of thirty feet or more to the broad pavement below. *Now there's a bonebreaker of a fall,* Georgie Jay would say...

Where was she? How far away were her friends? She knew she was still in London, because beyond the huge stuccoed houses that lined this wide square she could see slate rooftops and white church spires stretching away to the familiar golden dome of St Paul's. But there was no sign at all of the seething bustle of humanity that filled the noisy streets around Covent Garden. A solitary carriage was pulling up further down the road, and a footman held open the door to let out a beautifully dressed woman and a small girl.

The way the woman held the child's hand, and smiled down at her, with love, brought a sudden ache to Tassie's heart. Then her mind was filled with other emotions, because she'd suddenly realised that she was no longer wearing Moll's shabby old gown, but was swathed in a white lawn nightdress, with lacings at her throat, and with skirts that fell down to her bare ankles. She touched it with distaste and growing alarm. Who had undressed her, and put her in this? She couldn't remember a thing about arriving at the house! But she did remember those men last night. Marcus and his fancy friend Hal. Had they brought her here? If so, *why*? Why hadn't Marcus just handed her over to the constables? Then she remembered. And felt rather sick again. She sat suddenly on the edge of the vast bed, and recalled how Marcus and his friend had been discussing her hair, her voice, her skill with cards. Talking about her—as if she was for sale.

Moll's brash voice came back to her, as she warned, *'You must have seen the way men are starting to look at her! There'll be trouble soon if you don't look out...'*

She clasped her hands together tightly. Something told her that what the men Marcus and Hal had in mind for her could be a good deal more dangerous even than being hauled up before the magistrates. Frantically she started to search the room for her shoes, her stockings, the horrible gown she'd stolen from Moll; but it was no good. Every chest, every closet was quite empty.

And besides, the door was locked.

She stood very still in the centre of the room, trying to keep calm, trying to think what her friends would do. 'Stay in charge, Tass,' Georgie Jay was always telling her. 'Size up your enemy's weakness—and remember every card that's been played in the game.'

But her game so far, with the man called Marcus, had been a simple path to disaster. Again her heart quailed within her. She'd been stupid enough—yes, and ungrateful enough—to pick his temptingly placed pocket as he hid her from the Watch yesterday—and then, as if Fortune was wreaking revenge, she'd been challenged by him to a game of piquet at the Angel. She'd recognised him immediately, of course, with his thick dark hair and his lean, hard face and his limp. A little shiver had gone through her as he assessed her. But she still hadn't been able to resist cheating him, playing a dangerous game as ever; and if it hadn't been for the place being raided she'd have escaped with her winnings, despite the fact that the man called Marcus had realised she was cheating him. But the general alarm, the rush to get out, had meant that she was trapped, literally, in her enemy's arms. And then he'd recognised her as the thief who'd taken his wallet.

He'd also assumed that she was a doxy, and that Lemuel was her keeper. Lemuel, in charge of *her*! That was a joke, but nothing else about her situation was very funny at all.

Tassie curled up, shivering, on the big bed. She couldn't help but remember the moment when Marcus had pulled her against his long, powerful body—how he'd felt dangerously strong and full of hard-packed muscle. Then he'd kissed her, so casually, as if he'd done that sort of thing with women a hundred times before... She clenched her hands tightly.

And that wasn't the worst of it. The worst of it was that she'd been wildly disturbed. Her whole body had pounded with agitation. She should have pushed him away, should have defended herself, as she had that time with Billy, but instead she'd found herself melting treacherously in his arms.

She remembered all too vividly how her small breasts had tingled, her nipples growing hard, almost painful as they were crushed against his broad chest. And all the time, as he pressed his lips mercilessly against hers, all the time, as his strong hands played across her back for the benefit of the constables, pulling her even closer, she'd felt an insistent ache of longing, a melting in the pit of her stomach, as though a flame had been kindled there...

Worst of all, though, had been the cold, shivery feeling that engulfed her when at last he let her go, and insulted her so hatefully in front of those leering constables.

They had some plan afoot, the arrogant Marcus and his friend Hal—something to do with a man called Corbridge. Then when she'd tried to run away, they'd kidnapped her and brought her here. *Why?* Oh, this was playing deeper than she'd ever intended when she planned her stunt with Lemuel last night. She had to get out of here.

Just then she heard the sound of footsteps coming towards her door. She jumped up, her arms folded defensively across her breasts as she heard a key turning in the lock. Her heart thumped so heavily she thought she might choke. The door opened, and a woman glided into the room. She wore a black gown, edged frugally with lace; her brown hair was gathered tightly at the nape of her neck. She was young, yet she was dressed like a middle-aged matron. Was she perhaps the housekeeper here? Behind her followed a thin female servant, also in black, but with a starched white apron over her skirt and a white lace cap on her head. She carried a tray of food, and her expression was dauntingly grim. But the first woman smiled at Tassie and, to Tassie's astonishment, her unremarkable face was quite transformed by the kindness that shone from within her.

'My dear,' she said softly, 'you should not have got out of bed! You should still be resting.' She turned to the maid, who had put the tray down on a small satinwood table. 'That will be all, thank you, Emilia. You may go.'

The maid gave Tassie a far from friendly look, which Tassie duly registered. Then she left, and Tassie waited, tense, silent. 'You looked so ill, my dear,' the woman was continuing, 'when Hal and Major Forrester—Marcus—brought you here last night. You need to rest. And you need plenty of good, nourishing food.'

Major Forrester. An army officer. Tassie shut her eyes and opened them, both frightened and perplexed. If Hal and Marcus had brought her here, why hadn't they told this kind woman—who clearly had authority—that Tassie was a common thief and a cheat to boot?

'We thought you might enjoy a light meal after your rest.' The woman pointed encouragingly at the tray. 'What is your name, pray?'

Tassie took a deep breath. 'Tassie. That's all—ma'am.'

'Then welcome to this house, Tassie. Hal has instructed me to look after you until you get your strength back.'

Tassie muttered, 'Saints and fiddlesticks, I don't believe—' She corrected herself rapidly. 'I mean—*why*, ma'am?'

'Oh, you poor thing, of course, you'll hardly remember! You're here because Hal and Marcus found you, hungry and near-frozen with cold, out on the streets last night. You fainted; they couldn't just leave you there.'

Tassie blinked. So the two men hadn't told this lady anything like the truth, and the omission did nothing to reassure her. She glanced quickly at the door, wondering whether to make a run for it right now. 'They have acted very—nobly,' she breathed.

Her irony was completely lost on the other woman. 'Well, naturally!' She smiled. 'Hal is sometimes rash and impetuous, but he has a most generous heart. And so, of course, has Marcus. Gracious me, here I am, rattling on, and your food is growing cold! I'll leave you to eat in peace—but first, can I let anyone know you are here? Friends, or family?'

'No one, ma'am,' said Tassie in a small voice. No one at all—she should be used to it by now, but even so she was caught unawares by the sudden ache in her throat. 'But you are kind to think of it. My—my thanks.'

The lady in black frowned, her head a little on one side. 'Strange,' she murmured. 'Hal and Marcus said you were from one of the poorest quarters of the city, but your voice, your manner of speaking, give that the lie. Surely you have not always lived in poverty?'

'I was brought up in the country,' said Tassie quickly. 'I am an orphan.'

'Ah, one hears such sad stories about orphans… Were you treated kindly?'

Tassie shrugged. 'I was fed, and given a roof over my head, ma'am.'

'I see. Tassie. *Tassie.* What an interesting name. Well, enough of my questions. Enjoy your food. I will visit you later; no doubt Marcus will also.'

The lady left the room, closing the door behind her. Tassie, bracing herself anew at the sound of Marcus's name, heard her footsteps retreating softly down the corridor, and drew a deep, deep breath to steady herself. For the kind lady had helped her more than she would ever know, in that she had forgotten to lock the door…

Marcus, who had been restlessly pacing the first-floor drawing room as the afternoon sun sank low in the sky, turned questioningly towards the black-gowned Caro Blakesley as she came to join him. Hal's sister was one of the kindest, sweetest people he knew, and the death of her husband in a riding accident a year ago was a tragedy she had borne with dignity. Now he asked her, quickly, 'Is she awake, Caro? She's not ill, is she?'

'She seems well, Marcus. I think the girl slept for so long simply because she was totally exhausted, and weak with hunger, poor thing. I took her a hot meal and told her to rest. She was most grateful.'

Marcus's grey eyes narrowed. 'Grateful? Are you sure of that?'

'Yes! Contrary to what you said, she seems to me to have a shy but sweet nature. Her name is Tassie. I was quite enchanted by—'

Marcus broke in. 'Caro. You did lock the door to her room again, didn't you?'

Caro hesitated. 'Why, no, I did not. It seems so hard to keep her a prisoner, when she is such a meek, gentle thing! She was an orphan, you know, brought up in the country...'

But Marcus was no longer listening, because he was already heading for the hallway.

He caught Tassie at the top of the stairs. She turned to run, but he was on her in seconds, grasping her firmly as her arms and legs flailed amidst the loose folds of her voluminous nightdress. Breathing hard, a little too conscious of her strikingly feminine form beneath the enveloping garment, Marcus carted her back down the corridor and threw her on to the four-poster bed, then very firmly shut the door. Outside, the February dusk was gathering into chilly darkness; he quickly closed the curtains, and lit a candle from the low-burning fire, while Tassie lay there glaring at him.

He went to stand over her, his hands on his hips, and said in a voice calculated to frighten her far more than any ranting or raving, 'I was informed that you were resting.'

'Yes. Yes, I was!'

'Caro—like her brother, Hal—is good, and kind, and far too trusting.'

Tassie heaved herself up. 'Caro—that lady—she is Hal's sister?'

'Of course. Why, what else could she be?'

Tassie muttered, 'I thought she was p'raps the housekeeper here.'

'Housekeeper!'

'Well, how was I supposed to know different? Nobody said!' She felt her heart thumping rather hard again, but tossed back her loose hair defiantly. 'Any rate, one thing's for sure: Caro is kinder than you!'

'Certainly I'm not so easily taken in by a cunning trickster.' He smiled dangerously. 'Trying to escape, were you? Decided to do a runner?'

Tassie bit her lip. She certainly wasn't going to try to run past *him*, even if he did have a limp. She was nearly as tall as Lemuel, but this man towered over her, six foot of hardened muscle, shoulders forbiddingly broad beneath his riding coat, strong booted legs set firmly apart. Major Marcus Forrester. All ready for action, she thought rather faintly. His long dark hair was tied loosely back from his face in a way that only emphasised the implacable set of his jaw, the iron glint in his grey eyes. And she couldn't help but remember his kiss… One way or another, she really was in trouble. Time for desperate measures.

Slowly she pulled herself up off the bed. She let a couple of tears pool in her eyes, then, as soon as she guessed he'd noticed them, she looked away and swallowed. 'It's a bit difficult to explain. You see, I—I was just going to look for the serving maid who brought me my food. I was hoping she would help me. It is my monthly time, sir, and—and…'

Instantly Marcus's face was all concern. He said, 'Dear God, how stupid of me. You mean Emilia: I shall fetch her to you straight away, with all that you require.'

Tassie blushed shyly and glanced up at him from beneath demurely lowered lashes. 'My thanks.'

But then, suddenly, his eyes flashed with anger and he sprang towards her. 'By God, you impudent wench,' he roared, 'is there no end to your trickery?'

He'd grabbed her by the arm, and with his free hand was grasping at the deep pockets of her nightdress. And Tassie realised with horror that he had seen, outlined against the fine lawn fabric, the little silver mirror and the gilt scent phial that she'd hidden there. She grabbed for them at the same time he did, but she was too late, and as he scooped the precious objects into his hands, Tassie dived instinctively for the door.

A futile attempt. Thrusting the objects on to a nearby table, he hauled her back, and she was overpowered by the sheer masculine force of him. He was breathing hard as he fought her into submission: every plane and angle of his lean face seemed carved in granite, and there was a dangerous light in his eyes. 'You little thief!' he exploded. 'How could you steal from Caro, who has made you a welcome guest in her house?'

She cursed her survivor's instinct to take what she could, born of years of hardship. Trying vainly to still the wild beating of her heart, Tassie gazed up at him with despairing defiance. 'I didn't know this was her house, did I?'

'Even so, this goes beyond all bounds.'

'And so do you, you're a bully and a—a *prig*!' she declared, taking refuge in attack. 'You've no right to keep me here against my will, no right at all, and you will let me go, this minute!'

He shrugged, and to Tassie's surprise, a slow smile started to soften his features as he gazed down at her. He spread his hands wide. 'Playing the street minx again? I'm not stopping you.' A positively wicked grin curved his mouth. 'But you'd not be wise to go out on the streets looking like that, I assure you.'

Bewildered by his sudden change of heart, still breathless from her outburst, Tassie followed the raking line of his hard grey eyes and looked down at herself. To her utter dismay, she realised that in the struggle for the trinkets, the laces that fastened the neck of her nightgown had come undone, leaving her bosom completely exposed. He was watching her with cynical amusement, and she gave a horrified gasp and tried to pull the fabric back across her throat. But her fingers fumbled with the unaccustomed laces, giving him time to lazily reach out his hand and brush his palm across her pink-tipped breasts; and as her nipples pulled and tightened to his touch, Tassie felt a sensation flood through her so strongly that she could scarcely stand. Like his kiss, only—only... Her breasts ached almost unbearably, and her stomach churned with dark longing. She tried to back away, but her legs were weak; she was struggling for control, yet felt quite helpless as his long fingers toyed with those incredibly sensitive crests.

And Marcus, too, was shaken. God, but she was beautiful, this girl! Common thief she might be, but she was also a young woman, and all that any man could desire; that was why the heat seared his flesh and pounded between his thighs. *Watch yourself, Marcus,* he warned himself. *Douse that flame at your loins, man, she knows exactly what she's doing.* Aloud he drawled, 'A tempting doxy, indeed, in spite of that hot temper! Well played, my resourceful vagabond. You certainly know how to distract your opponent when caught in the wrong, don't you? But you should take care, you know. Not every man would react to your teasing with such restraint.'

Tassie almost groaned with shame. He thought she'd revealed herself to him deliberately! Desperately she tried to push him away, but he knocked her hands aside, then reached with almost dismissive casualness to catch at the laces of her nightgown and proceeded, with those same long, sensitive fingers that had just tormented her so wickedly, to tie the laces into perfect bows across her throat. Tassie slapped at him blindly, overwhelmed by his nearness. 'Get your hands off me,' she faltered. 'Or I'll—I'll…'

Marcus was in control again. An iron self-control he'd learned in battle. Obediently he took a step backwards and admired his handiwork. 'You'll what, minx? Call for the constables?'

Tassie, white-faced, let her gaze swing towards the door; Marcus quickly moved to block her path. 'Oh, no. No escape that way, my dear. At least—not before I've informed you of a proposition I've got in mind for you.'

Tassie pulled herself together with an effort. 'Indeed?' she flashed back. 'A proposition? And there was I thinking you'd already made several! Let me go now; give me back my clothes, or I'll tell that kind lady, Caro, that you've tried to kidnap me!'

He smiled, his teeth white and even in the shadowy light of the fire. 'Just as I could tell her you're a thief. Save your histrionics for the low-class dives of Covent Garden, Tassie. Yes, I know your name; Caro told me. Let me repeat that I'm not in the market for light-fingered doxies.' She flinched again; he pressed on. 'But you do happen to have several qualities in which I *am* interested. Firstly, you're obviously an expert at all forms of trickery—cards, thievery, and so on. Secondly—you're rather a good little actress, aren't you? I've noticed how quickly you're able to switch from ranting hussy to poor, beleaguered innocent, from spouting street cant to quite respectable English. Tell me, where did you learn to speak so well when you've a mind to it?'

Her heart thudded again, but she tilted her chin defiantly. 'Why, sir, it just comes natural to me!' she declared, putting her hands on her hips and deliberately adopting her ripest city slang. 'Anyone can speak proper when they choose!'

'That I take leave to doubt. But now I'll move on to my third point. You, as I see it, are in deep trouble. You stole my wallet, and were cheating at the Angel; by rights you should be locked up in Newgate. Not a pretty prospect, as I'm sure you'll agree.'

Tassie did agree. She'd heard about Newgate, and the very thought of being inside that foul place made her feel quite sick. 'I thought you were talking about a proposition,' she said in a low voice. 'But it sounds more to me like some kind of threat. And I warn you, if you turn me in I'll deny everything!'

He said evenly, in a voice that made her shiver, 'You could try. But I would advise against it.' He took a few uneven paces round the room, and paused eventually with one hand on the mantelpiece, and his booted right foot on the fender. The firelight flickered over his lean, vivid face and made sparks appear to dance in his disturbing grey eyes. 'Let me take you to the heart of the matter. There is a man in London on whom I wish, very badly, to be revenged. He has several weaknesses, and I intend to attack accordingly. Firstly, he is a gambler, who cannot resist a challenge when the stakes are high. And, secondly, he has a marked liking for pretty women who are skilled at card play.'

'So I'm ruled out for certain, surely, if you are looking for someone pretty? Since you make it quite clear that I am nothing of the kind!'

She saw a half-smile flicker across his strong mouth—a dangerous, all-male smile. 'Those weren't my precise words, minx,' he softly said. 'I think, in fact, that you could be very, very pretty.'

She felt the colour rising in her cheeks. 'You jest with me,' Tassie said flatly.

'I assure you, this is no jest.' No, indeed. His voice, his expression told her he was in deadly earnest. 'To put it briefly, Tassie, you and I could help each other out, quite considerably.'

Tassie clasped her hands together tightly. 'So far I've gathered that you want me to play cards with your cousin. Sebastian Corbridge.'

She'd taken him by surprise. 'How on earth do you know his name?'

'I heard you talking about him last night, with your friend—Hal.' She looked up at him directly. 'But why bother with *me*, Marcus? Fie, it would only take a skilled card cheat one night to fleece this man Corbridge, and you must know there are plenty of those in London town! Why not look one of them up, and leave me out—' she let scorn trickle into her words '—of your petty scheme of revenge?'

Marcus was silent for a while, but he was still assessing her with those iron-hard eyes that made her feel so uneasy. At last he said, 'This isn't about me, Tassie. Corbridge, you see, has cheated not me, but my godfather, a kindly, honest old man who has no idea how to protect himself against rogues. That is why I am acting for him. I want to lay a trap for Corbridge, I want him lured into deep, deep play; and I want you to be the bait at the heart of it.'

Bait. Tassie swallowed rather hard on the sudden dryness in her throat. His coat of dark grey broadcloth had fallen open as he talked, and the moulded softness of his white silk shirt did nothing to diminish the breadth or the power of his shoulders and chest. She found her gaze flickering with some agitation over the strong muscles of his thighs beneath his tight-cut breeches and remembered a little faintly how she'd felt, all too clearly, the evidence of his arousal as he'd casually fondled her breasts.

Bait. This man wanted to make a bargain with her. He

wanted to cold-bloodedly use her to trap an enemy he despised.

Oh, this was possibly the most dangerous man she had ever met. She would have to keep her defences up, every minute, until she got well away from here. She tilted her chin in defiance, though really she felt more alone and more afraid than she had for many years. 'And how exactly were you thinking of paying me, Marcus? By the hour? By the day? How do you usually hire your—your *sluts*, pray?'

He folded his arms across his chest. 'I thought I'd reassured you several times that you're really not to my taste. I was merely offering to pay you for your time, and skills—'

Her fear was banished by anger. 'Oh, this I will not endure! You think your fancy words and fine money give you the right to insult whomsoever you please—but you've truly picked the wrong person this time, believe me, Major Forrester! Now, I'd be extremely obliged if you'd give me back my clothes and let me go, this very minute.'

'*No!*'

There was a pause. Then Marcus said slowly, regretfully, 'It really is a great pity, Tassie, but I think you'd be wise to go along with my plan.'

Tassie paled. 'Why?'

'Unfortunately, some things are beyond my power. You see, the constables have got hold of that young red-headed scamp who was with you last night.'

She was shaking her head, feeling unsteady. 'No. Lemuel got away from the Angel, I know he did. You're lying!'

He shook his head. 'He made the mistake of going back to the Angel once the fuss had died down, to look for you; that was when the constables arrested him. Lemuel's not as clever as you, is he, Tassie? He's the kind who talks too much. If he's not released pretty quickly, he could get you and all your friends into serious trouble.'

Her heart was thudding again and she felt rather sick. 'So what must I do? To help him?' *Oh, poor Lemuel, always the most loyal of friends, and 'tis all my fault...*

Marcus's eyes were hard as granite. 'I have a certain amount of influence at the Bow Street office. I could get your friend out of there, without a charge. But only if you agree to help me with my plan against Corbridge.'

Tassie gazed at him, her heart aching with distress. 'So— so you're prepared to *blackmail* me now, are you, in order to get what you want?'

'Blackmail?' he queried sharply. 'Hardly. All you have to do is dress yourself up like a lady—in clothes which I will provide—and speak charmingly, as I know very well you can. When the time is right I want you to play cards with my cousin Lord Sebastian Corbridge, making quite sure that you win; in return, I'll help your foolish friend and reward you handsomely.'

'How much?'

'I'm willing to offer you the sum of fifty guineas.'

The ground rocked beneath Tassie's feet. She had never seen so much money in her life. *Fifty guineas...* She drew a deep breath and tossed her hair back from her face. 'Aren't you afraid that I might rob and cheat *you* again, Marcus?'

Marcus laughed, and in his laughter was a sudden chill. 'No, I'm not. Not in the slightest. You see, I'll be keeping a very close eye on you, Tassie. I hold all the aces this time. From now on, don't even think of getting the better of me.'

She would think of nothing else, Tassie vowed resolutely. But her answer had to be yes. Yes, she would accept his offer—firstly, because Lemuel was in trouble, and, secondly, because this man's money, so casually offered, could mean more than he would ever guess.

It might help her to find out who she really was.

Only a few days ago, back at the Blue Bell, Tassie had

asked Georgie Jay casually, 'How would you find out, Georgie? If there was some mystery about your past? If you wanted to know where you really, truly belonged?'

Georgie Jay had frowned. 'It's the same old story if you want anything, Tass. You need money. Money for fancy investigators—money for lawyers. You'd need a whole purse-ful of guineas to go down *that* road, girl. Not thinkin' about that place you ran from all those years ago, are you now?' She'd shaken her head. And yet she was always thinking about it, always. Now, in this bedroom, alone with Marcus, she swallowed down the sudden ache in her throat. She'd known for months that her time with kind Georgie Jay and his friends could not go on for ever. *You need money...*

Bait, Marcus had said. She'd be the bait in the trap; the lure to tempt his enemy Corbridge into a deep, deep game. But once Lemuel was safe, she, Tassie, would make very sure that *she* was the one deciding on the order of play. She faced Marcus squarely, hiding all her inner turmoil like the player, the trickster he took her to be. 'Fifty guineas, you said?'

'I did.'

'And you promise to pay me as soon as I've done what you want?'

'Most certainly I promise.'

'And you'll get Lemuel away from the constables...' Tassie thrust out her hand. 'We have a bargain, Marcus, you and I.' But the touch of his warm, strong fingers as he grasped hers unsettled her anew. She dragged her hand away quickly. He proceeded to tell her then that she would be staying here, with Caro to look after her, until the time was right to tackle Corbridge; and Tassie nodded coolly, as if it were every day that she made a bargain for fifty guineas with a complete stranger. But her heart was thudding against her chest like a caged bird by the time he finally left her. And after he'd shut the door, she heard the key being turned in the lock outside.

She sat down on the bed, in a state of turmoil. The plate of food, now almost cold, reproached her from the nearby table. She reached for a chicken leg, knowing she should try to eat, but the flesh, though tender, was like ashes in her mouth.

God's teeth, but the man was a detestable bully! Was she quite mad to make such a dangerous bargain? She let the chicken leg fall back on to the plate. She knew what the real trouble was. The trouble was Marcus. When he held her, and caressed her so—so *casually*, she felt all her strength, all her determination never to be any man's plaything, never to let any man possess her, melt away like frost in the morning sunshine.

She pulled herself up and reminded herself that it wasn't only the money; she was doing this for Lemuel. Marcus had promised to get poor Lemuel away from the constables. Marcus had given her his word of honour… *No, he hadn't.*

And she remembered now what the other man, Hal, had said outside the Angel: *I went after the girl's accomplice, but he bolted like a ferret.*

She stood up, her face growing stormy. Had Lemuel really come back to look for her, as Marcus said? Or—was Marcus *lying* about Lemuel?

It might have been some consolation to Tassie to know that Marcus was equally in a state of turmoil. He was no stranger to the favours of beautiful women; so how was it that he'd been aroused far more than was good for him by this girl of the streets, this streetwise, dishonest wench called—of all the ridiculous names—Tassie? All right, so it was an understandable male reaction to have instantly felt his loins stirring at the glimpse he got of her slender, burgeoning female body beneath her thin lawn gown, and at the way her small, high breasts responded to his touch even as she hurled insults at him. Yet he found her a complete paradox, for in spite of her scruffy appearance she gave an impression of utter innocence, and of underlying refinement as well!

But that illusion must be as false as the rest of her. She'd told him she was no whore; yet how could she be innocent, or of gentle birth, living the life she'd led? Marcus set his mouth in a hard line as he pulled on his greatcoat and prepared to go out. His tactics against her were perfectly justified; she was simply a clever minx, well taught by someone. His wits must have been addled by Philippa's betrayal. She too had been soft and sweet in his arms before he left for the Americas, and her kisses had been warm and full of promise.

Marcus pushed Philippa grimly to the back of his mind for now and turned his thoughts, as he left the big house, to Lord Sebastian Corbridge. Corbridge was the enemy against whom he must plan his tactics step by step, whatever the cost. And the wench Tassie?

Why, she would be the ace in Marcus's hand. Nothing less—and definitely nothing more.

Chapter Five

It was later that same night. The grandfather clock in the hallway of the house in Portman Square had just struck eleven, and Hal Beauchamp was in the ground-floor study, pacing anxiously up and down. He froze when he heard the slam of the big front door, then hurried quickly into the hall. 'Marcus. In here, man. What have you been up to?'

Marcus had already shrugged off his caped greatcoat and hung it on the mahogany coatstand. His leather riding boots echoed on the polished floor as he followed Hal into his study.

'Reacquainting myself with the London gambling haunts,' he answered as soon as Hal had shut the door. 'And I've learnt that Sebastian Corbridge has taken to frequenting Lady Amanda Sallis's fashionable little gaming house in Albemarle Street.'

Hal poured his friend a glass of brandy. 'The play there is deep, if I remember correctly. And Lady Sallis and her young female assistants are all extremely pretty, and use their wiles to encourage the punters. Tell me, what game does Corbridge prefer?'

Marcus took the brandy, but didn't drink. 'Piquet, for the

moment. They say he's playing carelessly. The other night he went under by almost two thousand, boasting as he did so that his expectation of Lornings in the autumn should cover any debts.'

'The devil he did,' breathed Hal softly. 'Still thinking of setting up the girl as bait, my friend?'

Marcus sipped his brandy, but his eyes never left Hal's face. 'Not having second thoughts, are you, Hal? After all, it was your idea.'

'I know.' Hal fingered the stem of his glass carefully. 'But I'm not at all sure that I was in earnest, I must confess. And Caro's been lecturing me. Keeps saying how sweet Tassie is, and how much she admires our honourable intentions regarding her—in other words, my sister hopes we aren't planning any mischief with the girl.'

Marcus said shortly, 'By rights the wench should be in Newgate. She'll have been play-acting again for your sister, doing her best to touch Caro's tender heart—' He broke off. 'You didn't tell your sister what we were planning, did you?'

Hal gazed at his old friend steadily. 'Oh, don't worry, dear boy. I've stuck to our original story—how the girl's a poor, starving waif without a home, and we've decided to keep her here for a few days until she's recovered her strength. I think Caro accepted all that, though she's uneasy. She says, and I know what she means, that in spite of everything, Tassie has a kind of underlying—*gentility*—'

'Oh, no. Oh, no.' Marcus shook his dark head and started his uneven pacing of the room again. 'Don't let your sister be taken in, Hal. Don't *you* be taken in! That girl is a devil of a fine actress, which is just what I want. Just what I *need* to wreck Corbridge's vile plans.'

'You're quite sure,' said Hal carefully, 'that she's willing? That she knows what's involved?'

Marcus laughed shortly. 'Oh, she's willing all right. The

mention of fifty guineas made her eyes light up, believe me.'
Marcus didn't mention his threat about Lemuel, because in
fact he and Hal hadn't seen Tassie's nervous young friend
since he'd hotfooted it from the Angel. Marcus felt uncomfortable about the lie, but it had served its purpose, hadn't it?
First thing tomorrow he'd tell Tassie that her lanky companion was free. And then—then, Marcus would set his plan in
motion.

The girl was a superb little trickster, no doubt about it.
She'd fooled Caro, and she'd—almost—fooled Hal. So much
the better for his plan. He would train her in the ways of the
gentry—she'd be a quick learner, of that he was certain—
then set her up in some tasteful satin-strewn boudoir as one
of those alluring, faintly mysterious ladies on the fringes of
fashion who ran their own discreet little gaming establish-
ments in town. And the trap for Corbridge would be set…

But already he'd underestimated his young recruit. For
just at that moment there was a knock on the study door;
Hal went to open it, and was surprised to see the housemaid
Emilia standing there, her sharp face agitated beneath her
lace cap.

'Sir,' she addressed Hal, wringing her fingers, 'it's that
young madam in the guest chamber, sir. Oh, I knew she'd be
trouble, the minute I laid eyes on her! And now she's—*gone*!'

Marcus became dangerously still. 'Gone?'

'Vanished, sir! Her room's empty, and that bed, it's never
bin slept in—I always said the young minx should never be
let inside this house.'

Marcus drew in his breath swiftly, remembering the valuables Tassie had earlier stuffed into the pockets of her gown.
Hal, looking bewildered, exclaimed, 'But she retired to bed
two hours ago! And I asked you to go to her, Emilia, to see
that she had everything she might require…'

'I did go up, Master Hal, I swear to God I did! Checked if there was anything she wanted, like you said!'

Hal said brusquely, 'You were kind to her, I hope?'

Emilia sniffed. 'As kind as one could be, sir, to a baggage like that. She said—quite rude to me, she was—that all she wanted was to be left alone, in peace. So I left her.'

'And you locked the door again, as we instructed?'

'Yes! I locked it real careful, sir!'

'You can't have done. You can't have done!' exclaimed Hal, pacing the room in agitation.

It was Marcus who said with an effort at calmness, 'All right, Emilia. Knowing the girl's tricks as I do, I rather suspect she'd have fooled any of us.' He turned to Hal. 'Let's go up and take a look around her room. You never know, there might be some clue as to where she's gone.'

But it was a waste of time, Marcus knew it already, as the two of them strode up the wide, curving staircase towards Tassie's empty bedchamber with Emilia fretting at their heels. If the minx had chosen to run off—in her *nightgown?*—he wouldn't put it past her—then there was nothing, absolutely nothing he could do to bring her back. She'd have returned to her low-life friends, of course. She'd find the lad Lemuel with them, safe and sound, and she'd realise that Marcus's threats had been lies.

Marcus knew that he'd make other plans, would find some other way to defeat Corbridge. But even so he felt ridiculously low in spirits as he gazed around that empty room. At least it didn't look as if she'd stolen anything, for the little silver hand-mirror and the scent phial were still on the dressing table where they belonged. For a moment or two he fingered the keyhole in the door that Emilia swore she'd locked. Then his eyes were drawn suddenly to something that glittered on the floor.

He stooped to pick it up. It was a hairpin, twisted into a strange shape. He said to Emilia, 'Is this yours?'

'It could be, sir!' She looked at him in some surprise at his question. ''Tis only a hairpin. They fall out all the time, they do...'

'Damnation,' muttered Marcus, 'damnation—' And then he broke off, because all three of them had become aware of an explosion of confused noise coming from somewhere below—the sound of the heavy front door banging shut, of running footsteps, of voices shrilly raised. And, incredibly, the sound of a bird squawking. Hal, muttering, 'What in God's name is *that*?' rushed out along the passageway to the top of the stairs and leaned on the galleried balustrade to peer down into the gloom of the great hall below. Then his shoulders started to shake with laughter.

'Marcus,' he called to his friend, 'you'll never believe this. Come and take a look.'

With a feeling of foreboding, Marcus hurried to Hal's side and gazed down. Chaos appeared to have broken loose. Anxious servants were pouring out from their quarters at the rear of the big house, some of them in night attire, waving their arms and shouting. One of them—Marcus thought it was the butler, Sansom—was even brandishing a broom.

Above them, wheeling and circling round the lofty hall with plumage as bright as a jewel and a squawk as piercing as a bullet, was a bird. A red-and-green parrot. And down below, in the big hallway, at the centre of the chaos, was the girl, identifiable immediately by her tumbling golden locks, though he couldn't see very much of the rest of her, because she was clad in one of Hal's elegant greatcoats, its hem trailing heavily over some outsized boots that quite dwarfed her small feet. She was pushing her way with determination through the mêlée of shouting servants, and striding up the broad staircase towards the airborne parrot, quite heedless of

Marcus and Hal gazing speechlessly down at her. Halfway up, where the stairs turned in a sweeping curve, she hitched up her coat and flung herself astride the banister. And there she perched, precariously balanced above a twenty-foot drop, while reaching out coaxingly to the cackling bird that flapped maddeningly just out of her reach. 'Here, Edward! Here!' she crooned.

Hal's laughter had died some time ago. 'God. She'll break her neck,' he muttered.

Marcus had already decided that was *not* going to happen—at least not in his good friend Hal's house. His face as dark as thunder, he leaped down the stairs two at a time, ignoring the frantic jarring to his wounded leg, but Tassie saw him coming and teetered dangerously as she made one last effort to reach out for the parrot.

Marcus got there just in time to grab her, and pulled her back so hard over the banister that she fell awkwardly against him.

'Let me *go*, you—you stuffed-shirt bully!' She pummelled furiously at his chest, hampered by the long sleeves of the greatcoat she wore. 'I almost had him then, but you frightened him, you great brute!'

'Not half as much as I'm going to frighten you,' said Marcus. He was aware of Hal hurrying downstairs past him to dismiss the gawping servants. Caro seemed, thank God, to have slept through it all—fortunate that her chamber was at the other side of the house. The parrot, muttering soft protests to itself at all the commotion, was now clinging agilely, almost upside down, to the massive gilt frame that surrounded an oil portrait of Hal's revered grandfather.

'That thing,' continued Marcus, nodding grimly at the bird's antics. 'How the devil did it get into the house?'

'He's not a thing,' declared Tassie, 'he's Edward, he's mine, and I won't, I won't be without him!'

Marcus was still holding her. 'I suppose you've been back to your low-life friends?'

'What if I have? I've done no harm, and neither has Edward,' she flashed back. 'I just meant to collect him and his cage and bring him back to that horrible, quiet room upstairs for company. 'Tis not my fault the place is in such a silly uproar!'

'The main door was locked for the night,' pointed out Marcus. 'As was the door of your chamber.' There was a silence; he gazed down into those green eyes that were so fathomless, so unsettling.

'Locks ain't everything.' She shrugged.

He'd been right, then, about the hairpin. Were there any tricks she didn't know? 'So you add the picking of locks to your other accomplishments, do you?'

'It comes in useful!' retorted Tassie defensively.

'I'll bet it does.'

'If poor Edward hadn't escaped from under my dratted coat as I opened the door—'

'I beg your pardon,' Marcus interrupted. 'That is Hal's coat, I think.'

'Very well, then, Hal's dratted coat. If he hadn't escaped—'

'You mentioned a cage. Why wasn't the bird in it?'

'He was!' She flung open the voluminous coat to reveal a small wicker carrier hooked to her belt. 'But look, he's pecked the door open, he does that sometimes, 'cos he doesn't like being locked up... Why, normally he's so quiet and peaceful, you wouldn't even know he was there!'

As the bird pranced around the portrait uttering devilish cackles, Marcus found this exceedingly hard to believe. 'Really? The bird certainly matches you in his squawking,' he observed.

The girl gazed up at him bitterly, her pointed little chin

raised in stubborn defiance. 'At least—at least I'm *truthful*, about really important things,' she declared.

'What on earth do you mean?'

'You said that the constables had taken Lemuel, and that if I helped you, you would get him out of trouble. But that was a lie, wasn't it, to force me to do what you wanted!' She put her hands on her hips. 'Aren't you ashamed of yourself?'

He knew she was a scoundrel and a thief, but, yes, he felt astonishingly guilty at that moment. In an effort to sound nonchalant he said, 'Well, if that's your opinion of me I'm surprised you bothered to come back.'

'Of course I came back,' she retaliated. 'We made our bargain, didn't we? About the money? We shook hands on it! Only—if you make me get rid of Edward, then I swear that I'll leave for good!'

He felt a curious sense of surprise, almost of pleasure, that she'd decided to return. She was obviously going to be trouble, but at least she was also proving a diversion. He said, 'Yes, we made our bargain. And I'm glad you've come back, even if you do intend to saddle me with that crazy bird.'

'I keep telling you. I couldn't leave Edward.'

Marcus suddenly realised that beneath her brazen demeanour, her face was quite white with tiredness. There were dark shadows beneath her huge eyes, and her voice trembled as she went on, 'He would pine to death without me. He'd think I'd abandoned him, you see. And—and I had to see Georgie Jay, to tell him and everyone else that I'd be away for a while, otherwise they'd worry...'

'Georgie Jay?' He gritted the name out. 'Is he another of your low-life friends? Whoever he is, I hope you didn't even think of telling him what you were up to, Tassie. Because if you did our agreement is off. Do you understand?'

'Yes! I understand!' she retorted bitterly. 'And I didn't tell my friends *anything*, you bully! Because that's what they are—friends. And Georgie Jay—he's like an older brother to me...' Her green eyes filled with sudden tears, and abruptly she swung her head away from him so that he wouldn't see them. She added in a low voice, 'How long before we can begin our business, Marcus? Will we start tomorrow?'

'Not exactly. We might have to wait just a little longer.'

She exploded at that. 'God's teeth, why wait at all for a session at card play? You know how good I am!'

'Firstly,' he answered steadily, 'you fooled Hal at the Angel, but you didn't fool me. I've got to make sure you're absolutely ready to play the part. Secondly, Sebastian Corbridge is going to be even more pressed for money than usual by the next quarter-day, because the rent on his expensive house in Brook Street will be due. So the prospect of easy winnings—presented by *you*, Tassie, armed with a purseful of guineas that I will provide as stake, and the promise of much more where that came from—will appeal to him at a time when he's most likely to be tempted into reckless play.'

Tassie frowned. 'When's quarter-day, Marcus?'

'The twenty-fifth of March. Lady Day.'

'Five weeks,' she breathed. 'Five whole weeks...' She looked almost—afraid. Oh, thought Marcus suddenly, she deserves a better life than she's led... And immediately his inner self reproached him: *Are you going to give her a better life, then, Marcus? Are you?*

Suddenly the bird, Edward, swooped down from the high picture frame, anointing the gloomy painting with a fresh deposit in passing, and glided to a practised halt on Tassie's shoulder. She reached up to stroke the bird's soft, turquoise breast. 'There, Edward, there. It's all right now.'

The parrot regarded Marcus with its head on one side, its bright eyes beady with dislike. *'The devil damn thee black, thou cream-faced loon,'* it cackled.

'*Macbeth,*' explained the girl tonelessly. 'It's one of his favourites. He knows a lot of Shakespeare, from old Matt.'

Marcus felt quite dazed. 'I'm sure he does,' he said. 'You'd better go to your room now, Tassie, and catch up on your sleep. We've got a lot to sort out tomorrow. One of my first tasks is to find you somewhere safe to stay.'

'You mean I'm not staying *here*?' The girl's head flew up and Edward hopped about, agitated, on her shoulder. 'I thought it was part of our bargain that I stayed here!'

'What, and plague my generous friends to death? I hardly think so.'

'But I don't want to be anywhere except London! I don't want to leave London!'

'Or Georgie Jay?' demanded Marcus. 'I'm paying you to work for me, Tassie, and paying you well. Does it matter where you stay?'

She shook her head, her dishevelled blonde curls rippling around the collar of Hal's coat in the shadowy candlelight. She said, 'No. No, I suppose it doesn't really matter where. I need the money, you see.'

She was turning to go up the stairs, dejectedly. But Marcus, a sudden thought striking him, caught her by the shoulder. 'Wait,' he said. 'You're not planning anything with your friends, are you? Not going to let them in secretly in the next night or two to strip this place bare?'

She gazed up at him with something very like scorn in her eyes. 'What do you take me for? Don't worry, Marcus!' She regarded him almost pityingly. 'You must be truly desperate to get this money back for your precious godfather, when 'tis plain you can scarcely bring yourself to tolerate me for an instant!' Suddenly her eyes opened, very wide. 'This money. The money of your godfather's, that you want to win back, from your enemy Lord Corbridge. Let me hazard a guess. It is to be *yours*, is it not? Yes, that must be it!' She clapped her hands together. 'It is your inheritance, and that is why you will do anything—even put up with *me*, whom you plainly despise—to get it back.'

Marcus said strongly, 'I want it for my godfather, to restore him to his rightful position.'

'But you are his heir, aren't you?' Tassie gazed at him with her bright, clear eyes. 'You do not deny it... Do you know, I almost feel sorry for your cousin Lord Corbridge.'

'Tassie—'

But she had snatched herself away from his grip. 'No need to lock me in,' she said in a low voice. 'I keep my promises, Marcus. I only hope that you do, too.' And slowly, with the big greatcoat trailing ridiculously at her heels and the bird perched precariously on her shoulder, she made her way up the remainder of the stairs and along the shadowed corridor to her bedroom.

Marcus felt as if he'd started a rash campaign and had just lost the first battle. As he went tiredly down the stairs, he saw that the bird had left tell-tale splashes not only on the oil painting, but also over the carved banister rail and the marble tiles of the hall.

Hal was waiting for him in the hall below. He must have overheard something of their conversation, because he said, 'You needn't take her anywhere, Marcus. You know we've always told you to consider this house your home.'

Marcus eyed some green feathers drifting in the candle-light and sighed. 'Your generosity, my friend, exceeds all bounds as usual. But if Corbridge heard from the London gossips that I'd taken a half-criminal little sharper under my wing, my plan would be all to pieces before it began.'

Hal nodded, frowning. Then his kind face brightened. 'Why don't we say that she's a distant relative of yours, a poor cousin perhaps, who's come for an unexpected visit?

They'd never realise her true past, or her skill at card play; and the story will keep the gossips away, if only for a while.'

'A while is all I need. A few weeks, no more.'

'Then she will stay.' Hal hesitated. 'She looked so tired just then, Marcus, and so—alone. Do you really think you can make this thing work?'

'I have to. I have to, for my godfather's sake.'

'And do you think the girl is capable of playing her part?'

'I do,' responded Marcus firmly. 'I'd guess she's already planning what to do with that money I've promised her. And she's a cunning little thing—an excellent actress, sharp and resourceful. Yes. I think we can do it.'

'I know you'll take care. But the girl—well, she might be a rogue, but nevertheless she could come to real harm in the kind of circles you're planning to place her in. You don't intend to...' he frowned '...to let Corbridge actually get his hands on her, do you?'

Marcus was surprised at the strength of his reaction to the thought of Sebastian Corbridge's notoriously lecherous hands going anywhere near the girl Tassie. 'I want her to play cards with him,' he said vehemently, 'not seduce him!'

Hal nodded, but his expression was still uncertain.

Tassie, too, was full of doubts. The fire in her room had died, and the sheets rustled with crisp unfriendliness as she climbed into the big bed. She longed suddenly for the constant racket of Drury Lane, the blandishments of the late-night pie-and-ballad sellers, the shouts of the sailors and young gallants as they tottered noisily from one alehouse to the next.

At least she had Edward. She'd fixed him up a perch beside the mantelpiece, using a coatstand, and now he was preening his feathers and crooning to himself in consolation for his earlier fright.

She'd lied to Marcus about saying goodbye to Georgie Jay, because in fact she hadn't seen Georgie Jay at all. By the time she'd got to the Blue Bell, it was late, for it had taken her a long time to fiddle the lock with the hairpin Emilia had dropped, and then she'd had to hunt for something to wear. Hal's coat and boots in the downstairs hall had been all she could lay her hands on. Easing open the heavy front door had been no simple task either as she tried not to disturb the silence of the big house.

She'd made her way to Covent Garden by a mixture of walking, running and tricking a couple of sedan-bearers into giving her a lift. She'd had to run really fast from the sedan-bearers, because they had been mad as hell once they realised she had no intention of paying them for the ride. And when she got to the Blue Bell at last, she found that Georgie Jay wasn't there. He'd gone—with Moll, naturally—to drink ale and eat mutton pie at Bob Derry's Cider Cellar. He wasn't even worried, it seemed, by Tassie's disappearance.

And Lemuel—Lemuel, who Marcus told her had been arrested by the constables—was in the taproom with Billy and old Matt, busy in a game of whist!

'Lemuel,' she'd breathed gladly, 'oh, Lemuel, you're safe!'

''Course I am,' he retorted, lifting his eyebrows in surprise at her outburst. 'Though I had to run like the blazes to get away from them Horneys outside the Angel! It were a daft idea of yours, Tassie—don't you involve me in anythin' like that again, you hear?'

Then he went back to his cards. She gazed at them, speechless. They didn't ask one question about how she'd escaped from the raid, or where she'd been ever since. All they were interested in was getting on with their game.

Then old Matt said in a kindlier tone, 'You look all in, lass. Best go to your bed, and get some rest before morning.'

'Aye,' put in Billy eagerly, 'there's someone comin' to see you tomorrow, Tass!'

Matt looked at him quickly, warningly, and Tassie caught that look. 'Who?' she demanded. 'Who's he talking about, Matt?'

Old Matt sighed and said, 'Well, you'll know about it soon enough. Moll's brother and his missus are coming up to London for a day or two. Moll told them about you, and they want to meet you. Just for a chat, that's all.'

Lemuel was looking at her a little forlornly now and pulling his hair into fierce red tufts. It appeared that Georgie Jay had decided her fate in her absence. Tassie felt a tight constriction round her heart. She smiled brightly at them all, as if she didn't care that her old world was falling to pieces. 'Very well,' she said. 'I'll leave you to get on with your game.'

And she'd gone upstairs, as if on her way to her bed, but instead she had fetched Edward in his small travelling-cage, and hurried down the back stairs so no one would see her. She made her way back to Portman Square, this time sneaking a ride on the rear of a heavy carriage rumbling westwards, while Edward grumbled away from under Hal's coat.

Nowhere to turn. Nowhere to turn, the big wheels had chided mockingly in her ears.

Now she stirred restlessly as the cold moonlight stole through a gap in the heavy curtains and cast alarming shadows across her bed. She had made a bargain with the man Marcus, and she was going to keep it. But the thought of being in Marcus's company day after day set up stirrings of unease all through her body. With burning cheeks she remembered the way he'd crushed her in his arms and kissed her; the way he'd brushed his palms across her breasts. He'd been a soldier, an officer; clearly he was used to being in charge, to making judgements about people. And he thought she, Tassie, was a low-life trickster. A slut, he'd called her.

She'd learned years ago what happened between men and women when their passions were stirred. When Georgie Jay's band had been staying on a farm, helping with the harvest, she'd been sent to fetch twine from the barn loft. Suddenly she'd heard soft womanly cries from below her and, peering down, she saw a dairymaid lying with a farmhand in the hay, her hands grabbing fiercely at the man's brawny back as he kissed her hungrily. Tassie had watched, frozen, as the man had loosened the girl's laced bodice, flicking his tongue and his lips over her breasts; then he'd fumbled with her skirts, and his own breeches, before beginning to thrust with rhythmic strokes against the woman's hips.

Tassie couldn't get down from the loft, or they'd have seen her. At one point the man had pulled away, muttering something, and Tassie had glimpsed, in full arousal, his rigid manhood—that part of his body that women were always whispering and giggling about. Then the dairymaid reached for him and stroked him there, making little sighing noises in the back of her throat before clutching him to her again, her eyes closed, her hips urging him on. Realising they were quite beyond noticing her, Tassie had bolted down the ladder outside into the blinding sun, and stood there trembling.

That night, as the farm labourers all had supper, she had heard the dairymaid dismissed as a slut—and the one who insulted her most was the very man who'd lain with her. From that incident, and from everything else that went on around her, Tassie had learned that it was dangerous ever to get involved with men. Men would flatter you and caress you until they got just what they wanted, and the gentry were no different. She had to remember that the kiss last night would have meant nothing to Marcus. Why, he might even be laughing about it now, with his friend Hal!

And yet—the money he had promised her. *You'd need a whole purseful of guineas for that, girl,* Georgie Jay had told her when she'd tentatively talked about solving the mystery of her past. Her mind full of fevered thoughts, she drifted at last into a light and restless sleep, dreaming that she was a child again, and there was some lesson she had failed to learn from her schoolroom books, and so she was to be beaten when daylight came; but she was wakened when she heard a strange noise somewhere in the distance. Ever alert to night sounds that could be a warning of danger, she sat up quickly and listened. The sound of footsteps, slow and uneven, going to and fro, to and fro...

Whispering to Edward, who was cocking one beady eye at her from his perch, to be silent, she went to her door and opened it softly. Someone in the hall below was as wide awake as she was.

She hurried to the banister and peered over. Marcus was down there, pacing the hallway; and his face was a mask of pain each time he put his weight on his left leg. She watched for a moment, her heart suddenly torn with instinctive pity. She'd already guessed he was the sort of man who would endure any amount of pain silently, and ask for no help. She watched him a moment longer, in the near-darkness—only a single candle burned, in a holder inside the big front door— and then she began to return, quietly, to her room. But he looked up. He had sharp hearing, even sharper eyes. She must remember that for the future. 'Tassie!' he called out. 'Is that you?'

She turned back reluctantly.

'It's all right,' he called again, more gently this time. 'I just wanted a few words. Come down here, will you?'

She walked down the stairs in her nightgown and stood facing him, her mouth set stubbornly in anticipation of fresh trouble.

'Can't you sleep?' he asked, almost kindly.

She was taken aback by this show of concern. *Be careful.*

Remember that he thinks he has bought you. 'I was asleep, yes. But—I heard someone walking around.'

'I woke you. I'm sorry. Confound it—' He sat down, rather suddenly, on one of the chairs placed against the wall, and she realised that his forehead was beaded with sweat.

'You're in pain,' she said swiftly. 'Have you seen a physician?'

'Of course.' He grimaced. 'It's just a matter of time, they say; they also tell me to rest, as if that were an option... Seems you're a light sleeper, Tassie, like me. Look, I've been wanting to apologise properly. About your friend Lemuel. It was wrong of me to lie. I'm sorry.'

She shrugged and looked away. 'I suppose—most people would do the same. If they wanted something really badly, that is.'

Still seated, he was gazing up at her intently. 'But would *you*, Tassie? Tell lies, I mean, to someone who trusted you?'

She hesitated. This was a different Marcus. A man she could almost be friends with. She replied steadily, 'You know already that I'll take advantage of people who've got money and who look down on me and my friends. But, no, I wouldn't lie to someone who trusted me.'

'I wonder how many people have *your* trust, Tassie? I wonder who, exactly, you are?'

She didn't reply, but her heart hammered a warning as his gaze held hers. *Street thief. Bait in the trap.* In the silence, the hall clock ticked steadily.

'Well,' he said at last, 'I've disturbed your rest and soon I'll be disturbing everybody else if I keep up my midnight marching. Off you go, back to your bed. And I'll see you in the morning.'

He stood up, but sat down again quickly, his face contracted with pain. 'Just a muscle,' he muttered, 'sometimes it seizes up...'

Tassie was instantly on her knees beside him. 'I can see it!' she declared. The long muscle of his injured thigh was jumping, the nerves on edge beneath his tight breeches. 'Let me ease it for you.' As she spoke she was already starting to knead his thigh, using her small, sensitive fingers to probe and soothe. 'Tell me if I hurt you,' she instructed him. 'Tell me at once.'

Marcus somehow managed to swallow his surprise at her unhesitating response. Managed to fight down, too, his reaction to such a sudden and intimate contact. Because the touch of her fingers was working magic; beneath her light but sure touch the pain was vanishing, and the sweet scent of her hair, so close to him, was intoxicating...

'You're not hurting me,' he said. 'Far from it.'

She gazed up at him with those clear lambent eyes. 'Were you injured in the war, Marcus?'

'Yes, it's a flesh wound, it's nothing; should have healed weeks ago...'

'You probably didn't rest it enough.' Tassie's hands were still busy manipulating the knotted flesh that had tensed with pain; her face was all concern. He realised she'd completely forgotten that he was a stranger who'd hired her. To her he was someone in distress, who merited her help. Unfortunately Marcus found himself battling to suppress his physical response to such a sudden and intimate contact.

'There!' she was breathing with satisfaction. 'I *think* some of the tightness has gone. This is what the Romanies do, when one of their kind is taken with this sort of pain...'

'Tassie.' His voice was curter than he'd intended. 'Tassie, you'd better stop. *Now.*'

She looked at him in dismay. 'Oh, Marcus, have I hurt you?'

'No. Far from it indeed.'

Her face was crestfallen. 'Then—is it because I mentioned my travelling days?'

'Your travelling days have nothing whatever to do with it.' Deliberately he moved her hand away, forcing a smile. 'And I'm grateful to your Romany friends. That's really much better, believe me.'

'Then I'll carry on—'

'No, damn it!' Her eyes were shocked. He stood up, trying his leg carefully, and went on, more gently, 'Thank you, Tassie. You're certainly full of surprises.'

She stood up also, embarrassed and shy. 'I don't like to see anyone in pain,' she muttered. 'Or any animal. Not ever.'

'I've grown rather too used to witnessing pain, I'm afraid. War toughens you.'

Her eyes were dark with sympathy. 'I suppose it *has* to, or you couldn't do what you have to do. But you went to war because you thought it was right, didn't you, Marcus?'

'Did I?' His question was mild, but his eyes were hard. 'That was the trouble: I'm not sure that it *was* right. I'm not sure that we should have been fighting in America. That country wants, and probably deserves, its freedom, and sooner or later it will get it.'

'So you're not going back, then, to be a soldier?'

'At the moment,' he said, 'they wouldn't have me, I'm not fit enough.' He put his hands gently on her shoulders—a mistake, her skin was warm and soft beneath her nightgown; he pulled away quickly. 'Listen, Tassie. About our agreement. I'll release you from it now, if you like. You don't have to stay. You don't have to do what we agreed. I lied to you, about Lemuel, and that made our agreement a false one.'

She froze then. 'But—I thought we had a bargain!'

'Of course,' he said hastily. 'I just wanted to say—'

'We agreed, Marcus. We decided. On everything!' She looked quite genuinely dismayed.

'A bargain, Tassie!' he vowed quickly.

Her expression instantly relaxed. He reached out his hand, and she took it, then snatched her fingers away as if his touch burned her. 'A bargain,' she breathed. And she went slowly off up the stairs, an upright, lonely figure.

Marcus watched her go, shaking his head in perplexity. Had she truly not realised what she was doing to him, when she stroked his thigh like that? She had lived her life in the company of the lowest of the low. And yet she had seemed, when she knelt at his side, genuinely innocent of what effect such an intimate touch would have on a red-blooded male... She was either innocent—or she was very clever. But would she be a match for Corbridge?

Sighing, he set off to his own bedroom, and realised that this was the first day for a long time that his thoughts had not been dominated by Philippa.

But he thought about her now. For two years, at war in a foreign country where the very soil had stunk of men's dying, his memories of Philippa and her sweet love for him had guided him homewards.

Oh, yes. He thought about her now.

It was a little after midnight that same evening, and Lord Sebastian Corbridge was at the exclusive little establishment in Albemarle Street that Marcus had mentioned to Hal. It was a popular destination among the gentry, with everything on offer that could contribute to a man's well-being: good wine, delectable suppers, and plenty of deep play expertly conducted by Lady Sallis's charming young hostesses, who would, for a certain rate of pay, provide rather more intimate companionship in the private rooms upstairs.

Sebastian Corbridge, who'd just gone down several hundred guineas in a game of piquet, was not in the best of moods. And his brooding thoughts about his cousin Marcus did not help.

Several of his acquaintances were here tonight, the same men who'd been in the club yesterday evening when Marcus had burst in and threatened Corbridge so vilely. Curse Marcus, for his damned impudence! People had been reminding him of the unpleasant incident wherever he went, and Corbridge had tried his best to shrug it off. But the memory of Marcus's hard, uncompromising face, of his primed soldier's hand ready and waiting on the hilt of his sword, continued to unsettle him.

'What are you going to do, Corbridge?' his cronies had probed avidly. 'Marcus Forrester insulted you in public. God's blood, man, he threatened you!'

'You should report him to the magistrates,' drawled another. 'Get him hauled up before the beaks and drummed out of town for disturbing the peace.'

Lord Sebastian Corbridge saw the light of malevolence in their eyes, and knew that secretly they were all enjoying his discomfiture, damn them. He'd worried all night about Marcus's reappearance in London. Sebastian knew only too well that the way he'd encouraged Sir Roderick Delancey, Marcus's godfather, to gamble his way into massive debt, then to sign that formal letter handing over the Lornings estate to Sebastian if Roderick couldn't pay off those debts by September, might not bear too close a scrutiny. Corbridge had planned on his cousin Marcus being away in the American war for much, much longer. Then Lornings would have been safely in Corbridge's hands, well before Marcus returned. If indeed he did return. Many did not.

But Marcus was back, damn him, and his injured leg certainly did nothing to reduce his formidable demeanour in Corbridge's worried eyes. Nevertheless Corbridge had reacted nonchalantly to his friends' probing questions. 'I wouldn't dream of lowering myself to his level,' he'd drawled, taking a delicate pinch of snuff.

'But he challenged you to a duel,' Viscount Lindsay maliciously reminded him.

'A duel? A tavern brawl is more his scene. And it certainly isn't mine, my friends. Why…' and he smiled round at them all '…think of the damage he might do to this coat of mine. The Mechlin lace alone cost two hundred guineas!'

Unfortunately this sally was received with frowns, not laughs. 'But surely you won't just let him get away with it, Corbridge?'

'No,' breathed Lord Sebastian Corbridge, 'no, my friends, I *won't* just let him get away with it.'

In fact, he'd already made up his mind that if Marcus proved too troublesome, he would pay some city toughs, perhaps some ex-Bow Street Runners who knew what they were doing, to rough him up and spoil that handsome face of his for good. For Marcus was, undoubtedly, handsome. And a reminder of that fact was the last straw in a long and difficult day.

Corbridge had just been debating whether to risk another game or cut his losses and leave, when the proprietress of this discreet establishment, Lady Sallis herself, came over to him. Corbridge's spirits rose, until he realised she'd come to ask him about bloody Marcus Forrester.

'I hear that your military cousin is back in town, Lord Sebastian,' she'd said softly, moving her fan just a little to one side so he could see the dimples that had intrigued many men adorning her knowing smile. 'Perhaps you would arrange a meeting for me.'

'With *Marcus*?' Corbridge hadn't troubled to keep the scorn from his voice. Scorn mingled with disappointment, because he'd had his eyes on Lady Amanda Sallis himself. She was a wealthy, intriguing widow, not yet thirty, with raven curls and mischievous if rather hard blue eyes; and everyone knew that alongside her rather successful private gaming establishment she was not averse to conducting spirited adventures of the amorous kind with a favoured few. 'I hadn't realised, my lady,' Corbridge went on rather bitterly, 'that you had a taste for the low-life.'

Lady Sallis lifted up her finely arched eyebrows in mock surprise. 'Come, now, Lord Sebastian,' cajoled Lady Sallis. 'Major Marcus Forrester is hardly what could be called low-life, surely? He is your cousin, after all. His great-grandfather—as you never cease to remind everyone with reference to yourself—was the illustrious Earl of Stansfield.' She wafted her fan gently. 'And he is *remarkably* handsome.'

'I suppose he is,' replied Corbridge with studied acidity, 'if you have a taste for ex-army men with no culture or manners, who stride—or rather limp—around all day in boots and greatcoat as if they'd just got off their horse.'

'Oh, yes,' said Lady Sallis rather dreamily. 'Some of us *do* have such tastes, you know. He is a fine figure of a man. And a slight roughness around the edges adds a certain pleasure to any encounter…' She gazed rather pointedly at Corbridge's slight figure, undistinguished in spite of his expensive tailoring. 'So introduce me, will you? After all, I hear he's fancy-free now that Miss Philippa Fawcett is having second thoughts about him.'

Corbridge said rather shortly, 'I imagine you're quite adept at making your own introductions, Lady Sallis. You've certainly had no difficulty in other quarters.'

'Steady now, Sebastian.' Her smile was still bright, but those blue eyes had suddenly narrowed. 'I would advise you to tread carefully. You gained yourself no friends by ruining Marcus's godfather, you know. And everyone's talking about the way Marcus had you spluttering like a plucked chicken when he accosted you at your club last night. Don't underestimate him.'

'He's a rash, warmongering fool!'

'Really? One way or another, he seems pretty able to look after himself.'

That was just the trouble—Lord Sebastian Corbridge knew that already. He was frightened of Marcus, of the cold steel in his eyes, as well as in his hand.

Lady Sallis moved away from him after that, in a cloud of perfume and rustling silk, to talk and laugh with her favoured guests and to ensure that her pretty female assistants were playing their parts dutifully at the gaming tables. Corbridge left the house shortly afterwards, considerably agitated.

He was worried about his finances. The bills incurred in his extravagant way of life strained his resources badly. Sir Roderick's letter of security was of no use till the autumn, and on quarter-day—a mere five weeks from now—the rent on his expensive house would be due.

He needed more money soon, and badly.

Chapter Six

When Tassie came down to breakfast the next morning, there was no one around. It was the stony-faced butler who eventually directed her to the breakfast parlour, while making it quite plain that he thought she had no business being there. Tassie hoped fervently that he had no idea just how lost and vulnerable she felt in this big house. Last night Marcus's apparent kindness to her, when they were alone, had unsettled her deeply; it was almost as if he had some respect, even liking for her. Yet she must remind herself always that his sole intention was to use her to lure his enemy into a trap. The term he'd used was *bait*.

She'd dressed herself that morning in a plain grey gown brought in to her by Emilia, had brushed her hair with a mixture of apprehension and defiance, lifted her chin in a haughty stance, and swept down the staircase—only to find herself alone.

'Major Forrester and Mr Beauchamp went out early,' the butler Sansom told her stiffly in response to her query, as if it were none of her business what her betters got up to. Tassie gave him her best haughty nod in return, and seated herself with a flourish at the damask-covered table. Then she saw how the table was groaning under dish after dish of the most delicious food she had ever seen in her life, and her spirits began to lift. A maid younger than Emilia brought her a plate, and she gazed rather dizzily at the hot dishes of eggs and sausages, sautéed kidneys and bacon and golden kedgeree sitting before her. At least it seemed that she could trust Marcus and his friends to feed her well.

The butler Sansom was hovering nearby, his face disdainful. Probably watching to make sure she didn't steal the silver. 'Coffee or tea—ma'am?'

'Coffee, if you please, Sansom,' she said, echoing the butler's haughty tone and actually starting to enjoy herself.

The butler took a dainty china cup and saucer and filled it from the big pot with a silent pursing of his mouth. And as he passed it back to her, he let go of the saucer too soon; Tassie grabbed for it, and the scalding brown coffee splashed across the pristine white tablecloth.

'Oh, *no*!' Tassie cried.

Just at that moment Caro came in, and gasped as she saw what had happened. Tassie saw Sansom smirking behind his hand as he sternly ordered one of his maids to clear up the mess; and Tassie knew then that he had done it deliberately, to make it look as if it were her fault. Caro—whom Tassie had assumed was the housekeeper, a mistake that caused her cheeks to burn—was all kindness, assuring her that it didn't really matter, but Tassie found that her appetite had quite gone. No good trying to blame the butler; no one would believe her. 'I am very sorry,' she muttered to Caro. 'You must wish me at Jericho, I'm sure.'

'Why, of *course* not,' Caro protested. 'We are all truly glad to have you here, my dear.'

All of you? queried Tassie inwardly, biting her fingernail. For the sour-faced Emilia had just come in, and she, like

Sansom, shot Tassie a look of downright dislike, as if to say, *Whatever makes you think you belong in a grand place like this, you slut?* Then Emilia bobbed a quick, respectful curtsy to Caro.

'Begging your pardon, ma'am, but there's a lady to see you. Miss Philippa Fawcett.'

Caro set off quickly towards the entrance hall, and Sansom had gone off to the kitchen for fresh coffee, so Tassie, all alone in the breakfast parlour, put down the piece of toast she was buttering and turned round slowly in her chair to gaze through the open door. In the hallway she saw Caro talking to a poised young woman in a hooped pink gown and matching fringed silk shawl, with an elaborate straw bonnet perched on her shining curls. Chestnut curls. *Yours for ever, Philippa...*

'Our carriage is waiting outside, so I cannot stay, dearest Caro, for longer than a few moments,' the newcomer was saying in a bright, cultured voice. 'I declare, I never realised that our stay in London would be so very hectic! I feel quite weary at the thought of all the invitations we have received this last week alone... I have called only to return this book that you lent me.' She held out a slim volume. 'And to ask—is it true that Marcus Forrester is staying with you?'

Tassie didn't miss how Caro seemed to stiffen at the other woman's question. 'He is, for a while at least, Philippa. But he went out early this morning, with Hal—for a ride, I think.'

Philippa looked disappointed. Then she gave a bright little smile. 'You have probably heard, dear Caro, that Marcus and I have had—a certain—misunderstanding.'

'Really?' Caro spoke very gently. 'Marcus does not confide in me, of course.'

Philippa was toying with the strings of her pink silk reticule. 'No. But—I did hear some talk, that there may be some prospect of poor Sir Roderick's fortune being restored after all. Is that true, do you know?'

'I really don't know, Philippa. Again, it's none of my business.'

'Will you tell Marcus I was asking after him?'

Tassie had moved closer to the doorway of the breakfasting parlour. She heard Caro say, in her usual kindly way, 'Of course I will tell him, as soon as he returns.'

'My thanks... Well, my carriage is waiting.' Philippa rearranged her lace-edged shawl, nodded and was turning to go, all pink silk and ruffles, when she caught sight of Tassie in her drab gown. Her nose wrinkled in disdain. 'Dear Caro, who on earth is *that*?'

'This is Tassie,' said Caro quietly. 'She is a friend—a distant cousin of Marcus's—who is staying with us for a few days.'

'Really? You should be careful, Caro, one hears such dreadful stories of people being taken in by obscure relatives...'

Tassie sighed inwardly. Then her spirits picked up. Time for a bit of fun. 'Pleased to meet you!' she declared, stepping forward to make a ridiculously exaggerated curtsy. 'Fresh from the country, I am, miss, only they don't speak of my side of the family much, seeing as how we was poor folk living off the land, sheep and pigs we had, but at least I know what's the genuine article and what's not, and that goes for people as well as porkers...'

'*Tassie!*' The icy male voice cut like a sword through Tassie's jaunty banter. 'That is considerably more than enough!' It was Marcus, who'd just come in through the front door. Slamming it behind him, he stood there, clearly furious, looking more than usually formidable in his long riding coat and boots, with his dark hair drawn back from his hard-boned features. Tassie's heart was thumping as he looked from her to Philippa.

'Tassie,' he went on, 'apologise this instant.'

Tassie nodded meekly and turned to face Caro. 'I'm truly sorry, Miss Caro. That was rude and—*rustic* of me.'

'I meant apologise to—' But Marcus, clearly, could see from Tassie's expression that this was one battle he would win at too great a cost. Better to cut his losses. 'Philippa,' he said, giving her a cool bow. 'This is an unexpected surprise.'

Philippa shot a look of sheer dislike at Tassie, then turned to Marcus, her face all smiles. 'Why, Marcus,' she said, 'our carriage was just passing, so I thought, having heard you were staying with dear Caro and Hal, that I would call to see how you were.'

Marcus bowed his head. 'I am honoured.'

'And...' she lowered her voice, glancing again at Tassie '...Marcus, do I have to speak in front of this—creature?'

'Pretend I ain't here, miss,' suggested Tassie helpfully. 'Like you'd ignore the riff-raff on the street.'

'*Really...*'

Marcus took Philippa's arm and guided her a few feet away. 'What were you going to say, Philippa?'

Philippa's voice was rather tight. 'I—I wanted to tell you, Marcus, that Mama is holding a soirée next Wednesday. Naturally Caro and Hal are invited also. There will be many of your old London friends there...'

Tassie began to softly hum the tune of a popular street ballad. She couldn't help but notice that Marcus was not overwhelmed by Philippa's invitation. 'I'm really not sure, Philippa,' he was saying. 'You see, I'm rather rusty at soirées. And I might already have an engagement.'

'I shall consult with Hal, Philippa; your soirée sounds enjoyable,' interrupted Caro, stepping forwards swiftly to cover the awkward silence that followed. 'Pray thank your mama for us!'

Philippa twitched her pink shawl and looked one last time at Marcus, as if hoping for some reaction from him. When none came, she turned to go rather abruptly, saying, over her shoulder, 'Please do try to attend, Marcus. I think you might enjoy mingling with the kind of company to which you are accustomed.' She cast a final cold look at Tassie, who grinned and bobbed a mocking curtsy. Philippa said, 'Well, really!' and made for the door with Caro following in her wake to show her out.

Tassie decided it was rather a good time to make her exit, up the stairs to her room. But Marcus had other ideas entirely. Marching swiftly up behind her, he reached out with one strong hand and pulled her back to face him. In a voice of steel he rasped, 'Acting the part of a country simpleton was *never* part of our bargain. Do you understand me, Tassie?'

Tassie nodded fiercely. 'I do! But that *person*—she had no right to talk to me as if I was something out of—out of the gutter!'

'Perhaps she did not. But there are other ways to deal with such misapprehensions. One way would be for you to speak, and behave, as if you were a lady of quality.' His glance fell caustically on the coffee stains that still adorned her drab gown. 'I must also point out that you should attempt to eat your meals with an effort at decorum.'

'God's teeth, Marcus,' she said indignantly, 'the butler did that to me, the spilt coffee was not my dratted fault!'

He brought his fist down on the hall table with such force that the ormolu clock rattled and Tassie jumped. 'One final thing. Your language is atrocious. You swear like some of the toughest old troopers I've had under my command, and I won't have it, whatever the provocation, not in Hal and Caro's house. Do you understand me?'

She clenched her hands, and said in a voice that trembled

with passion, 'I have promised to keep our bargain, Marcus, and I will do so. But perhaps 'tis you who should reconsider it, for I cannot pretend to be what I am not. Though you would do well to remember that sometimes even fine ladies flaunt themselves and lie for profit!'

'What do you mean? *Who* do you mean?'

'I'm saying that at least I'm honest, in telling you I'm after your money! At least I've promised to earn it! Why was she here, that—that creature in pink silk and ruffles, if not to ask Caro after your godfather's estate?'

'I hope you're not making all this up, Tassie.' Marcus's voice was dangerously quiet.

She met him with her clear, calm gaze. 'Why should I lie? She wanted to know, from Caro, if there was still a chance of your godfather—Sir Roderick—getting back his fortune now that you are back. She's come snuffling round like a cat after cream.'

'Stop. I mean it, Tassie. Enough.' Marcus was breathing hard. But she was right to warn him. Just for a moment, when he had come in and seen Philippa there, he'd hoped that what had been between them still existed, regardless of his expectations. More fool he. This outcast of the London streets had once more shown herself to be in many ways wiser than he was.

'Very well,' Tassie said steadily. 'I'll stop. But I tell you this—I'll put up with no more insults from your fancy friends or from you. You have made a bargain, too, Marcus, with me. If you think I am not fit to play it through, then tell me, now, and I will take Edward and go from this house for good!'

There was a long, tension-filled silence, during which Tassie's heart thumped so loud that she was sure he must hear it. She was suddenly afraid that she had really gone too far.

Then Marcus nodded, as though a moment of crisis had

been reached and passed. 'Our bargain still stands,' he said. 'Come and have some coffee with me.'

So she followed him back into the breakfast room, and, feeling slightly shaky, sat down again while Marcus poured them both some coffee.

'I'm sorry, Marcus,' she said quietly at last. 'It was wrong and stupid of me, to act as I did. But are you *really* going to tell people I'm your country cousin, like Caro said to—to that woman?'

'That's right.'

Tassie's eyes rounded. 'I suppose you have to tell them *something*. Otherwise they might think I'm your lightskirt. Mightn't they?'

Marcus started to laugh then. In fact, he laughed so much, he almost choked on his coffee. 'I'll make quite sure they don't, believe me.' Tassie frowned down into her cup. What stupid things she came out with. But his face changed so much, when he was amused by something, it was as if he was a different person. It was the same last night, when he'd spoken to her like—like a friend... He couldn't be in love with that Philippa creature, he couldn't!

'So I'm to be your cousin,' she went on airily. 'What kind of cousin, Marcus?'

'A very distant one. And definitely not a pig farmer.'

'Very well. But really, Marcus, you must want to restore your godfather's fortune very badly to concoct such a Shrewsbury tale! I suppose your prospects of inheriting will help you get that Philippa woman back, though why you should wish to marry someone who is such a milksop, and no doubt throws fainting fits whenever she is thwarted, is quite beyond me—'

'Enough!' he roared, and Tassie jumped up again, gripping the edge of the table. 'Allow me to inform you, Tassie,' he went on, 'that I'm not paying you to pull apart my private life. I have plenty of acquaintances more than willing to do that for free, believe me.' And then his stern mouth twitched with amusement. 'Also let me tell you—since you are so concerned about embarrassing this household—that I have this morning been making arrangements for you to visit a fashionable but discreet *modiste* who will dress you in a more becoming manner. Caro will accompany you, and check that you have everything you need, and so will Emilia.'

Tassie said anxiously, 'They won't try to make me look like a painted doll, will they? I don't want no pink silk and ruffles.'

'Pink silk and ruffles wouldn't suit you in the slightest, my dear. And besides, you will be leading a quiet life for the next few weeks. No adventures in public places where Sebastian Corbridge or his cronies might see you.'

So he wasn't going to throw her out, then. But the prospect of the shopping expedition lowered her spirits, because she knew the frosty-faced Emilia didn't like her one bit, and Caro was frighteningly virtuous. All in all, her new life seemed rather overwhelming. 'Are—are you coming, too?' she asked hesitantly.

He sipped his coffee as he contemplated her. 'Hardly. Ladies' fashion shops are not exactly my usual haunt. But I shall be back this evening to hear all about it. You won't try to run away, will you?'

'No,' she declared, 'of course not! We made a bargain, remember? But, Marcus…'

'Yes?'

'What exactly do I have to win off Lord Corbridge?'

'Just a letter. But it's a letter that signs away my godfather's estate come September.'

A letter, that was worth so much… 'What does it look like, Marcus, this letter?'

'Look like? The usual kind of legal document. Parchment, rolled and tied with pink ribbon, a seal.'

Tassie sighed a little, then she unexpectedly let a smile dimple the corners of her mouth. 'I warn you, Marcus. I'll play cards for you, but I'll run away for sure if they try to put me in pink silk and ruffles!' Then she bowed her head to concentrate on buttering more toast.

'Remember,' Marcus admonished gently, 'not to eat as though you're actually *hungry*,' and she froze, then lifted up a delicate slice of toast to her lips in the perfect, mincing manner of a lady of fashion.

Just then Marcus heard Caro out in the hall. He rose from the table and went to join her. Though Philippa had gone, he was still aware of the delicate floral scent of her perfume lingering in the air. He ran his fingers through his hair, knowing Caro was watching him anxiously, and said absently, 'The girl, Tassie. I've told her to behave herself, and mind her manners while she's out with you...'

Caro moved closer. 'I'm sure she will! Oh, Marcus. Won't you even talk about Philippa? If only I could in some way help. You and she were once so close...'

He said, 'She was asking you about my godfather's fortune, wasn't she? Unless Sir Roderick's prospects are restored, I think my chances of being *close* to Philippa again are negligible.'

Caro's eyes softened. 'I'm sorry, Marcus. I hadn't realised that money played such a large part in the match.'

'Neither did I.' He smiled rather bleakly.

'Yet she invited you to her mother's soirée...'

'Philippa's mother let me know in no uncertain terms, when I called the other day, that she is trying to bring Sir Robert Lawdon up to scratch. He is wealthy—you will know him—and she assured me that Philippa was not averse to the match.' Marcus's voice tightened. 'So my guess is that Lady Fawcett is encouraging all her daughter's various admirers, including myself, to attend on her, in order to increase Philippa's desirability in Sir Robert's eyes. Hence the invitation.'

Caro murmured, 'You were not always as bitter as this, my dear. I'm sorry you have been hurt.'

'Don't be. I should have been better prepared, that's all.'

'Well, I shall not go to the soirée then,' Caro declared. 'And neither will Hal. He finds these affairs an atrocious bore. Now, listen, Marcus, I must talk to you about Tassie. Hal tells me you want me to ensure that she is taught how to behave in polite company, and I shall do it with pleasure, because I like her extremely; she has considerable spirit. But I need reassurance. She is also very pretty, though I don't think she realises it yet. You're not going to lead her into any—any kind of possible *harm*, are you?'

'Far from it, my dear! In fact, with your help, I can make her quite presentable, and even give her some prospects in life.'

Caro looked far from convinced. 'But why, Marcus? Why take her up like this?'

'Believe me, I'm not planning a life of vice for the girl. Let's say—it's because of a debt of honour, Caro.'

'So long as the price is not too high. For Tassie, or for you.' Caro gazed at him a moment longer, then went on, more lightly, 'Well, whatever you plan for her will, I am sure, be an improvement. She does not seem to have had much of a life, the poor thing.'

'Oh, I don't know. It seems to have been remarkably colourful to me. At least she could never complain of boredom.'

'That's true, I'm sure. Now, I wonder what you have in

mind for her future—she is intelligent, and could, I suppose, with a little training, become a nursery governess, or a lady's maid?'

Marcus pressed her hand. 'Leave it with me.'

'Of course. Well, the carriage should be here shortly, to take us to Bond Street. I'd better go and persuade her to leave the breakfast table.'

He took her hand and touched it with his lips. 'Dear Caro. You are simply the kindest person I know.' Caro smiled, and went into the dining room. A few moments later she emerged again with Tassie at her side. The minx threw Marcus a glance of wary defiance as she walked jauntily past him towards the stairs, humming a tune under her breath; and Marcus grinned back, prompting a flash of merriment in those spirited green eyes. Over the next few weeks Tassie would doubtless stretch his patience with her mischievous ways, but he could deal with her tricks, and put them to good use. What *did* worry him was that she was even prettier than he'd at first realised.

She presented an image of natural grace that no one would expect from an outcast of the streets. And in that flimsy nightgown yesterday, with her blonde hair piled up in ringlets that threatened to tumble round her shoulders any minute, and those huge green eyes flashing scorn, she'd presented a tempting morsel indeed, whether she was aware of it or not. Did she play such tricks on him deliberately, to try to snare him? He began to wonder if he had made an elementary mistake, one all army officers were warned against: *No involvement with any of your troops!* Especially as in this case his prime lieutenant in dealing with Corbridge was to be not a rough soldier, but a rather delectable, and surprisingly appealing, young woman of considerable spirit.

He'd not give her the chance to distract him again. He would treat her with firm, detached coolness, and make quite sure that she had no chance to try her mischief on anyone else—except his enemy, Lord Sebastian Corbridge.

Marcus's ponderings were rudely interrupted by a loud shout from the direction of the breakfast parlour, where the butler was collecting the dishes. The shout was followed by the clatter of breaking crockery.

Marcus went quickly to investigate. 'For God's sake, man. What is it?'

Sansom just stood there, shaking with rage, a jumble of smashed china scattered around his feet. 'Sir, the marmalade dish,' he spluttered, almost incoherent. 'Someone's coated the sides of the dish with butter. It's that hoyden, that street-girl—it slipped right out of my hands. She should be whipped—'

Marcus strode back into the hall. 'Tassie!' he roared.

Tassie had reached the top of the staircase with Caro, but she halted suddenly, gazing down at him with expressionless eyes. Caro flew down to be at Marcus's side. 'Marcus. What is it?'

Sansom was starting to clear up, his face still black with fury. Marcus explained quickly and angrily to Caro. 'In truth, the girl deserves the back of my hand. I'll make arrangements for her to leave your house immediately. I cannot subject you and Hal to this sort of behaviour any longer—'

But Caro interrupted him, her hand on his arm. 'No, Marcus, no! Sansom was extremely rude earlier to Tassie. I thought at the time that it might have been *he* who deliberately caused her to spill her coffee… The poor girl was getting her own back on him in the only way she knew. Leave it with me. I will speak to Sansom. Do not be harsh with her.'

With that, Caro went quickly into the breakfast parlour. Marcus looked up again to the top of the stairs, but Tassie had fled.

Rather wisely, he decided grimly to himself. And he was

pretty sure that was a brothel ditty she'd been humming just then. Caro was unfailingly kind, but how long at this rate before the minx outstayed her welcome?

Chapter Seven

During the next few days, Tassie found herself taking unexpected pleasure in her new surroundings, though she would have died rather than let Marcus know it. Caro was like the kindly older sister Tassie had never had; and Hal also proved unfailingly generous. One morning, when Marcus was out on his usual round of visiting people who might be able to help his godfather, Hal offered to take Tassie to the park in his new curricle.

Tassie hesitated, puckering up her little nose in that way that Hal found extremely endearing. 'I do not think Marcus wants me to be seen out in society.' No doubt her conduct during Philippa's visit had reinforced his opinion. 'After all, I am only supposed to be a country cousin. A *very distant* country cousin.'

Hal reassured her swiftly. 'Tassie, specifically he doesn't want his enemy—Corbridge—to see you. And there's little danger of *that*—Corbridge keeps the fashionable hours, he's never in bed before four in the morning, and never out of it until well into the afternoon. There's no chance of bumping into him in the park, believe me.'

Tassie was torn, afraid of Marcus's disapproval, yet yearning to be out in the fresh air, to ride behind Hal's beautiful horses. Apart from her visits with Caro to the dressmaker's shop, Tassie had not gone far from the house. Hal saw how her eyes gleamed with longing, and laughed. 'Come along. Marcus made no rule against enjoying yourself! And he bought you a new riding habit, didn't he? Now is your chance to wear it.'

So Tassie scurried upstairs to change into her new habit, one amongst several items she'd been able to purchase ready-made at the dressmaker's because, the assistant confided, the lady who had ordered them had suddenly found herself unable to pay her bills. Gambling debts, Tassie had decided, shaking her head at such foolishness.

Now, dressed in the burgundy velvet outfit and the little feathered cap, she felt unexpectedly bashful; but as Hal helped her up beside him, she quite forgot her shyness as she gazed at the beautiful horses, and absorbed Hal's skilled handling of them. And Hal, glancing sideways at her as the breeze ruffled her golden ringlets and brought some colour to the soft curve of her cheek, thought, *Why, she's a beauty. Quite a little beauty.*

'You like horses, don't you?' He smiled at her.

'Oh yes,' she breathed, her eyes shining. 'I learned to ride years ago.' With Georgie Jay's band of travellers, on a gypsy pony, though she thought it best not to add that.

The only thing that spoiled her outing was Marcus's anger when they got back to Portman Square. 'I'd rather you didn't make a public display of yourself, Tassie,' he'd said coldly.

Hal interrupted quickly, 'Hold hard, Marcus, dear boy. It was my idea.'

Marcus said, 'Was it?' as if he clearly still thought it was all Tassie's fault; and then he'd read Tassie a lecture on obedience, and how their bargain was off if she caused any more trouble.

Instead of retaliating, as she usually did, Tassie had gone very quiet, finding to her horror that she had a big lump at the back of her throat because he was scolding her so roundly and making her feel wretchedly stupid. Tearing off her feathered cap, she stormed up to her room, leaving him staring after her mid-sentence. She slammed the door shut and pulled off her riding habit, her fingers tangling hopelessly with all the buttons, while Edward squawked in sympathy. And then she caught sight of herself in the mirror in her white chemise, saw how the lace edging emphasised the swelling curve of her breasts, and she pressed her hands to her burning cheeks.

Once all this was over, she would have her fifty guineas. She would be free to follow her own fortune. Every night, she made her plans.

But in the meantime—how *dare* Marcus speak to her like that? How dare he?

Tassie did not go down for lunch, calling out that she had a headache when Emilia rapped on her door. She lay on her bed till the afternoon shadows lengthened, but then there was another knock at the door, and Caro came in. 'We are going to the theatre tonight, Tassie,' she said in her gentle voice. 'You will come with us, won't you, my dear?'

Tassie pulled herself up defensively. 'Marcus will not want me there. I will spoil it for him.'

Caro said quietly, 'It was Marcus who asked me to come up and invite you.'

Tassie registered disbelief. 'But he doesn't want anyone to set eyes on me at all, let alone at a public place like the theatre! And besides—you will all be ashamed of me.'

Caro said, 'Nonsense. You will look lovely. I will help you to dress.'

And she did, helping Tassie into a new gown that had arrived only yesterday from the dressmaker's. It was a hooped polonaise of pale blue silk, with a matching fitted jacket of darker blue trimmed with cream ribbons, and a cream bonnet with a half-veil. Tassie had never worn anything like it, and her heart thumped with apprehension as she walked carefully down the wide staircase in her full skirts and saw Marcus waiting for her there in the hall, his eyes dark and assessing.

Because he was so quiet, she assumed there was something wrong, yet again. 'What is the matter this time, Marcus?' she said in a tight little voice. 'Am I not dressed properly? Caro said this would be suitable for the theatre...'

He stood there a moment longer, looking as imposing, as disturbing as Tassie had ever seen him in his dark grey topcoat and slim-fitting breeches and lace-edged cravat. For heaven's sake, she thought rather faintly, what on earth had possessed her to tangle in the first place with such a formidable man? She waited, silently, for the rebuke she was sure would come.

But he just said, 'You look very well, Tassie. Come. Hal and Caro are waiting for us in the carriage. Remember, won't you, that if anyone should speak to you, you are in town for a few days only, a distant relative of mine; you must say as little as possible in reply. And Caro is your chaperon; you must never, ever leave her side.'

She tilted her chin. 'What if Sebastian Corbridge is there?'

'He and his friends are out of town for a few days.'

Ah.

'And the veil on your bonnet...'

'Yes?'

'Use it.'

The play was an unexpected delight to Tassie. She could not help but remember how in winters past she'd sung and danced on the cold pavement outside the theatres as old Matt played his fiddle, to earn a few pence for herself and her friends. And now here she was, in a private box! She half-expected people to stare at her, to laugh at her in her finery, but she made a huge effort to remember to keep her bonnet with its half-veil demurely covering her hair and the upper part of her face, and to talk but little in a low, polite voice. And Marcus looked on her almost approvingly.

If only he would be kinder to her, as Hal and Caro were. Most of the time he was distant, almost severe: rebuking her at mealtimes when she used the wrong fork, scolding her for curling up on a couch, or for chewing her fingernails, or for keeping dice in her pocket to practise with. He treated her as if she was foolish and stupid, which she wasn't. She suddenly realised that she was almost looking forward to meeting Sebastian Corbridge, and rooking him of his money, just to show Marcus what she could do.

During the interval, Caro left them briefly to visit some friends in a nearby box, and Hal and Marcus talked between themselves, often breaking into merriment over some private joke. They were most likely discussing the pretty actress who played the heroine and showed far too much of her dainty ankles, thought Tassie acidly. Suddenly, she became aware that a plump, powdered gentleman in a neighbouring box was staring at her rather intently. Her first impulse was to stare back and tell him in no uncertain terms that he ought to keep his roving eyes to himself; but then she remembered that she was meant to be a lady. And perhaps he was a friend of Marcus's or Hal's. Uncertain, she dimpled demurely up at him from beneath her half-veil; and the man, giving a delighted grin, lifted his pince-nez and leaned forward to scrutinise her even more frankly.

Tassie coloured, hot and uncomfortable beneath his gaze. He looked very finely dressed, but he was rather portly, and his beady eyes gleamed from his rotund face. She turned away quickly, glad of her veil, wishing he would stop staring, wishing Marcus would do something; but Marcus was still deep in conversation with Hal, who was on the point of going to find Caro and her friends.

She was relieved when the staring man got up at last and left his box; but her relief turned to dismay when, Hal having just gone, there was a light tap at the door of theirs, and the portly man himself, resplendent in satin and lace, came in and made a low bow. He spoke to Marcus, but his eyes were on Tassie.

'Well, Major Forrester,' the man said, 'I heard you were back in town; gather you've been rather busy. Going to introduce me to this pretty young filly, hey?'

Instantly Tassie knew there was something wrong. Marcus moved quickly to stand in front of Tassie's seated figure and said coldly, 'Your servant, Viscount Lindsay. You mistake the matter, I think. This young lady is a relative of mine, making a private visit to town under the protection of Hal's sister Mrs Caroline Blakesley, who will be rejoining us shortly.'

'Really?' Viscount Lindsay grinned. Taking no notice of Marcus's forbidding posture, he sidled closer to Tassie and reached for her hand, lifting it to his mouth and kissing it. Tassie felt herself shivering, because his lips were plump and wet as they lingered on the back of her hand. Also she didn't like in the least the way his hot eyes were roving over the bodice of her gown. She snatched her fingers away.

'Must say you've been keeping mighty quiet about your young—relative, Forrester,' said the man directly to Marcus, with a leer that implied he didn't believe his story in the least.

'That is because,' said Marcus through clenched teeth, 'she is only here for a few days, Viscount Lindsay. She has not yet been properly introduced into society, hence our seclusion in this box. Now, if you'll excuse us, I think the second act is about to begin.'

'So it is, so it is,' replied Lindsay genially. 'And no doubt there'll be even livelier entertainment later on with this little lightskirt, won't there, Forrester? Who's she for, you or your friend Beauchamp? Or will you share her?' He grinned and let his hand brush very deliberately along Tassie's shoulder, fondling her through the filmy fabric of her gown. And he nipped her, lightly with his fingertips, so he didn't get a reply from Marcus, because Tassie, leaping to her feet, had slapped him hard across the face. 'God's teeth, take your filthy hands off me, will you?' She'd sent her flimsy chair flying; the man, likewise unbalanced, staggered back against the wall of the box, clutching at the velvet draperies for support. Marcus was on him immediately, grasping him by his arm, while Tassie set her chair straight and sank into it, trembling with fury.

'You'd best get out of here, Lindsay,' said Marcus flatly. 'And take your bawdy-house manners elsewhere, damn you.'

The portly Viscount Lindsay dragged himself away from Marcus's grasp and started towards the door. His eyes were narrowed and malevolent. 'I'll not forget this, Forrester. Or that tantalising little doxy over there. A *relative*? She smiled at me, you know, beneath that saucy veil of hers; as good as invited me over. Watch her, Forrester. She'll bring you trouble.'

'Not half as much as I'll give you if you don't leave now,' drawled Marcus softly.

On hearing raised voices, people were starting to turn and stare into the darkness of their curtained box. Lindsay, faced with Marcus's fists, slunk away; Marcus lowered himself into the empty seat beside Tassie. Dear God, she was such an innocent in so many ways in spite of her streetwise earthiness.

Lindsay was right; if he was not careful, she would bring him trouble. He said, more sharply than he intended, 'Is it true, Tassie? Did you smile openly at a man you didn't know?'

For a moment she flinched at his coldness as if he'd struck her, but then she shrugged in her old manner and retorted, 'What the devil was I supposed to do, Marcus? He was sitting there staring at me, looking me up and down as if I were a prime bit of horseflesh, but I assumed he was a friend of yours, so, yes, I smiled at him!'

Marcus said with dangerous patience, 'Tassie. *Tassie*. If you were with your old friends, in some tavern or other, and a man you didn't know smiled at you and looked at you like that, would you smile back?'

Some of the colour was returning to her cheeks, but her voice was still a little shaky as she replied, 'God's teeth, no. But I was trying to be a lady, Marcus.'

Marcus suddenly saw that she was trembling again, and tried to soften his voice. 'I don't think he'll recognise you again. But you intrigued him—and I'm very much afraid he will talk about you. One of his friends is Sebastian Corbridge.'

Tassie paled again. 'Does—does this mean you wish to cancel our bargain?'

'No.' He sighed. 'But I perhaps need to reconsider our strategy.'

She gazed at him. 'Whatever you say.'

He touched her hand. 'Tassie. Are you all right?'

'Of course! Please do not make such a silly fuss—and be sure that I have learned my lesson!'

The curtain was about to come up again just as Hal returned, with Caro. Tassie gazed at the stage with bright, unseeing eyes, because Marcus's touch had burned her, and the look of sudden pity in his eyes had unsettled her far, far more deeply than his anger.

* * *

For some days now Marcus had been toying with the idea of releasing Tassie from her bargain. He reminded himself constantly that she'd lived in rough, semi-criminal company. And yet her wary but delighted, almost innocent eagerness for every treat in store—her new clothes, her enjoyment of good food, the ride in the park—had got under his guard in a way he'd never anticipated. *No involvement with any of your troops...*

But during those few days in London he had come to the end of the line in trying to see if there was anything he could do to revoke, or at least call into question, Sir Roderick's debts to Sebastian Corbridge. He'd visited one law office after another in the vicinity of Lincoln's Inn, questioning dry and sometimes shifty attorneys about the business till his hands longed to fasten round their equivocating necks... but the answer was always the same. The agreement could not be cancelled—and if Sir Roderick didn't surrender his estate to Sebastian in September, he would be thrown into a debtors' prison.

All this went through Marcus's agitated mind as the play ran its course on stage. And with the final curtain came another blow. As Caro led the way from the theatre, with Tassie at her side, Hal confided in Marcus that his sister had received an invitation to go and stay with some close friends of hers near Bath. Marcus felt his spirits plummet anew. 'Dear fellow,' went on Hal in a low voice, 'Caro doesn't want to leave you in difficulties. She knows Tassie can't possibly stay in the house without her as chaperon. So naturally she's turned the invitation down.'

Marcus's brain was whirling as they followed Caro and Tassie out to their waiting carriage. Caro must go to Bath. But Tassie? She couldn't stay here—and he couldn't let her go. Because he couldn't let Lornings fall into Corbridge's evil hands.

The cold night air, as he stepped outside, lashed his flagging spirits like a bucket of iced water. *Of course.* He would take Tassie to Lornings.

Marcus told Hal of his plan later that night, as they shared a brandy together in the firelit study. At first, Hal was shocked.

'You're really taking her to your godfather's house? Is he ready for her, do you think?'

Marcus grinned. 'Could anybody be ready for Tassie? Strangely enough, Hal, I think that she and Roderick might get on rather well. He's got a way with waifs and strays—after all, he took me in when I was without a home. And it will also give me the chance to maybe help him out in various ways, without him feeling that he can't do anything for me in return.'

'You know that Caro would gladly delay her visit to her friends if it helped.'

'I know, and I'm more than grateful. But tonight showed me that I can't run the risk of Tassie catching anyone else's eye in such a fashion, and it will be a few weeks yet before I can put my plan into action. Let Caro go to Bath. Tassie and I will go to Lornings.'

'She's too deuced pretty to stay out of trouble in London for long,' Hal agreed. 'But, Marcus, do you still think you can make this plan of yours actually work?'

'It's certainly worth a try,' responded Marcus firmly. 'She's got her eye set firmly on the money I've promised her. And in a way Lindsay's attention has helped to make up my mind; she's got what it takes to draw Corbridge into the trap I plan for him. Yes, I think we can do it.'

He suddenly remembered Sir Roderick's sad, weary face, and he knew that he had no choice but to make his plan succeed.

Marcus told Tassie the following morning that she would be travelling to his godfather's house, and he was more abrupt than he meant to be. She was eating her breakfast, in a somewhat less desperate manner than she used to, when he came in to see her.

'Is it—is it in the country?'

'It's in the country,' he replied flatly, tired because he had slept little that night. 'I've been out already this morning to hire a travelling chaise for you. It will be arriving within the hour, so I suggest you complete your breakfast swiftly and make yourself ready for a long journey.'

'Is Caro coming?'

'No, she's going to visit friends in Bath. It should take you three days to get there; you will be staying at posting inns along the way. We have decided that Emilia will accompany you.'

Tassie found that her appetite had gone completely. Emilia didn't like her at all! Besides, the thought of the countryside in February made her spirits sink utterly, bringing back memories of mud, and bare trees, and biting winds that sliced through thin clothing. And she guessed Marcus's godfather to be an angry, embittered old man because of all the money he had lost to Sebastian Corbridge... Suddenly it all seemed rather overwhelming.

'Does your godfather know about me?' she asked Marcus suddenly. 'And the part I am to play in your plan?'

'No,' he said emphatically. 'Any talk of the matter would distress him. I will tell him what I've told everyone else—that you are a distant relative who has come temporarily into my care. And you will be able to see, at first hand, just how much the Lornings estate means to him.'

And to you, thought Tassie swiftly. She swallowed, feeling rather sick with apprehension. Aloud, she said in a nonchalant voice, 'So it's all arranged. I don't suppose you're coming, too?'

He sipped at his freshly poured coffee, contemplating her reaction. 'As a matter of fact, I am. Not wishing to impose you on my godfather without any kind of explanation, I shall be riding on ahead of you.' He gave a half-smile. 'Don't tell me you're pleased, minx.'

'Why on earth should I be?' she retorted.

But suddenly, inexplicably, she felt relieved. At least she wouldn't have to face his grim old godfather on her own. 'And Edward?' she added quickly. 'Edward's coming with me, isn't he?'

Marcus had anticipated there would be great trouble if he didn't. 'Edward is coming, too, provided he stays in his travelling-cage throughout the journey. Do you understand?'

She gave a little sigh of relief and nodded. She would be more than a match for old Sir Roderick and the frosty-faced Emilia. But—a match for Marcus? She wasn't quite so sure. 'I understand.'

He went on, 'It will still be cold up in the Cotswold hills at this time of year, so make sure to pack your warmest clothes.'

It will still be cold in the hills at this time of year. Something she almost remembered, but not quite—a half-vanished picture, a fading voice... No. She was mistaken, as she had been mistaken so often before.

'Tassie,' Marcus was saying, 'Tassie, is something wrong?'

His voice came as if from a long way away. She shook her head firmly. 'Why, no. I was merely considering what I need to take, that is all.' After that she went swiftly up to her room.

It was Caro who had encouraged Tassie to borrow some books—'Reading is a ladylike pursuit, my dear!' She'd lent Tassie a romance, which Tassie found unbearably tedious, wanting only to shake the foolish heroine into some sense. But one afternoon, while passing Hal's study, Tassie had slipped in and found, on his shelves, a slim pocket-book containing maps of the English shires.

She kept it well hidden. Every night she had pored over it, looking for the place she had run from, so long ago. She'd walked for miles, avoiding any towns, sleeping in hedgerows; then a passing carter had offered her food, and given her a lift. She wasn't sure where he was bound, and it didn't much matter at the time; all she wanted to do was get as far away from the big house as she could. But as night fell she'd grown afraid of the carter and ran again, hungry and footsore, with no idea where she was, a lost child on the verge of exhaustion by the time Georgie Jay and his friends found her at the side of the road.

The big house was called Wychwood. That was all she knew. And she could find it nowhere in Hal's map book; she hardly expected to, for sometimes she wondered if it only existed in that cold, unhappy region of her past that she had put far, far behind her. But she found the Cotswold hills, close to Lornings, in Gloucestershire. *It will be cold up there...*

She put the book away thoughtfully.

She had heard Caro talking to Marcus about her. 'The girl is sweet-natured and intelligent,' Caro had said, 'and could, with a little training, become a nursery governess, perhaps, or a lady's maid!'

Tassie had slipped away quickly. Oh, no. Oh, no. She had her own plans to make; and it seemed that destiny, in the rather formidable shape of Marcus Forrester, was leading her onwards.

* * *

Lord Sebastian Corbridge was on his way that same morning to his carriage maker in Long Acre to see about a new town chaise, when he heard that Marcus was making arrangements to travel to Gloucestershire. It was his friend 'Piggy' Lindsay who told him about it. Lindsay accompanied him to the carriage maker, mainly to take the opportunity to grumble about some ridiculous slight he'd received at the hands of an impudent lightskirt in Forrester's box last night, but Sebastian took no notice of that—served Piggy right for trying to move in on another man's property, especially a dangerous man like his cousin. He was secretly relieved to hear that he wasn't the only one to be made a fool of by Marcus Forrester. But Sebastian was disturbed by the news about Marcus leaving for Lornings.

It was Lindsay himself who said slyly, 'Best watch out for your claim on that place, Sebastian. Marcus and his godfather, Sir Roderick Delancey, are thick as thieves—they might well be planning to strip Lornings bare of its contents before it falls forfeit to you in the autumn.'

As Sebastian checked through the bill for his new carriage, and realised that pretty soon he would be in Queer Street if he didn't pull back on his spending, his mind flew to the splendour of Lornings. The great hall was now empty of inhabitants, its furniture covered with dustsheets, but, damn it, Lindsay was correct. The place was packed with treasures—silverware, fine porcelain, historic paintings— that were, by rights, his; he couldn't legally act on that fool Roderick's debt till September, but a man had to have something on account...

He smiled at last, but his smile was brittle, and his fingers worked restlessly over the diamond signet ring he wore. 'Rest assured,' he said softly, 'I shall deal with Marcus Forrester.'

* * *

During the course of that morning, the big hall of Hal and Caro's house filled up relentlessly with cases and portmanteaus. Edward sat inside his wicker cage, glaring at them all, especially Marcus, while the frosty-faced Emilia made it clear what she thought of travelling with Tassie. Tassie was in her room, with the kindly Caro helping her to pack the last of her things. Marcus had expected resistance, but Tassie was being remarkably quiet and obedient; Marcus would have been less reassured had he known that she was secretly slipping in her old, comfortable buckskin breeches and shirt, and a sharp little pocket knife, together with several packs of pristine playing cards and a bale of dice that were guaranteed, in the right hands, to throw a double six every time.

Everything was going well, thought Marcus. The travelling chaise would arrive soon, and Hal had offered his chief coachman to drive it. Soon Tassie would be on her way, following him to Lornings.

But then, the messenger arrived.

He was dressed in military uniform, and he requested a word with Major Forrester, urgently. Marcus disappeared with him into the small ante-room off the hall, then rejoined Hal a few minutes later.

'So much for my plans, Hal! I'm wanted at the War Office.'

Hal frowned. 'They're not forcing you into that recruiting post after all, are they?'

'No, nothing like that. Do you remember when I travelled unofficially into North Carolina last autumn? I gave a full report at the time, but apparently the War Office wants to ask me again about the enemy strongholds there.'

'I'd heard rumours that our generals are hoping to get a foothold in the Carolinas, in case New York should fall... This is bad timing, dear boy. They'll be wanting to interrogate you for more than an hour or two this afternoon, if I know the War Office. You won't be going to Gloucestershire for another few days at least… What about the girl?'

Marcus hesitated. Then he said decisively, 'Tassie must travel as we planned. I'll send a letter on ahead, with all speed, to my godfather, so he will be expecting her. I should be able to follow her within a few days. She'll come to no harm with Emilia to look after her.'

Hal relaxed. 'And our coachman, Hugh Roberts, is a good, reliable man. The girl will manage without you for a few days.'

Would she? Marcus wondered. Or would she run at the first opportunity, with whatever she could steal? But then, he remembered. She'd made her promise, and he felt strangely certain that she would keep it.

Tassie was wildly, desperately miserable when Marcus came up to her room to tell her that he couldn't come with her to Lornings after all. Still clutching the fringed shawl that she was folding into her bulging portmanteau, she gazed up at his familiar figure as if he was betraying her.

'Then I'm not going,' she said flatly.

'Where are you going, then?' Marcus replied equally bluntly, his arms folded across his broad chest. 'You can't stay here without Caro to chaperon you.'

Tassie pulled a face. 'And who, pray, will—*chaperon*—me in Gloucestershire?'

'There is an elderly housekeeper who will watch over you. And besides, my godfather keeps very little company.'

Tassie felt her heart quailing at the thought of travelling to this new, strange place and facing yet more hostile strangers. 'Do you know, Marcus, I feel like a pawn in a chess game.'

'I am paying you!'

'Yes,' she muttered, pushing the last of her things into the valise that Caro had lent her. 'And I agreed. So 'tis all my own doing.'

Just then Caro came into the room with a warm cloak for her, and now she opened her mouth to speak, no doubt to yet again offer to postpone her trip to Bath. But Marcus silenced her with a look, and Caro left, frowning. He was aware that Caro, who knew nothing of his real plan, thought he was being cruel to the girl—Hal, too, perhaps. Damn it, sometimes he himself thought he was being cruel, even though none knew as well as he that Tassie would, in normal circumstances, as soon rob him as help him. But the die was cast. He said reasonably, 'Look, Tassie. I'll follow you to Lornings in a few days, I swear. In fact, I've already sent a message post-haste to my godfather, so he'll be expecting you. And you won't be travelling alone.' He tried a smile. 'You'll have Emilia for company.'

'I don't *want* Emilia for company! And I feel quite certain that she doesn't want me!'

Marcus sighed. 'You mean you'd rather have *me*?'

'God's teeth, no!'

Marcus laughed at that, but not unkindly. She spoke with her usual vehemence, yet to Marcus she looked lost and bewildered as she faced her totally unknown future. She wore a dark brown travelling outfit, which with its well-cut skirt and little jacket emphasised her slender elegance, her golden hair. It was hard, at times like this, to believe that she had tramped the countryside with a band of rogues for years. He said again, almost gently, 'Tassie. You know, I hope, that I wouldn't force you into anything against your will.'

Tassie knew she had no other option. The money he'd promised her was her only chance to make some sense of her past, of her future. She said in a low voice, 'We have made a bargain, Marcus. I will go, and do what I promised.'

Marcus hesitated. Then, much to Tassie's astonishment,

he touched her cheek almost tenderly and said, in a softer voice, 'Very well. Take care of yourself, minx. Do you know, I think I'll miss you.'

Tassie scowled and stepped back rapidly. But her skin still burned from his light caress as he turned to leave the room.

During the journey to Gloucestershire, Tassie rapidly came to the conclusion that she would rather have walked than ride in so uncomfortable a conveyance. The chaise was heavy, and wallowed in the mired ruts of the early March roads; the constant lurching motion made her feel ill, and Emilia's disapproval of everything she did depressed her spirits constantly. Edward travelled in his cage on the floor of the coach, grumbling incessantly; every time they hit a rut, he would let out a loud, complaining squawk, at which Emilia would glare as if she would like to throttle him.

During the afternoon, Emilia dozed off, and Tassie lifted Edward's cage onto the seat beside her. 'It'll be all right, Edward,' she whispered to him through the bars of the wicker cage. 'You and me have been through worse, much worse than this, haven't we, now?'

Edward muttered something in reply, and Tassie, pressing her ear to the side of the cage to hear it, sighed deeply. 'You're supposed to say something sensible to cheer me up, Edward. "Pieces of eight" is no use at all.'

That night, in the posting inn, on learning that she was expected to share a bedroom with Emilia while Edward was assigned to an empty stable at the rear of the building, Tassie took matters into her own hands. Feigning sleep, she waited till Emilia was snoring. Then she got dressed again and crept down to the stables herself. There, she wrapped herself in her cloak, pillowed her head on some hay intended for the horses, and slept at the side of Edward's cage.

The grooms made a bit of a fuss when they found her

there in the cold, chilly light of dawn; but Tassie quickly distracted them by showing them some of Edward's clever tricks. By the time a distraught and angry Emilia had finally tracked her down, she was sitting happily with the grooms on the floor of the stable, showing them how to trickle the dice by the light of a glimmering lantern, while Edward pecked gleefully at a crust of buttered bread that one of the grooms had found for him.

Emilia, after complaining bitterly to the coachman Hugh about Tassie's wild, termagant ways, turned on Tassie herself.

'You're a shameless jade, that's what you are!' she declared. 'It's not right that I should be forced to keep company with the likes of you!'

Tassie, white-faced, clutching Edward's cage close, said, 'It wasn't my choice that you should travel with me, Emilia, believe me.'

'Oh, I realise that!' jeered the other woman. 'You were hoping Master Marcus would travel with you, weren't you? You wouldn't have slept in the straw of the stables then, oh, no! Everyone in Portman Square, me and Sansom and all the rest, guessed immediately how you were after bedding him from the moment you set eyes on him. All that carousing round in the night with that parrot of yours, clad in a man's clothing, looking like a back-street bawd; and then you've the nerve to dress yourself like a fine lady, and go off to the theatre with him and Master Hal!'

'Darling Marcus! Darling Marcus!' squawked Edward suddenly.

Emilia looked at the bird in downright horror; then back to Tassie. 'Indeed you won't get Major Marcus Forrester in your clutches, let me tell you that now! He's promised to a real lady, he is, to Miss Philippa—oh, they've had a little disagreement, but they were childhood sweethearts, and she'll be back to him soon enough, soon as she realises his worth, so you keep your sticky little hands off him, madam!'

As soon as she realises his worth? thought Tassie. Yes, as soon as he's restored the prospect of his godfather's inheritance, which he is paying me to attend to.

Edward was quite silent now. Tassie looked down sadly at her chewed fingernails, and hands which were indeed greasy from feeding Edward his buttered bread. 'Perhaps you'd better go back to London, Emilia,' she said in a low voice. 'What Edward said—it was a joke. I think I ought to continue this journey on my own, don't you? It's a journey I have to make, because of a promise, you see.'

Emilia eyed her narrowly, suddenly uncertain. Bother the girl. If she wasn't careful, Tassie would twist her round her little finger as well, just as she'd got round Master Marcus, and the Beauchamp family at Portman Square, and even those grooms she'd found her with, dicing in the stables, at six of the clock this morning.

Funnily enough, the girl truly didn't seem to realise how pretty she was. Well, thought Emilia a little enviously, if she could only see herself as others did! The soft bed and wholesome food at the house in Portman Square had had their effect; she was as lovely as any lady Emilia had ever seen, in a wild sort of way, with those big green eyes that were almost too large for her delicate face, and thick golden curls that tumbled in sleep-tousled disarray around her slender shoulders...

Emilia hadn't missed the way those grooms had looked at her. Some ripe ideas going through *their* minds, no doubt. Yet even they had treated her with respect, bringing her coffee and fresh-baked rolls from the kitchen and hanging avidly on her every word as she explained how to trickle those dratted dice.

No hint of any bawdy mischief there, though in all truth,

with anyone else in the world, there should have been. Darling Marcus, indeed.

'I'm not leaving you alone, miss,' declared Emilia truculently at last, 'to get yourself into even more mischief! Besides, I promised them at Portman Square that I'd look after you. But when Major Marcus arrives, you leave him alone, you hear? He's not for the likes of you.'

Tassie said slowly, 'I've told you. I wouldn't want Marcus Forrester if he was the last, the very last man on earth.'

Emilia nodded, almost satisfied. They travelled after that in a state of armed truce, with Emilia complaining about her headaches instead of about Edward, and earning a promise from Tassie that she would find her some tansy—an old country cure—and make a brew of it for her as soon as they reached their destination. Then the sun came out, warming the chilly air; and Tassie, unable to bear Emilia's fretful worries about footpads and highwaymen as they drew further away from habitation, asked Hugh Roberts the coach driver if she could sit up on top with him.

At first Hugh thought she'd be a nuisance. So he was relieved when she sat quietly, her attention on the unfolding rural landscape, with her infernal bird in its cage wrapped in her cloak against the cool breeze. And he was unexpectedly pleased when he saw how the fresh air brought a little colour to the girl's pale cheeks.

Nevertheless, Tassie's quiet demeanour hid a state of turmoil. Emilia's stark accusation about her designs on Marcus still thundered in her ears. Had the servants guessed? Had they known about Marcus kissing her, about that awful scene in the bedchamber when he'd taunted her for being half-clothed?

What she'd replied to Emilia was still, in a way, the truth. Certainly, when she'd first had the misfortune to meet Major Marcus Forrester, she hadn't liked him one little bit.

How could she, when he was arrogant, and disdainful, and accused her of being a thieving little doxy? And yet things had changed during the vivid time she'd spent with him in London. She'd found herself actually enjoying being with him. Oh, they still sparred and insulted one another, but she felt he was—her friend.

She tried very hard not to think about the way he'd kissed her that night outside the Angel. But she couldn't help but remember it when she was halfway between sleep and waking, or when she caught him watching her with those vivid grey eyes. And the thought of what else his lips and hands might do to her made her pulse quicken strangely, and her blood race in her veins.

Was that what Emilia meant? Had the hostile maidservant seen it straight away? Tassie almost blushed with shame as she remembered Emilia's vicious accusation: 'Everyone guessed immediately how you were after bedding him from the moment you set eyes on him...' *Bedding him.* Suddenly something she had never really troubled to think about in relation to herself seemed very real when she thought of Marcus. She remembered the way he smiled at her, remembered the warm strength of his powerful body, the heart-stopping touch of his fingers, and she felt the colour rushing hotly to her face.

The coachman said, in a kindly voice, 'You comfortable enough out here, missy? Not too cold for you?'

Tassie pulled herself together with an effort. 'Not at all. I'm truly comfortable, thank you, Hugh. The fresh air suits me.'

Hugh nodded sagely. 'Aye. Sensible of you to get away from Miss High-and-Mighty in there. Don't you worry about her—you'll be safe enough from her bad tempers when Major Forrester catches us up. He's a good 'un, is Major Forrester.'

Bother the man Marcus, why did everyone go on about

him so? With a slightly dizzying feeling of horizons opening out rather too rapidly before her, Tassie gazed out at the
bleak fields, scattered with sheep, the bare-branched trees,
the stark ploughlands. Yet Hugh the coachman was right. She
felt she could trust Marcus, had felt it from the moment she
made that stupid bargain with him; knew that beneath his
autocratic, challenging demeanour he was basically a man
of honour. The thought crept into her mind that she *did* feel
safe with him.

If the coachman hadn't been there, she'd have chided herself aloud. Safe, with Marcus? Far from being safe, he was
possibly the most dangerous man she had ever met. Anyway,
he was still hoping for Philippa's hand—wasn't that what all
this was about? And how could she possibly waste so much
time thinking about a man who was in love with such a silly,
vain creature? Oh, drat and blast Major Marcus Forrester.
Darling Marcus. She would go mad if she couldn't turn her
thoughts to something else.

Suddenly, looking around, she realised how much she
was missing Georgie Jay and her old, familiar companions.
These were the sort of country roads she had walked many a
time with them. They'd lightened every journey with stories,
and jokes, and merry quips… She sighed. She doubted they
would miss *her*.

She turned to face the coachman suddenly, and her green
eyes were dancing again. 'Are you a gambling man, Hugh
Roberts?'

He turned to look at her in surprise, his face weather-
roughened and good-natured. 'I likes a wager now and then,
missy, as well as any honest fellow.'

Tassie grinned. 'Then listen, Hugh. Over there, beyond
that ploughed field, I can see a lonely seagull in the sky. I'll
wager you one whole shilling that before we get to the next
bend in the road, there'll be a cluster more.'

The coachman stared after her pointing finger. 'Nay. It be going away from us, that bird, for certain, lass! There'll be no more gulls this far inland, not this time of the year.'

'A shilling,' repeated Tassie, her eyes glinting.

'Very well, lass. You're on!'

A few minutes later, a horde of crying gulls rose into the air, and Tassie threw the coachman a look of pure triumph.

'You got me there, girl,' he admitted, looking almost pleased at her victory. 'But I'd appreciate the chance to earn my shilling back. Tell you what. In quarter of an hour or so, we should meet up with the mail coach from Oxford. I'll wager you the leading nags will be greys. How about it?'

'Greys? Fie, what nonsense. They'll be bay, most definitely bay. I trust you've got a good store of shillings on you, Hugh?' responded Tassie merrily.

And so the journey proceeded in a flurry of light-hearted banter and wagers, with Tassie gradually accumulating several of Hugh's shillings, and Hugh, openly entranced by his unusual passenger, only too pleased to hear her gleeful laugh. They were travelling through rural Oxfordshire now; and Tassie, even as she chattered with Hugh, never ceased to absorb the unfolding landscape with every fibre of her being: a church here, a stretch of woodland there, an ancient stone bridge over a fast-flowing river... The sense that she had been here before gripped her more strongly with every passing mile.

After one more night, which they spent uneventfully at a roadside inn just outside Cirencester, they reached the gates of the Lornings estate at eleven in the morning. Tassie knew she was in unfamiliar territory now; and, though still perched up beside the solid and reassuring figure of Hugh, she found her heart beating with apprehension as the carriage rolled along the sweeping drive.

Early lambs gambolled in nearby fields, and the blue sky

arched high above acres of parkland set in a fertile valley between the rolling Gloucestershire hills, but Tassie saw none of it. Instead she gazed at the vast, imposing mansion that was drawing steadily nearer, the mansion that was to have been Marcus's inheritance. She said at last, to Hugh, 'Is that where Marcus's godfather lives? It looks so big, so cold...'

'Not there,' said Hugh gruffly. 'Not at Lornings itself. He's had to move out, the old fellow has. In Queer Street, they say; so it's all closed up. Over yonder—' and he pointed with his thumb '—*that's* his home now. The Dower House.'

Tassie shivered as they pulled off the main drive and Hugh guided the horses along another, narrower track towards a stone-built old house that lay in the shelter of a copse of beech trees. It looked a twisted, ill-kempt place, with tall chimneys, and secretive gables, and a daunting multitude of stone-mullioned windows. She could picture only too well the kind of cross, bad-tempered old man who must inhabit a place like this. She bit her lip, then turned to Hugh. 'I don't suppose—I don't expect—that he'd be *too* disappointed, if I didn't arrive just yet, would he? If I waited somewhere nearby for a day or two, till Marcus arrived?'

Hugh grinned down at her. 'Always one for a jest, aren't you, lass? Course he'll be expectin' you. Master Marcus sent a message ahead, didn't he? Hup, Beauty! Hup, Starlight!' He drew his big horses to a halt a little way from the house, by the stable block. 'Down you get, now, and take that bird of yours with you. I reckon old Sir Roderick will be real glad to see you.'

Tassie slid down with Edward's cage in her hand and went slowly, with dragging feet, to knock on the big front door. She heard voices inside. A man's voice, slow and resentful, then a woman's, grumbling sharply. 'You go to the door, then, blast you, Jacob. I've got my hands a-full as it is with all this washing.'

'No, you go, woman! Who the devil can it be anyway, this time of day?'

Tassie's heart, already low, sank even further as the door opened slowly and a plump, short, cross-faced woman in her fifties stared first at her, then at Edward, and snapped, 'Be off with you! We don't want no tramps and beggars here!'

Then, before Tassie could reply, the woman saw the carriage with Hugh at the horses' heads and gave a start, calling back shrilly over her shoulder, 'Jacob! Jacob! Fetch the master, will you? Seems we've got visitors, though I'm blowed if I know who they are—oh, Sir Roderick, you're here already...'

The woman bobbed a curtsy and stood back as an elderly gentleman with faded blue eyes and a shock of white hair made his way slowly to the door, aided by a stick. He looked down at Tassie and then at the carriage with a puzzled frown on his lined face. 'What's this? What the deuce is this?'

Tassie, her heart shrivelling within her, said in a very small voice, 'Oh, dear. You're not expecting me, are you?'

In the back room of the Blue Bell, Georgie Jay had gathered his anxious band together. 'Well, boys? Any news?' He'd been out searching all day, and so had Lemuel and Billy. As each day went by they grew more anxious about Tassie. Georgie Jay had been furious with them for letting her go that night when she'd come back for Edward.

'We didn't know she intended runnin' off, Georgie!' Billy had protested. 'And anyway, no one's better than our Tass at lookin' after herself.'

'We've let her down badly, and that's the truth of it,' Georgie Jay snapped back. 'Now perhaps I'm to blame as much as any of you, but the fact remains that we can't be easy till we've found her!'

And then old Matt came in, bursting with news. 'Georgie,

I've tracked down the gent that Lemuel saw playing cards with our Tass at the Angel! Marcus Forrester is his name. *Major* Marcus Forrester. And the news is that he's recently sent a lass who sounds like our Tassie in a chaise to Gloucestershire!'

Billy was on his feet. 'I'll get 'im! I'll get this Marcus, for snatchin' our Tass!'

Georgie pulled him back down. 'Be easy now, Billy. Do you know exactly where, Matt?'

'No. But we can follow her path!'

'Indeed.' Georgie Jay nodded, a look of satisfaction spreading across his face. 'There we have it, lads. To Gloucestershire we go. And God willing we're in time.'

Chapter Eight

It was late at night when Marcus finally left the government offices just off the Mall and swung astride the horse that Hal was holding ready for him.

'God's blood, Hal,' he exploded to his friend as he gathered up the reins, 'It's no wonder we are losing the war in America if everything takes as long as this.'

His business with the War Office had been cumbersome and slow. For every hour he had been in the company of someone important, he had to spend at least two hours sitting chafing with impatience in some vast, firelit anteroom, heavy with furnishings and gloomy with portraits of England's past leaders.

'It's not our problem, Marcus,' responded Hal gravely. 'We're out of it now, remember?'

'Yes, but those wretched foot soldiers in the line regiments aren't. They're the ones who've got to put up with the incompetent fools dictating to them from three thousand miles away. Hal, it's enough to make me want to go back there and sort things out, I swear to you!'

'They won't have you, dear fellow, remember? You've

been discharged as unfit for active service. Anyway, I rather think it's as well for your godfather that circumstances forced you home.'

Marcus nodded slowly; and Hal, looking at the handsome but chilly set of his friend's features, thought to himself that someone should have warned Lord Sebastian Corbridge just what he was up against.

Caro had left for Bath, and the house was quiet. They all, even Sansom, Hal suspected, missed Tassie's bright if disruptive presence; and Hal was still privately worried about what Marcus planned for her. Only the other night, Marcus had suggested to Hal that they pay a visit to Lady Sallis's select little gaming establishment in Albemarle Street, where Sebastian spent much of his time and his money; Hal had agreed to go, but his unease was plain.

'I trust you're not thinking of getting Lady Sallis to take Tassie on,' Hal said bluntly. 'Her girls are on offer to the punters, Marcus, just as blatantly as the gaming tokens.'

'I've told you to rest easy on that score,' replied Marcus, but once they were there, Hal could not help but notice how intently Marcus took everything in; how he listened to every word as Lady Sallis herself, pleased at their interest and fluttering her lashes at Marcus, upon whom she clearly had designs, showed them round her Mayfair gaming rooms.

So it was with more than a little relief that Hal heard Marcus say now, as they rode home from the War Office through the darkened streets that led to Portman Square, 'My business in London's at an end, Hal. Tomorrow I'll leave for Lornings.'

Hal buttoned up his greatcoat against the frosty chill. 'Then of course I'll come with you.'

'No need for that!' Marcus was surprised. 'I'm grateful for your support, but I'll manage on my own.'

'Always did better together, though, didn't we?' grinned

Hal. 'Remember the action at Stony Point, when we made the enemy run? Besides, the house is too quiet without Caro. I'd rather come with you for a few days.'

'To the wilds of Gloucestershire? Are you quite sure?'

'Try keeping me away,' replied Hal wryly. 'I can't wait to see what sort of havoc that damned parrot's caused.'

'Dear God, don't remind me.' Marcus realised to his surprise that he was actually looking forward to seeing Tassie again.

Not only that—he *needed* to see her again. Because away from her bright, quicksilver presence, his plan to enmesh Sebastian at the card tables and cancel Roderick's terrible debts seemed a forlorn hope indeed, although he would never admit it to Hal.

Dusk was starting to gather above the rolling Gloucestershire hills as Tassie, sitting cross-legged on the big couch in her comfortable shirt and breeches, gathered up her cards and gazed thoughtfully at her opponent.

''Tis your turn to discard,' she pronounced. 'Let us hope the play runs more evenly this time, shall we?'

The white-haired old gentleman who faced her across the card table grinned delightedly. 'My dear girl,' he said. 'It has nothing to do with luck, and well you know it. You are an expert player. I thought I had a repique in that last hand, but your clever retention of the knave quite spoiled it.'

Edward, who was perched close by, lifted his head to give a knowing cackle. 'Well,' replied Tassie modestly, 'I think perhaps I had the balance of the cards.'

Sir Roderick chuckled openly. 'I haven't enjoyed a game of piquet so much in years. You are twenty points ahead; pray, don't feel guilty. But tell me. How do you do it?'

Tassie looked at him sideways. 'It isn't exactly *cheating*, you know…'

'Go on,' said Roderick, fascinated.

'There are ways, you see, of calculating the odds, depending on the level of the bids. But you must remember that a bid can only be overcalled by raising the number of tricks to be won or lost, do you understand?'

'Oh, dear,' sighed Sir Roderick. 'I can't really say that I do. If I manage to avert a rubicon, I shall be most gratified.' But his eyes twinkled with pleasure.

Tassie had been here for several days and nights, and to Sir Roderick it was as if a little sunshine had come into his life. He'd been surprised, certainly, to see the big travelling coach drawing up, with the girl, and her parrot, for the message Marcus had sent forewarning him had indeed gone astray; but the letter Emilia brought from Marcus, with the promise of his own arrival very soon, put his mind at rest, and he'd taken instantly to the girl. She was a distant relative, Marcus had explained somewhat vaguely, who was in need of a quiet retreat for just a little while. Well, she would have it. The girl, Tassie—what kind of a name was *that*?—had seemed frightened and lost, especially when the coach turned back, taking the sour-faced maid with it; but she'd put on a brave face, keeping the parrot with her at all times in its wicker cage. She'd eaten the food Peg brought her slowly, carefully, as if she didn't expect to get any more, and looked around her all the time, absorbing everything. Sir Roderick had gone to sit by her when she'd finished her meal that first night. 'My dear,' he said, 'please make yourself at home. Any friend of Marcus's is a friend of mine.'

Her big eyes had opened wide. *Why, she's lovely,* thought Roderick, *quite a lovely girl...* 'Well,' she began hesitantly. 'I wouldn't say we were exactly friends...'

'There's no need,' he'd said quickly, 'to tell me any more. You will stay.'

'Edward, too?' Seeing his hesitation, she pointed to the bird. 'Ah.'

'He goes everywhere with me. He knows Shakespeare and all sorts. *Macbeth* is his favourite.'

'*Macbeth?* How delightful. Edward can stay, too.' Sir Roderick had smiled. 'But—*Tassie*? You were not christened by that name, surely?'

She looked quickly up at him, her eyes shadowed with something that was almost fear. 'I am Tassie now,' she said.

'Very well,' he nodded gently. 'Tassie it shall be.'

Peg and Jacob had grumbled at first, about the extra work their guest would bring. But the next morning Tassie had been up bright and early, helping Jacob in with the logs and sweeping out the parlour. Then, when Jacob announced he was going to help with the milking at the home farm, Tassie asked if she could come, too. 'I used to work on farms in the summer,' she explained.

Peg's brother, Dick Daniels, ran the Lornings home farm for Sir Roderick. It was a small place, holding just a dozen cattle and some breeding ewes, but there was always plenty of work to be done, and Tassie proved herself useful there also. As for Sir Roderick, since losing so much of his money he'd retreated into himself, bitterly ashamed of his dreadful foolishness and of what he'd done to Marcus. But Tassie's arrival was a diversion, and a welcome one; she played cards with him every afternoon over tea, for tokens only, while Peg prepared the evening meal. Sir Roderick hadn't enjoyed himself so much for a long time. The girl brightened up the house. He looked forward now to Marcus arriving, but he was apprehensive, too. She was a distant cousin, Marcus said. But Roderick knew of no such relative. The girl was beautiful, special—where had she come from? Roderick trusted Marcus like a son; but if his motives towards the girl were anything less than honourable, Roderick knew he would have to challenge him.

And now, as the afternoon's shadows lengthened and the smell of Peg's delicious cooking came from the kitchen, the girl was sitting facing him, curled up on a comfortable couch in the breeches and shirt she seemed to prefer to dresses. She was casting him a mischievous glance as she threw down her last card, saying, almost apologetically, 'I'm afraid you haven't averted a rubicon, Sir Roderick. Will you cut for the deal?'

Sir Roderick laughed. 'I think, my dear, that my pride has suffered enough for one evening. We'll finish there, shall we?' He gathered up the cards, still smiling as he remembered the skill of her play.

She was silent for a while. Then she said, almost hesitantly, 'I don't suppose you've heard from Marcus? About when he'll be here?'

Roderick rested his kindly blue eyes on her upturned face. 'No, m'dear, I haven't heard. But he promised, in his letter, to come as soon as possible, and I trust him. Don't you?'

Tassie looked, just for a moment, disconcerted. Then she ran her hands through her loose blonde curls. 'Oh, yes. Of course,' she said airily.

But Sir Roderick wasn't sure she meant it, and he wondered, again, how things stood between her and Marcus.

Jacob knocked then on the parlour door, and came in. Usually by this time he was out doing his rounds, checking that everything was secure before dusk fell, not only here, but over the way, at the big, empty hall.

'Begging pardon, sir,' he said, 'but a couple of heifers have got out where the fence is down, and Farmer Daniels is needing someone to help round them all up before dark. Should I send for a lad from the village?'

'What about Will?' frowned Roderick. Will was Farmer Daniels's son.

'Will's up on the hills, with the sheep. He'll be on his way down now, but he can't bring them heifers in on his own, sir.'

Tassie had already jumped to her feet. 'Let me take one of your horses, Sir Roderick, and I'll help bring them in!'

Roderick frowned. 'You, Tassie? Oh, I know you can ride,' he added quickly. With his permission she'd taken out the grey palfrey in his stables, several times. 'But—bringing heifers in? That needs someone who knows what they're doing. And besides, it's starting to rain.'

She was already heading for the door. 'No matter,' she assured him, eyes sparkling. 'I've rounded up heifers lots of times. Don't worry. I'll make sure they're safe before darkness falls.'

Two hours later Tassie cantered back towards the Dower House, riding astride in her breeches behind Will Daniels, the farmer's son, holding him tightly round his waist as his sturdy cob covered the rough ground. Dusk was starting to enfold the hills, and the promised rain was now falling steadily, but she didn't care. It had been a grand afternoon.

Will had arrived on the scene soon after she did; together they'd dealt with the straying calves without difficulty. They'd cut hazel switches with the little knife Tassie always carried, and Tassie helped Will drive the heifers back to their field, swinging her switch authoritatively. 'Hup, hup. Now, Bonnie. Now, Silky. Get along there, you great beasts.'

Then Will repaired the broken fence with Tassie's help, hammering in a fresh post just as Georgie Jay and Lemuel would have done. Unfortunately Tassie's grey palfrey had cast a shoe, so she left her at the home farm to be seen to, then hitched herself up behind Will on his cob, to be taken back to the Dower House.

'You were amazin', Tass!' grinned Will back over his

shoulder. 'I'd never have managed those heifers without you, and that's for certain!'

Tassie's heart swelled. When Marcus finally deigned to put in an appearance, he would hear nothing but her praises, of that she'd made quite sure; and, truth to tell, none of her good deeds had caused her much hardship. She'd taken to Sir Roderick quickly, and was hugely grateful for his kind, unquestioning acceptance of her sudden arrival. She was relieved too that he appeared to know nothing of Marcus's plan to use her to win back his terrible losses. Jacob was an old dear, in spite of his fierce black beard and his scowl; and as for Peg, why, the plump old housekeeper had even started slipping morsels from the kitchen into Tassie's hand: slices of pie, dainty cakes, freshly buttered rolls, saying, 'Go on, girl. Get this down you. Lord knows, you need fattenin' up!'

At the thought of Peg's delicious baking, Tassie's stomach rumbled. She was soaked through, and her thin cambric shirt clung coldly to her body, but she was warmed by the certainty that there would be a roaring log fire and a hot meal waiting for her. 'Soon be back, Miss Tassie!' called Will, and she gripped him tighter, whistling a cheerful tune to herself as the cosy, lighted windows of the Dower House beckoned.

She didn't notice the two horsemen until they were almost at the house. But Will had seen them, because they were swinging their big horses round to block his path. 'Now, who the devil—?' muttered Will. Tassie peered round from behind Will's shoulder. They wore long greatcoats, with their collars turned up against the rain that was driving in from the hills...

Marcus, and Hal. Her heart gave a little warning jump. Hal looked the same as ever, but as for Marcus, she had forgotten how formidable he was, with his strong jaw and his glinting dark grey eyes and his long black hair drawn back from his face. And as she swiftly slid off the back of Will's horse, she saw that Hal was looking sheepish, almost embarrassed, while Marcus, why, Marcus looked absolutely furious...

Standing there, in her wet shirt and breeches, she lifted her chin defiantly, though her heart sank to the bottom of her boots, which were already half-full of water. God's teeth. What had she done wrong now? 'Well, Marcus,' she began with feigned cheer, 'this is a surprise—'

Marcus leaned forwards, towering over her from the saddle of his big roan. He said, flatly, 'Tassie. I think you'd better get inside, don't you? And get changed—*straight away.*'

Will protested, 'Sir. Sir, she was only tryin' to help—'

It was Tassie who cut in swiftly. 'It's all right, Will. I don't need you to defend me. Don't you think, Marcus, that you ought to find out *exactly what's going on,* before you start acting as if you owned us all?' She swept back her wet curls as the rain poured down relentlessly.

'It's quite plain to me what's going on,' said Marcus. 'And unfortunately your behaviour—careering around the countryside like a gypsy girl—doesn't surprise me in the least.' His expression was so hard, so grim, that Tassie, who hardly ever cried, felt an unbearable ache well up in her throat. She'd wanted so much to surprise him, with everything she'd done! But he was glaring down at her with narrow, disapproving eyes as if she was the stupidest creature on earth, and she wasn't going to explain now how she'd actually gone out to save his precious godfather's cows from being lost for good...

She swallowed hard, her eyes over-bright, and lifted her chin defiantly. 'I'll go in and get changed as soon as I've thanked Will properly for giving me a ride back.'

'You'll go inside this minute and make yourself decent, my girl!'

Will rode off quickly. She couldn't blame him. Biting her lip, Tassie walked with as much dignity as she could muster into the house. Then she ran blindly up the stairs to her little room under the eaves, where she flung herself face down on the bed, heedless of her wet hair, her soaking clothes.

She hated Marcus Forrester. He was arrogant, and cruel, and stupid; she must have been mad to agree to all this. She lay there in the darkness and felt as if her heart would break.

She didn't know how long she'd been up there when she heard all-too familiar footsteps coming unevenly yet purposefully up the wide oak staircase. Edward started to squawk wildly from his corner; she jumped to her feet to fling the cover over his cage just as the door swung open.

'I expected you to be changed by now.' Marcus stood there, his forbidding frame filling the doorway.

'Oh, you did, did you?' She put her hands on her hips defiantly. 'Come in, then, Marcus, do, and I'll get changed *now*! Why, you can tell me exactly what I should wear—since you seem to think you *own* me!' In a fever of wild rebellion, she started to tug at the buttons of her shirt; she had undone just two of them by the time Marcus had covered the distance between them and grasped her wrists. She had quite forgotten how strong he was, how powerful. She struggled against him, feeling suddenly afraid.

He tightened his grip, saying in a voice that was harsh with emotion, 'I sent you here to learn to be a lady. And I discover you riding pillion behind a farmhand. Whatever you wear for careering round the countryside, it shouldn't be *this*. Do you really not know why? Do I really have to show you?'

Tassie gazed at him, stunned. She had never seen him look quite so angry, quite so dangerous; every feature seemed etched in granite, and his black hair, wet from the rain, seemed to emphasise his hard strength. Her pulse thumped heavily, warningly; her throat was suddenly dry. She shook herself free. 'Since you make no secret of your—contempt for me, in whatever I do, then, yes, perhaps you'd better show me, Marcus. Feel free!'

He did. Before Tassie could even think of retreating, or crying out, he'd reached out with his strong hands to cup her breasts, gliding his palms flatly against the still-damp fabric of her shirt. Tassie gasped in shock as his heated touch sent flames through her whole body, and the crests of her nipples leapt traitorously in response. She froze, unable to move, unable to speak. He continued stroking devastatingly as he spoke, and it could have been the touch of the devil himself, so tumultuous were the sensations he aroused in her.

'When Hal and I arrived just now,' he gritted out, 'and saw you riding astride, behind that farm boy, you could almost have been naked, Tassie, for all the covering that your damp clothing gave you. I am not paying you to put on such a wanton display for my godfather, his servants, my friends. Didn't you see that Hal was speechless with embarrassment at the sight of you?'

Somehow Tassie pulled herself away from him, her fists clenched, her cheeks burning. 'My own horse cast a shoe. And how was I to know it was going to rain?' she breathed. 'Confound it, you blame the weather on me now, Marcus?'

She was pressing herself back against the wall, but there was no help there. His expression was hard, implacable; he advanced on her once more, circling his hands round her tiny waist, pulling her relentlessly towards him; and she realised, most dangerous of all, that her will to escape seemed to be vanishing fast.

'Very well,' he was saying, in a quiet voice that was even more punishing than his biting anger. 'The rain was not your fault. But other things are. Your breeches, charming though they may be, leave very little to a man's imagination. Your feminine figure, your slender limbs, are all too clearly outlined.' His strong hands were sliding down her hips, cupping her buttocks, pulling her remorselessly closer. 'There are women in Vere Street, I believe, who charge their rich clients a great deal of money to see them dressed in such a fashion…'

Tassie, almost beside herself at his touch, at the sweet ache of longing that assailed her whole body, pushed frantically and uselessly at his solid shoulders. 'Then perhaps I should seek my fortune in that way, and forget the mad, stupid bargain I have made with you, Marcus! Though I would not reckon much to my success in Vere Street, seeing how you've told me I am scrawny, and not to the taste of any gentleman of fashion!'

Marcus's grey eyes darkened almost to blackness. While one hand still clasped her hips, he used the other to cup her chin, to tilt her face towards him; and Tassie wanted to cry out in despair as his long, lean finger touched her cheek. Oh, he tormented her. He humiliated her and scorned her at every turn. Yet in his presence she wanted something, something she couldn't put into words, so very badly that she felt sick with longing.

And Marcus, too, gazing down at her expressive, passionate face, was overwhelmed, just as he had been when he'd seen her clinging behind the young farmhand on his sturdy cob with all her lovely hair curling about her cheeks, and her proud young breasts with their dusky areolae clearly visible beneath her soaking shirt, and Hal at his side breathing huskily, 'By God, Marcus, she's a beauty. A real beauty…'

Marcus had been harsh with her, he knew, but it was because his own male passions were raging unchecked, and the tightening at his loins told its own story. It maddened him that she still feigned not to know the effect she was having on men all around her, even as her sweet breasts thrust against his palms. He cursed inwardly as she continued to gaze up at him, her face so dazed, so expectant. Now was the time to leave, but instead his hands tightened round her waist as he grated out at last, 'Perhaps I was ill advised, minx, to tell you that you were not to my taste. Perhaps I will have to teach you yet another lesson...'

He bent to kiss her, meeting no resistance except, perhaps, a little tremor of shock. Her mouth was sweetly delectable as his tongue explored her parted lips, gently at first, then more strongly, thrusting and probing at the warm, velvety recess of her mouth. He heard her give a little sigh; she seemed to sway involuntarily against him, and then he forgot to think as he caught her in his arms, crushing her exquisitely feminine body against his own hard strength, deepening his kiss.

Tassie was fighting a losing battle against the tide of sensation that engulfed her. She'd felt shock, at first, when his tongue intruded into her mouth, and stiffened in resistance; but then its warm masculine strength, sliding so insistently between her lips, began to beguile her, and seduce her with its honeyed caresses. She wanted more, indefinably more; and a low insistent throbbing, a half-pleasurable, half-painful ache had set up at her loins, where the tightness of her breeches caressed her most secret parts. In truth, she felt as if her legs would no longer hold her. Desperately she clung to Marcus, her mouth lifted like an open flower for his kiss. She could feel the iron strength of his shoulder muscles beneath her fingertips; his shirt was no barrier at all; her breasts were pressed against his chest, and she could feel her nipples tingling and hardening anew, in a way that sent pleasurable yet shocking sparks of delight arrowing down to her abdomen. At the same time she heard him give a low, possessive growl deep in his throat, and before she realised what was happening his hand had slipped inside her open shirt and he was caressing one aching breast, enfolding its soft ripeness and gently rolling the nipple between finger and thumb so that dark passion started to shiver with increasing hunger through her trembling body.

He drew her to him with his other hand, more fiercely this time, cupping her slender hips and deliberately pulling them against his loins. She gasped as she felt the virile hardness there, shocked by the blatant evidence of his arousal, shocked yet swept along even further on a heightening plateau of desire. As his kiss deepened, her tongue twined with his with an intimacy that swept fire through her veins, at the same time flooding her with a deliciously pleasurable languor. She arched herself against him, nestling yet closer into his embrace, wanting to be nowhere else on earth…

'Ah, little temptress,' she heard him murmur, his voice husky with passion. 'Whoever taught you to kiss like that? What other delectable tricks do you know, I wonder?'

Tricks. Bait, to lure his enemy Corbridge. Feeling sick, Tassie pushed him away with a force that startled them both. 'You think—you think that I have been *taught*?' she breathed. 'At least, Marcus, I have learnt one thing today. I thought perhaps you were different from other men, but now I know that you are just the same as all the rest of your kind!'

He was controlling himself with a visible effort. His breathing was still ragged, and dangerous sparks burned in his eyes. 'You have a low opinion of men.'

'Indeed,' she replied bitterly. 'Men are always ruled by their physical passions—doesn't every woman on earth know that?'

Marcus caught his breath. He knew, of course, that the girl had lived wild. But the thought of another man kissing those sweet lips, tasting her yielding softness, set a blazing anger burning deep within him.

He stepped back from her and said, in a voice he forced to be cold, 'Never fear, Tassie. I will not touch you again. But now, perhaps, you see why you shouldn't dress as you do.'

Oh, thought Tassie blindly, he was blaming her, blaming her for all of it. And why should he not? Hadn't she melted in his arms, and let his burning kisses scorch her very soul? Didn't she still wish, even now, with the sparks of their passion still smouldering, that he would pull her into his arms, and kiss away her tears?

She found her voice with a huge effort. 'Oh, yes? So 'tis all my fault? Perhaps you shouldn't *look* at me like that!'

He said sharply, 'It would be hard for a man not to look at you when you are half-naked, woman, as you surely know. Garb yourself in some decent attire, before I'm forced to take you in hand and beat you for your disobedience as I would an impudent stable boy!'

Tassie faced up to him scornfully. 'So that's your fancy, is it, Marcus? I've heard the rich gents pay handsomely for *that* in Vere Street as well.'

'Put your clothes on,' he repeated flatly. 'And do something about that hoydenish hair of yours, will you? Then we'll try to forget that this ever happened.'

He went out, banging the door behind him. Tassie went blindly over to the window, hugging her arms over her breasts, biting her lip as she gazed out at the driving rain sweeping across the night-enfolded valley. Out there in the darkness lay Lornings Hall, Roderick's silent, empty, lovely home. Lornings was all that Marcus thought about; he wanted Lornings for himself, and, of course, for Philippa.

She turned back to face her little room, and this time the tears rolled hotly. She'd known he was dangerous, known from the moment she first set eyes on him in the Angel. He stirred something deep within her that she was totally unequipped to deal with; just how ill-equipped, she'd only now learned. He could have bedded her just then; just like that farmhand she'd seen making love in the barn to the dairymaid he'd later called a slut. Love was the wrong word for a foolish, almost brutish act, she used to think, but when Marcus had held her, and kissed her, the sensations he aroused in her had been strangely, compellingly wonderful...

Little temptress... The worst of it was that he'd assumed she'd done that kind of thing often. She was deeply, bitterly hurt by his assumption. It was what he *wanted* to believe of her, she supposed. It made him feel happier about treating her as he had.

Oh, what fools men were. What a fool *she* was. Tassie scrubbed the threatening tears fiercely from her eyes with the back of her hand. She'd keep her side of the bargain, and play her part to perfection in winning back the letter that promised Sir Roderick's estate to Sebastian. Then she'd take her fifty guineas, and she'd walk out of his arrogant life, to begin a new life, her own life, and never see him again...

Edward was grumbling again under his cover. At least it had protected him from Marcus. She wished she could protect herself as easily. Her stupid tears began to roll hotly again as Marcus's last stinging comment rang viciously in her ears. 'Do something about that hoydenish hair of yours...'

She pulled her sharp little knife out of her boot and carefully fingered its gleaming edge.

Across the valley in the village of Hockton the local inn was all astir, for a little earlier a traveller had arrived, a slender, immaculately clad London gent with powdered hair, who cursed the bad roads, and the food at the inn, and said he and his servant would stay for the night only because there was nowhere else within miles. As twilight fell this traveller, from the window of his bedroom, gazed across the rainswept landscape at the distant outline of Lornings Hall, magnificent as ever. Then there was a knock at his door, and in came his servant, Silas Jenkins, whom the underworld of London knew as a locksmith, famed for his skill and his discretion.

He carried his workman's bag; his fingers bore traces of oil, and specks of rust. 'All done, me lord,' he intoned softly. 'And there's some other news. There's travellin' folk come recently to these parts. And everyone knows travellin' folk to be thieves....'

Lord Sebastian Corbridge allowed a cold smile to lighten his features. 'Really, Silas? That is convenient indeed,' he breathed.

Chapter Nine

After his argument with Tassie, Marcus had stormed downstairs in a turmoil of fury and scarcely restrained arousal, cursing himself bitterly for sending the girl here. He joined his godfather and Hal, who were seated at the big dining table ready to begin their evening meal. Savoury scents wafted enticingly from the joint of sizzling mutton that Sir Roderick was starting to carve; Peg was bringing in a dish of golden roast potatoes and a jug of gravy, but Marcus hardly noticed them. It was some moments before he started to listen properly to the conversation around him.

'She's a real treasure, that girl,' Sir Roderick was saying to Hal as he passed him a thick slice of meat. 'Yes, from the minute she arrived, she's been cheerful, helpful, polite. The only trouble is that when she leaves, Peg's going to demand a girl to replace her!' He chuckled.

'She's a treasure indeed, sir,' echoed Peg, beaming as she lowered a bowl of buttered parsnips to the table. 'And she's proved a proper little helper to my brother Dick Daniels at the farm, and to young Will, his son as well.'

'That's true enough,' nodded Jacob sagely as he set down

a decanter of claret. 'Farmer Daniels says she knows everything as well as his Will, who was brought up to the life! She helps with the milkin', and the feedin', and even helped stable the beasts the other night when Will was out with the sheep.'

Marcus, astonished, gazed at Hal, who looked back, his fair eyebrows faintly raised in echoing surprise.

'Tassie?' Marcus was saying incredulously. 'Tassie knows about milking, and livestock?'

'Indeed, sir!' responded Jacob. 'Why, only an hour before you arrived, Major Forrester, she went a-dashing off at full tilt, not even bothering to cover her pretty head against the rain, to help Will bring in some heifers that had broken loose—just as well, because otherwise we'd have lost 'em for good, I'm thinking.'

Marcus, his plate heaped with succulent mutton, suddenly realised he'd lost his appetite completely. *'Heifers?'* And then Sir Roderick joined in.

'Yes, Marcus, I suppose I shouldn't have let her go, really; but Tassie was so anxious to help. She's an excellent rider, so I wasn't worried about her, though it was unfortunate that her palfrey cast a shoe... I was glad, though,' he added quickly, 'that you sent her upstairs straight away to get changed out of those wet things. So often, she has no thought for herself.'

Marcus was allowing Peg to pile potatoes on to his plate without even seeing them. As Peg moved on, Hal took the opportunity to lean quickly over to Marcus and whisper, 'Weren't too hard on her, were you, dear fellow? For galloping round the countryside, looking like a rather delectable country maid?'

'Yes,' replied Marcus rather bitterly, 'yes, I'm afraid I was.'

Just then Peg mused, 'Now, I'm wonderin' where our

Tassie is. It's not like her to miss her food, especially when she peeled all those potatoes herself.'

Marcus could stand no more. Feeling as if heaps of burning coal were being piled on his head, he jumped up and said abruptly, 'I'll go and see what's happened to her.'

He took the stairs two at a time and rapped hard at her door. 'Tassie. Are you there? Look, Tassie, I'm sorry. I was an idiot and a brute to speak to you as I did. Come down to dinner, Tassie, please.'

No reply. He knocked again, his heart sinking, for silence was the only response. Then he opened the door to her room, knowing he would find it empty. Her still-damp shirt and breeches lay forlornly across her little bed, reproaching him. Even her damned parrot was silent, gazing at him with beady, implacably hostile eyes. Of Tassie herself, there was no sign.

And then, on the floor, he saw it. Hanks of curling golden hair lay scattered on the scrubbed floorboards, reproaching him with their brightness. Dear God.

He went back downstairs quickly. 'She's gone,' he said curtly to their expectant faces. 'It's my fault. I—I was harsh with her.'

'Gone?' Their faces were astonished; Sir Roderick looked the most upset of all. 'You mean you think she might have run away? But wherever to, Marcus, at this time in the evening?'

Jacob said suddenly, 'Beg pardon, Major, but I wonder if she might have gone over to the Hall, to Lornings, I mean? She's been with me several times when I do my rounds—likes looking at the pictures and things, she does.'

'But the Hall will be locked, surely,' said Sir Roderick. 'And I have the only key.'

Marcus said slowly, 'Keys and locks have not hindered Tassie before. I'll walk over to the Hall and take a look.'

Hal said anxiously, 'Do you want me to come with you, Marcus?'

Marcus shook his head. 'My thanks, Hal, but if she's there, I want to speak to her alone. I have certain amends to make.'

He took the key, and pulled on his greatcoat, and set off by himself up the lane that led to the Hall.

How many memories this place brought back for him. The rain had stopped, but black clouds still drifted raggedly across the moon, and all around him the bare-branched beeches moaned softly in the night breeze. Lornings Hall stood before him, its stark turrets etched against the sky. He gazed at the big old house, recalling every door, every staircase, every room, like the back of his hand.

By September, all this would belong to Sebastian Corbridge. 'Not if I can help it,' Marcus breathed aloud. 'Not if I can damn well help it.'

Here, in Lornings' expansive grounds, he had learned to ride and to shoot under Farmer Daniels's eagle eye. He remembered Peg, the housekeeper, up to her arms in flour in the kitchen; black-bearded Jacob, too, grumbling but loyal. There'd been an army of under-servants to look after the great Hall then; he remembered parties, at Christmas and in the summer, with carriage after carriage rolling up the long drive, and the house filling with laughing, glittering people, including Philippa and her parents, who came over often, from their nearby estate at Caytham. The house was a part of his life.

And was all this justification for what he was doing to Tassie? a little voice suddenly asked him. He remembered the stark pain in her expressive eyes as he chided her so sharply. Yes! Yes, of course it was. They'd made a bargain, hadn't they? She was getting exactly what she wanted—her fifty guineas. It was just that he, Marcus, hadn't bargained for the surges of swift, almost violent emotion she stirred in him whenever he got too close to her...

Don't be deceived by her, he told himself grimly. *She knows exactly what she's doing. She's travelled wild with her tinker friends for years, and you're deceiving yourself if you think she's been protected from the realities of that kind of life.* Yet her kiss had been wild and sweet, her wide eyes full of innocent wonder—and she had aroused him more than he would have believed possible.

He climbed the wide steps to the imposing front door— only to find it locked. There was no tell-tale flicker of light, no sign of life. If Tassie had got inside, then she was lying low. Carefully he undid the iron-studded door with the big key, swung it open, and stepped into the vast, stone-flagged hall. Lighting one of the candles that stood in a holder on a brass-bound oak table, he picked it up and slowly mounted the double-branching staircase to the long gallery, where the flickering light sent dancing shadows across the dark-panelled walls, the dusty coats of arms, the ancient tapestries depicting hunting scenes and battles of long ago.

Suddenly, he saw a taper burning at the far end of the gallery, where it opened out into the adjoining banqueting hall. Tassie was there, gazing up at the oil portraits that lined the walls; her dark green cloak was draped across the nearby balustrade. If she knew he was there, she pretended not to. She looked pale, but composed.

Which was more than Marcus could say for himself; because as soon as he saw her he felt his body jar with shock. She'd changed into one of the dresses she'd purchased with Caro; and as if to highlight the enigma she was, the green velvet gown with its elegant tapered sleeves and sweeping skirts reminded him that she would pass anywhere as a lady of gentle birth.

But her hair!

Marcus felt a stab somewhere in the region of his heart when he saw how it clung to her head in ragged, rebellious golden curls. She must have hacked it off herself, savagely, in minutes. Yet she still, somehow, looked so vulnerably, achingly lovely that he felt his heart wrench dangerously within his breast.

Marcus knew, in that moment, that if Lornings were ever to be removed from Sebastian's clutches by using this girl as his weapon, then he must take care lest the weapon turn on himself.

Tassie turned to gaze at him, outwardly composed, although in fact her heart was thudding against her chest, because something about Marcus's harshly masculine figure, the gleam of the candlelight on his purposeful features as he strode up those wide stairs, unsettled her badly. *He will not cancel our agreement,* she told herself shakily. He will not send me away; I am too useful to him.

She drew herself up and tilted her chin. 'Well, Marcus?' she enquired calmly. 'What have you come to chide me about this time, pray?'

Marcus put down the candle on a nearby oak chest. She spoke so well when she'd a mind to it! Where did she learn to talk like that? Not from her vagabond friends, that was for sure. 'Well, minx,' he answered with equal calmness, 'you gave them all a fright, over at the Dower House. Roderick said you never, ever missed your dinner, which is something I can well believe. So, as they all blame me for your disappearance, I thought I'd better come and look for you.' He kept his voice deliberately light, though there was a curious ache in his throat, because of her shorn hair.

'How did you guess I was here?' Her eyes were dark with wariness, her voice cool—but what else had he expected?

'Jacob told us you sometimes came over here with him. Roderick was worried that you hadn't a key, but I told him I didn't think that would be a problem.'

A flicker of guilt crossed her face, followed quickly by

defiance, and he saw something of the old, vagabond Tassie re-emerging. He was astonished at how glad he felt.

'Fie, it's scarcely my fault if the catch on the pantry window needs fixing!' she responded tartly. She added defensively, 'Oh, I secured it again once I was in. I always do.'

'I'm glad to hear it,' he responded with suitable gravity, though his mouth twitched a little at the thought of her scrambling, in that velvet gown, through a pantry window. 'I've come to escort you back, Tassie. They're keeping your dinner hot for you.'

She hesitated, then said with an effort at nonchalance, 'I rather thought you'd come to tell me our bargain was off, Marcus.'

He shook his head. 'Far from it. I've come to say I'm sorry, Tassie, for my behaviour earlier. It was stupid of me.' He ran his hand over his thick dark hair. 'A simple physical reaction, I fear, a mindless male response. That is no excuse, I know—but at least it's an apology. And I assure you it won't happen again.'

Tassie's eyes flashed. 'Then you'd better remind yourself, Marcus, the next time you're overcome by your—your *mindless male response*—that really you much prefer your women to simper, and wear pink ruffles, and send you scented love notes with locks of their hair—'

'God's blood, woman!' roared Marcus, 'I came here to *apologise*, don't you understand? Why do you always make everything so damned difficult?'

She clenched her fists and blazed back. 'An apology? You call this an apology, when all you do is hurl insults at me?'

Marcus drew a deep, steadying breath. 'Very well. I will say it again, as plainly as I can. I am sorry. For so misjudging you, for scolding you, for reacting in such a crudely masculine way.'

She contemplated him coolly. 'You must want Lornings very badly, to grovel so to someone like me.'

'I don't want to see my godfather ruined, and Sebastian getting his grasping hands on his estate. I am doing all this for Roderick.'

'But of course,' she murmured witheringly.

He controlled himself with an effort. 'I have told you, Tassie. I will release you from our bargain whenever you wish.'

'No, you won't,' she replied softly, with a challenging gleam that threw him completely. 'Because I don't *want* to be released. I want the fifty guineas you promised me. After all, I'm nothing but a greedy, rough vagabond—*ain't I*? Fifty guineas, Marcus. That's the only reason I'm here.'

'Well,' said Marcus, his eyes the colour of rain-washed slate, 'well, at least we know where we stand.'

'Yes, we do, don't we?' Tassie answered brightly. 'And now, do you think you had better escort me back to the Dower House? Before your friends begin to think that perhaps I am—in the brazen way of a *temptress*—trying to seduce you?'

He gritted his teeth. 'By God, minx, you're enough to try the patience of a saint! I wish I had taken my hand to you back there!'

She laughed, but her emerald eyes flashed warningly. 'Now, now, Marcus. Control yourself. In case you succumb to—what was it?—your mindless male urges again.'

He was momentarily speechless. Then he picked up the candlestick and said, 'It's time to go back. Perhaps you would deign to accompany me in the conventional fashion this time, Tassie. Through the front door, that is.'

'I will, and gladly,' she replied tartly, picking up her cloak and slipping it on. 'Though I would suggest you move rather quickly, Marcus, because that dripping candle wax is about to burn your fingers.'

'*Damnation*—' Quickly he put down the dying taper and lit another from its dwindling flame. Then, still grim-faced, he gave her a formal little bow and escorted her downstairs, and out through the front door. After locking it, he left her briefly to go round the back. 'Just to check everything's secure,' he said pointedly.

'I told you, I locked the pantry window once I was inside,' she retorted. 'But check if you must.' And, perching herself on the low stone wall that bordered the courtyard, she pulled her cloak more tightly round herself and began to whistle 'The Bold Ploughboy' as loudly as she could, just to annoy him.

But as soon as he was out of sight and out of hearing, she stopped, and gazed up at the cold moon as the clouds danced across its pale, pure light. Her heart ached so badly it felt as though someone had taken it out, and bruised it, and given it back to her with 'Marcus' etched scornfully all over it. Darling Marcus.

She stared with wide, unseeing eyes into the darkness. He had dismissed the kiss that had shaken her to her very core as nothing. And yet she had never in her life dreamed that she could feel as she did when Marcus took her in his arms, when he pressed his lips to hers...

She realised, with a stabbing pain at her heart, that she was in love with a man who, if he felt any emotion for her at all, despised her for the way she had lived. For being what she was.

Then she jumped to her feet, because she could hear footsteps coming back around the side of the house. 'Saints and fiddlesticks, Marcus, what took you such an age? I am almost freezing to death out here...'

But the words died in her throat, because the man she was looking at was not Marcus at all, but—Lemuel!

She blinked. 'Lem—what on earth—?'

He put his fingers to his lips. 'Hush, Tass,' he breathed. 'Thank God you're safe!' He pressed a scrap of paper in her hand, and then he scuttled off on his long legs into the blackness of the overgrown shrubbery. Tassie, startled beyond measure, gazed after him. In the name of Methuselah, what was *he* doing here? Were Georgie Jay and the others with him? How on earth had they found her here at—*Lornings*?

She jumped again as she saw Marcus approaching, with that slightly uneven stride that was the only vulnerable part of him. She crumpled the note quickly and thrust it beneath her cloak.

He looked at her, frowning. 'Are you all right, Tassie? You look very pale.'

She shrugged. 'No wonder. I've probably caught my death of cold, waiting for you. And that wouldn't fit in with your plans at all, would it, Marcus?'

He suppressed an exclamation of annoyance; then he set off towards the Dower House, and she sauntered along behind him. But inwardly she was badly shaken by this new complication. She dreaded to think how Marcus would react if he knew her London friends were close by. Her fingers tightened round the note in her pocket; she longed to read it, yet feared what it might say. What were they *doing* here?

Such was her consternation that she quite forgot to tell Marcus what she'd been meaning to tell him. That since her last visit to the Hall a few days ago, some of the paintings from the banqueting hall had disappeared.

Marcus was not the most popular of people at the Dower House that night, whereas Tassie was warmly welcomed to the table to eat her own belated meal. She merrily pretended to everyone that she'd cut her hair on a whim. But Peg kept glancing at her cropped curls as she cleared away the dishes, clucking under her breath, 'Like a shorn lamb, she be. A shorn lamb...'

After dinner, the four of them played whist. Apart from Tassie's brittle gaiety, the atmosphere was forced; and Marcus knew, when everyone but he and Hal had retired for the night that he was in for a rough ride.

'Ye gods, Marcus,' exploded Hal as he paced the room, 'what did you say to her? What did you do, to make the girl hack off all her lovely hair?'

Marcus spread out his hands. 'All right, it's my fault. I accept it. I scolded her for riding around in unseemly attire, and she took it ill, and cut it off in a fit of pique.'

'You—*scolded* her. Is that all?' queried Hal suspiciously.

Marcus stopped and faced his friend. 'I was harsh with her, Hal. I told her she looked like a strumpet, and could expect to be treated like one if she went around galloping pillion to a farm hand.'

'A strumpet...' Hal shook his fair head. 'All right, so she was in breeches, and clinging on to that farm lad to stop herself falling off—but she looked so genuinely pleased to see us, Marcus! Until you started to go on at her, that is! I'd swear she didn't realise that—that...'

'That she was revealing her feminine charms in a rather obvious manner?' intervened Marcus harshly.

'Oh, I don't know,' said Hal, perplexed. 'You're the expert on the fairer sex, Marcus. Does she seem to you like a woman of experience?'

Marcus ran his hand tiredly through his hair. No. No, she didn't in the slightest. And that was just the trouble. She'd lived in the company of travelling rogues for years, with no such thing as a guardian or chaperon to protect her blossoming beauty. And yet—when he'd kissed her, when he'd

drawn her close against him and moulded her soft curves to
his own hard frame, she'd trembled at his every caress, as if
he was revealing dark and delectable secrets to her for the
very first time... Dear God, she was a mixture of innocent
and temptress that haunted his senses! Normally, Marcus
was well able to control his passions. He wasn't some ardent
green lad, wildly excited by a fumbling kiss. Yet if it hadn't
been for a supreme effort of will on his part, he'd have been
tumbling her to the bed, all caution thrown to the winds. He
had a sudden vision of her clouds of golden hair shimmering
around her naked, lissom body; of her slender arms clinging
to him as he pleasured her; of her tender breasts peaking
in his mouth, and her soft lips murmuring his name... He
groaned inwardly.

'Look,' he sighed at last. 'She's either totally naïve, or
possessed of a cunning that makes fools of both of us. Either
way, it's no use getting sentimental over the girl. I need to
get on with this business as soon as possible, and prepare
her for her encounter with Corbridge.'

Hal frowned. 'Your damned card game. What if she
doesn't beat him?'

'Of course she will. Do you remember how easily she
duped *you*, at the Angel?'

'Must say I'd prefer not to,' acknowledged Hal ruefully.
'But I still don't like it, Marcus! Even someone with her skills
is subject to the vagaries of fate; some day her luck will run
out for certain.'

Marcus, suddenly exasperated, lifted his head up at that.
'Luck, you call it? Did you notice, Hal, how thoroughly Tassie
and Roderick trounced us at whist this evening?'

'I did, but of course that was because you and I constantly
had the worst of the cards!'

'Not a bit of it, my friend. The girl you feel so sorry for
was using the Kingston Bridge trick in as polished a fash-

ion as I've ever seen—bending all the trumps very lightly each time they passed through her extremely nimble and not so innocent hands.' Marcus's face suddenly broke into a grin. 'I didn't mention it, partly because her partner—Roderick—was enjoying winning hugely, and partly because I'd no desire to add further to my reputation as a persecuting monster of innocent females.'

Hal's blue eyes danced with amusement. 'Maybe you're right about her twisting us all round her little finger.'

'I am right about her, believe me. She's completely charming, I know, but the scheming little minx knows exactly what she's doing. Even the cutting of her hair was done to make me appear a black-hearted oaf. She's enjoying all this, Hal, enjoying sharpening her wits on us.'

'Two guineas,' Hal was breathing. 'Two guineas I lost in that game this evening...' He looked with sparkling eyes at Marcus. 'Maybe you're right. Maybe she is a match for anyone, even Sebastian. Yet—you'll take care of her, Marcus, won't you?'

'I will,' said Marcus, in an unexpectedly gentle voice.

But Tassie, who had been listening at the door, didn't hear this last bit, because she couldn't bear to hear any more. *Scheming minx...looking like a strumpet...*

Her cheeks burned as Marcus's insults rang in her head. In the darkness she swiftly found her way to the stone-flagged kitchen and pulled open the heavy door that led out into the yard, where the night air cooled her heated skin. Closing the door behind her, she hurried across the yard and hitched up the heavy skirts of her green velvet dress so she could sit on the stone wall that linked house and stables. Confound the man. She'd only helped Sir Roderick win the game because she thought it would make him happy! She ran her fingers rather distractedly through her ragged crop of golden curls.

'I do believe,' she said softly into the darkness, 'that I have had enough of this miserable bargain.'

She pulled out the little note Lem had given her from the pocket of her gown and read it once again. *Tassie. We are staying near the village they call Hockton. If you are able to get away, then come to the big oak at the crossroads there, behind the churchyard. We will keep watch for you every night, after dark.*

She would go to them now. It would take her only minutes to run to her room and change into her old, comfortable clothes; then she would pick up Edward, and ride to Hockton, and beg her friends to take her away. The occupants of the Dower House would not even notice she was gone till the morning; Marcus would rant and rave, perhaps, for a while, but he would soon get over her loss. Nay, she thought, he would be *relieved.*

There were slow footsteps coming across the courtyard towards her. Scrambling from the wall, she pushed the crumpled note back in her pocket. Don't let it be Marcus. Please don't let it be Marcus.

It was Sir Roderick. He saw her and stopped in surprise, then smiled at her, resting one hand on his stick. 'Why, my dear. You should not be out here, in this chill wind, all alone.'

Tassie said quickly, 'I was over-warm inside. I just needed some fresh air.'

He nodded sympathetically. 'I understand. I come out here every night, to look out over the valley and take my fill of the Hall yonder. Don't you think it is the most beautiful house?'

'Yes,' said Tassie with heartfelt emotion. 'Yes, Sir Roderick, it truly is.' Watching him as he gazed at the moonlit mansion through the trees, she saw how his faded blue eyes were warm with memories.

'It has been my life, you know, that house,' he said. He turned towards Tassie. 'Marcus tells me that he has a plan to save Lornings for me. I do not know the details, but he has given me hope; and I am so very, very grateful to him.'

Tassie caught her breath. 'Of course,' she said. 'Marcus wants to see you back in your rightful home, Sir Roderick.'

He smiled. 'He is the very best of godsons. And having you here as well does me so much good, my dear. Will you play one last game with me, before I retire?'

An owl hooted somewhere in the darkness, an omen, as Tassie felt the trap closing around her. '*Now*, Sir Roderick?'

'Yes, now.' He chuckled. 'It's a good time for you to teach me some of your tricks, for Hal and Marcus are at present shut in my study trying to untangle the estate's accounts for me. The dear boys, I would so love to beat them again. Unless, of course—' he looked anxious '—you are weary of my company, which I would quite understand.'

'Of course not,' Tassie declared. Then her mouth dimpled in a smile. 'If you like, Sir Roderick, I'll teach you some of my—*special* tactics.'

'Really? What tactics, my dear?'

'Well,' Tassie began to explain, as arm in arm, they walked back towards the Dower House, 'next time we play Marcus and Hal you must watch my right hand.'

'Your right hand. Yes.'

'And if my first finger is outstretched, you must put down a diamond. If it's my second finger, then play a club, my third a heart, and my fourth, why, then, a spade!'

Sir Roderick's eyes gleamed with mischief as they crossed the yard. 'High or low, m'dear?'

'When I raise my eyebrows, thus…' she arched them delicately '…high. If my glance is cast down at the table, then—low. You see?'

'Diamond, club, heart, spade,' he was muttering gleefully. 'Diamond, club…'

Tassie grinned as they reached the door. 'Tomorrow we shall wipe the floor with them, dear Sir Roderick!'

He chuckled with delight. And Tassie followed him back inside, all thoughts of flight dismissed for now, because how could she break her bargain, and all but destroy the kindly old man who had taken her in, who trusted her?

She had cast deep. She would have all on, now, to play her way out of this one; and in the meantime she had to get a message to Georgie Jay and his band, to tell them where her present duty lay.

Chapter Ten

On rising the next morning, Tassie dragged a brush through her shorn curls and tussled impatiently with the side fastenings of her plain morning gown of grey dimity, smoothing the skirts awkwardly over the hoop. Saints and fiddlesticks, what a stupid garment, she muttered, casting a longing look at her breeches, which lay over a chair nearby. The grey gown enveloped her securely from ankle to neck, giving little hint of the slender figure beneath; perhaps that was just as well, for no man, not even the objectionable Marcus, could accuse her of setting out to be a whore in *this*.

Feeling ready, almost, to face the person who was the cause of her wretchedly sleepless night, Tassie went downstairs, drew a deep breath, and entered the low-beamed breakfast parlour. The morning sun shining through diamond-paned windows dazzled her for a moment, then she saw Hal and Marcus, already tucking with soldiers' appetites into the thick slices of fried ham and freshly baked bread that Peg had laid out on the big oak table.

Relieved that she was not alone with Marcus, Tassie nodded to them both as they quickly got to their feet. 'Good morning to you, Hal. Good morning, Marcus.' She was pleased to see some astonishment on their faces. Excellent. She had wrong-footed them already, with her ladylike attire and her polite greeting. 'I trust you have both slept well?' Then, before they could even catch breath to reply, she held out her hands, and deposited several shillings on the table. ''Twas a little jest of mine, to assist Sir Roderick in trouncing you both at cards last night. I hope you bear me no ill will?'

Hal laughed. 'No ill will at all, dear girl. I'm glad to know that your talents have not deserted you. As, I am sure, is Marcus.' Marcus frowned as Hal hurried quickly round the table to pull out a chair for the waiting Tassie. 'Allow me to help you. Some breakfast? A dish of tea?'

Marcus had sat down again, and was pouring himself more coffee. He watched all this suspiciously, expecting to see Tassie carve for herself a great hunk of crusty white bread, and smear it thickly with butter before cramming it greedily into her mouth. But instead, she said, with the merest flicker of her demurely lowered eyelashes, 'Tea, yes; and perhaps you will just cut a small—a very small—slice of bread for me, if you please, Hal. A lady never has much appetite, you see, first thing in the morning.'

Marcus almost choked over his coffee. 'Tassie,' he said, 'Tassie, it's only us, you know. Are you sure you're feeling quite well? Normally you devour half a loaf at breakfast.'

She flashed him a look that held daggers. 'You wish me to be a lady,' she said coolly. 'And so I would thank you, Marcus, not to mock my efforts. Would you pass the dish of butter, Hal? My thanks.'

She ate a few tiny sparrow-like mouthfuls and sipped her tea while Marcus and Hal watched, dumbstruck. Then she dabbed at her lips with the damask napkin and said airily, 'I have a fancy to go out for a brief morning ride, Marcus. I take it you will not object?'

Marcus's eyes narrowed. Ah, now, this was more like it. The wench was planning something—he'd wager a soldier's monthly pay on it. 'Not at all,' he said smoothly, 'I take it you've no objection if I accompany you?'

He knew, by the flash of disappointment that crossed her expressive face, that his guess was right. He'd foiled her in some way. But she merely said, 'Then I had better go and change into my riding habit.'

He stood and gallantly pulled back her chair, giving a slight bow as she rose from the table and left the room. Hal, grinning, pointed out, 'She's up to something, Marcus. Watch your pockets, my friend.'

'You think I didn't realise that?' Marcus sat down again, a little apprehensively. 'Dear God, sometimes I wonder what I've let myself in for.'

He wondered that even more when Tassie rejoined him, still pale, but looking bewitchingly, dangerously pretty in her burgundy velvet riding habit, with the matching feathered hat perched on her cropped golden curls. Her air of slight self-consciousness, her shyness, made her all the more endearing. He cautioned himself inwardly as he led her out to the stable yard.

'Your hair looks well,' he said.

'Oh, that.' She shrugged. 'Peg followed me upstairs just now and neatened it up with a pair of kitchen scissors.' She turned her bright gaze on him. 'Do you want a curl of it, Marcus? Tied up in a blue silk ribbon?'

He caught his breath. 'I'll let you know,' he said. 'I don't actually keep a collection.'

Jacob had the horses ready for them. Marcus, of course, was to ride his big roan, Dancer, while an elderly bay mare had been fitted with a side saddle for Tassie.

He saw her face fall. 'Is that for me?' she exclaimed. 'But I cannot possibly ride in that silly fashion!'

Marcus said, with dangerous patience, 'You must accustom yourself to riding side saddle, Tassie, as every lady should.'

She tapped her full velvet skirt impatiently with her riding crop. 'Oh, of course. What else?' she said, smiling sweetly up at him. But he heard her cursing rather colourfully under her breath as Jacob led the saddled mare to the mounting block and held it steady as Tassie swung herself up into the unaccustomed perch. 'Fie and fiddle, Marcus,' she exploded, 'how on earth is one supposed to gallop in a contraption such as this, pray?'

Marcus, comfortably astride his own big horse, stifled his grin and said, 'In Hyde Park, Tassie, ladies do not gallop. They walk, sedately, so they may talk genteelly to their companions. At the very most, they trot.'

'It sounds,' Tassie said, gritting her teeth as she struggled to position her right leg more comfortably, 'like the most drattedly boring thing I have ever heard of.'

'Dratted is not a term a lady would use, Tassie.'

She turned her calm, unsettling gaze on him. 'But I am not a lady, Marcus. As you keep reminding me.'

Marcus, tight-lipped, led the way out of the yard. Why did she always make him feel so damnable guilty, when she was here of her own free will, when she'd openly admitted that she was motivated purely by his money? He sighed. At least the girl had spirit; she was urging on her slow mare with some skill, managing even to get a trot out of the old beast. As he allowed her to draw ahead of him, Marcus assessed her with a practised eye, approving the neat clinched-in velvet jacket, the full, flowing skirt, the little laced-up half-boots that peeped out from beneath the hem. Then he reined in his roving thoughts abruptly as he realised he was seeing not the clothes, but the delectably slender female body that lay beneath it. He remembered how it had felt to hold her in his arms. Damn it, he told himself angrily, but the minx would be enticing half London at this rate, let alone Corbridge!

He felt his blood run cold at the thought of Sebastian. What if the loathsome creature tried to seduce her? That, Marcus would not tolerate. The girl was to relieve Sebastian of Sir Roderick's fatal letter promising him Lornings—no more. If his treacherous cousin laid one jewelled finger on her, Marcus would shake him by the throat until his snake-like face turned puce and his diamond buttons rattled...

The force of his reaction startled him. He tightened his hands on the reins and concentrated on the morning ride.

Tassie led the way up to the ridge of the nearest hill, from whence the whole, glorious estate could be viewed. On the far side of the winding silver river, Lornings Hall glittered in the morning sun, nestling amongst the winter-bare trees as if it had been there for ever. Tassie found momentary relief in the beauty of the scenery, the illusion of freedom; but it was an illusion, because really she was trapped. And the nearness of Marcus, who'd told her that last night's kiss meant nothing, disturbed her more badly than she'd have believed possible.

Think of the time after this. When Marcus is no longer in control of your life. For you have plans of your own, too long laid aside, that can then be acted upon... He was catching up with her now; she drew a deep breath and turned calmly towards him, holding on to her hat with one hand as the light breeze threatened to dislodge it.

'In which direction does Hockton village lie, Marcus?'

He pointed eastwards. 'Two miles or so yonder, beyond the woods. Why?'

She said airily, 'Oh—nothing.'

Marcus drew up his restless roan and said flatly, 'I trust you're not thinking of going *anywhere* by yourself, Tassie.

You're in my care, and I intend to keep it that way. Jacob says there are a few unsavoury vagrants around the area at the moment, quite possibly up to no good.' Tassie had opened her mouth to argue, but he'd already swung his horse round as if that finalised the matter. 'Time to head back,' he said over his shoulder. 'It looks like rain.'

Tassie gazed at him rather bitterly and turned her own mare after him. 'Sometimes you are such a confounded prig, Marcus. Those vagrants you dismiss so cruelly are probably just looking for work. They'll have been pushed off their own land and have nowhere to go.'

'Whatever the case,' said Marcus firmly, 'I don't want you riding about by yourself.'

She gave him a stony look. 'What, I wonder, will you do with yourself when you no longer have me to order around? Please remember I'm not one of your infantry, *Major* Forrester!' Then she urged her horse on ahead of him, whistling loudly just to annoy him. She succeeded; Marcus told her off, then wished he hadn't, because she became icily silent, and he was sorry for it. He found himself mentally resolving to let her take Dancer out, soon. That should liven her spirits again. She was a gallant little rider, whether perching side-saddle or—clinging on behind a farmer's boy.

By the time they were back in the stable yard, Marcus was finding her silence increasingly oppressive. 'A lady is permitted to smile, you know, Tassie,' he reminded her as he lifted her down out of the saddle. Almost instantly he wished he'd summoned old Jacob to attend to the task, because the slenderness of her waist within his hands, the close softness of her wind-flushed cheek beneath that absurd little hat—all these things were in danger of unsettling him completely.

As he set her down on the cobbles of the yard, she looked up at him, her emerald-green eyes wide and haunted. 'Even

ladies, presumably, only smile when they have reason to be happy about something. Don't they?' she whispered.

She smiled with Hal, Marcus noted. And she continued to maintain her model behaviour throughout the afternoon, by settling herself in Roderick's parlour by the fire with a piece of embroidery Caro had given her. But this was one skill she did *not* possess; Marcus, who was trying to explain to Sir Roderick his accounts for the last year, had to conceal his amusement at her smothered oaths as she stabbed, sometimes furiously, at the cloth in her candle-lit corner.

They dined at six, and afterwards, when the chill spring wind swept around the rambling old Dower House, and the windows rattled in their casements, and the log fire in the inglenook hearth leaped and danced as the draught whistled down the chimney, Hal and Tassie played at piquet—a pursuit far more to her taste than embroidery—while Sir Roderick questioned Marcus about his soldiering days; though truth to tell Marcus's attention was not entirely on the conversation, for he kept being distracted by a girl's merry laugh, and by the sight of a charming golden head bent with determination over the swift-moving cards.

After a while Peg brought in a tray of tea and some gingerbread still warm from the oven. Hal and Tassie paused briefly for refreshment, then returned, avidly, to their game. Sir Roderick was watching them now, enjoying the sight of them laughing and talking beneath the soft light of the candelabra. He said quietly to Marcus at his side, 'You say the girl is a distant relative. Is there really no one but you to look after her?'

'She's an orphan,' replied Marcus truthfully.

'What have you got planned for her, then, Marcus?'

Marcus caught his breath. What *had* he got planned for her? He was going to use her to trick his dastardly cousin, and win back Lornings for Sir Roderick, just as it had been lost, at the gaming table. But he couldn't tell his godfather that, because he guessed that Roderick would detest the idea of putting the girl at risk.

'She is under my protection, sir,' he replied quietly. 'And I mean it to stay that way.'

He was interrupted by a fresh gurgle of amusement from Tassie, as Hal, with some clumsiness, bungled the attempt he was making at the Kingston Bridge trick and sent the cards flying across the table. Her laugh was merry as Hal made some typically droll comment about his own ineptitude, and Marcus realised that she looked happier than he had ever seen her. Marcus went restlessly to put more logs on the fire, and when he returned to his seat, his godfather said to him, 'She needs a good man, that one. A kind, brave man with enough strength to give her all the tenderness she needs. She would repay him a hundredfold.'

Yes, thought Marcus, she needs a man. Even as he thought it, he saw Tassie suddenly looking at him, so wistful and defenceless, yet so beautiful that she took his breath away. He thought, rather dazedly, *I must press on. I must press on, with my plan...*

They all played whist together after that. Tassie told them she would on no account be cheating; but Roderick, her partner, looked so crestfallen that she must have relented, for together they beat Marcus and Hal quite soundly, much to Sir Roderick's delight. Afterwards Tassie insisted on helping old Peg wash up the supper dishes, then she came back into the parlour where the others were gathered, to plead weariness and announce that she was going to bed early.

Sir Roderick and Hal expressed immediate concern. Tassie, making swiftly for the door, did not notice that Marcus's expression had suddenly changed. His eyes narrowed, in a familiar, speculative look that the soldiers in his command had come to know only too well. A few moments after Tassie had gone, he stood up and said casually, 'Think I'll just take a turn in the fresh air, Hal.'

'Do you want me to come with you?' said his friend quickly.

'No,' said Marcus. 'I won't be long.'

Once Tassie was in her room, with her door firmly locked, any pretence of weariness vanished. Edward had set up a lively squawking to welcome her. 'Hush, Edward,' she pleaded, 'oh, hush,' as she hurriedly pulled off her gown and shrugged herself into her breeches and shirt. In the end she draped the cloth over his cage to silence him, then dragged on her warm coat and boots, finally cramming a cap on over her curls. Hurrying to the window, she wrenched open the stiff frame and groaned at the rasping noise it made.

'Drat the man,' she muttered fiercely under her breath. Marcus's wide-shouldered figure as usual seemed to completely fill her mind and vision. 'Drat him, for keeping such a wretched eye on me all day and all evening!'

Swiftly she scrambled out of the window, shivering in the bitter night wind. By hanging on to the stone ledge she was able to lower herself down on to the outhouse roof, then landed catlike in the yard. Her friends had said they would keep watch for her, by the Hockton churchyard each night after dark. She must see them, and tell them she was all right.

Her heart thumping, she hurried round the side of the rambling house to the stables. She saw Dancer first, and her eyes lit up, but, no, that would be really asking for trouble. So she decided on the old cob instead, who was not impressed by the prospect of a ride; but she spoke to him coaxingly as she struggled to haul his saddle from its peg and on to his back. 'Quiet, boy. I'll bring you six lumps of sugar tomorrow if you'll only carry me, as swift and silent as you can, to Hockton!'

As Tassie rode out of the yard, crouching low over the cob's mane, talking soothingly in his ear, Marcus, standing in the deep shadows just beyond the kitchen door, watched her go.

He'd developed a sixth sense where Tassie was concerned. It was quite simple: if he couldn't see her, she was up to no good. He prepared, grimly, to follow her.

Tassie heaved a huge sigh of relief as her eyes scoured the darkness around the churchyard and she saw red-haired Lemuel hurrying eagerly out into the road, raising his hand in greeting. She flung herself off the cob's back, and realised with a glad heart that the others were appearing from the shadows behind the trees. Lemuel was almost hugging her, Billy was grinning from ear to ear, old Matt was pumping her hand, and Georgie Jay was saying, 'Tass, girl! 'Tis good to see you, and that's a fact!'

'And 'tis good for me to see you!' she replied, her face warm with happiness. 'But how on earth did you find me? How did you know I was here?'

'That night you disappeared from the Blue Bell,' declared Georgie, 'we thought you'd be back the next day, boasting of your adventures. But when you weren't back, no, nor the next day either, we grew mighty worried, I tell you.'

Tassie's lonely heart swelled and warmed anew. So they'd missed her! Georgie Jay was continuing, 'Then we heard— wonder of wonders!—that you'd been seen travellin' out of London in a private coach. We were truly alarmed then, lass, thought you'd been maybe snatched away. So we followed your trail, and here we are! Ready to take you away again, back with us where you belong!'

Tassie shook her head. 'I cannot come with you, Georgie.'

'That you can, Tass!' put in Lemuel eagerly. 'Let's go, now, before someone misses you!'

'Aye,' said old Matt, nodding. 'Whatever trouble it is you've got yourself into, girl, we'll get you out of it, never you fear.'

Billy, clenching his big fists, said, 'If anyone comes after you, I've got my knife ready! I've seen that dark-haired gent, ridin' around the place. I'll drive it between his ribs if he tried to stop you leavin', Tass girl—'

Tassie's heart lurched rather sickeningly at the thought of Marcus dead. 'No!' she broke in. '*No*, Billy!' They looked at her in surprise. She went on, more quietly, 'You don't understand. You see, I—I *agreed* to come here. I'm not a prisoner.'

'Then why in the name of heaven,' frowned Georgie Jay, 'are you staying with those two fancy gents in that big place? What have they promised you, girl? What have they threatened you with?'

Tassie said desperately, 'It's a little hard to explain, Georgie Jay! They're kind to me, really they are. And I'm ever so grateful to you for finding me, but I've got to go back to the house now. It's a matter of honour, you see. I've made a promise, and I must keep it.'

'Doesn't sound very honourable to me,' stated old Matt baldly. 'You look worn to a feather, girl. And what the devil's happened to your hair?'

Tassie reached self-consciously to her shorn locks. 'Oh, that—I cut it myself. It's more convenient like this. Really, I'm all right. But listen, you must all be very careful—the people round here are suspicious of strangers, and they might try to make trouble for you.'

'That so? Well, we could make trouble for *them*,' scowled Billy, his slow brain having difficulty working through it all. 'What about that fancy big Hall you've been visiting,

Tassie—that Lornings? I'll wager there's lots of fine treasure in there that no one'd miss—'

'*No!*' said Tassie hurriedly. 'You mustn't even think of it, Billy! You'd get yourself into bad trouble, and me, too, do you understand?' She turned with fresh anxiety to Georgie Jay. 'When did you arrive at Hockton, Georgie?'

'Got here just yesterday evening,' he said steadily. 'In time to see you goin' into that Hall with the dark-haired man following. Soon as you came out and the man disappeared for a bit, Lemuel here, being swiftest, ran out to slip you our note.'

Tassie heaved a sigh of relief. *Yesterday evening.* So it couldn't possibly be them pilfering from the Hall, for it was a few days since she'd noticed the pictures were missing. 'I'm so glad to see you,' she declared with feeling. 'But really, I'm quite all right.'

All right except for the stupid, nagging ache at her heart that started up whenever Marcus, her tormentor, was near.

'We'll be around for a week or so yet, girl, we've got some work layin' hedges at a farm a couple of miles yonder,' said Georgie Jay. 'Leave us a message if you need us—the three crossed twigs, as usual—just at the foot of that forked oak over there.'

'I will,' promised Tassie, comforted by the thought of their nearness. 'Be sure that I will!'

'And soon we'll all go back to London together!' old Matt added. Tassie smiled back. But she knew, now, that things could never be the same.

She turned towards her horse; but just at the last moment, as the others were turning back towards Hockton, Georgie Jay came swiftly to her side. 'Tass,' he said in a low voice, 'I did wonder if you might be after finding out about that place you ran away from all those years back.'

Her heart started hammering again. 'What do you mean, Georgie?'

'Didn't you realise? How close the old place is?'

And then her heart almost did stop. The places she'd recognised. The faint stirring of sad memories long suppressed. 'No! And, Georgie, I didn't realise you knew where I was from! I'd been wandering for days when you found me…'

Georgie Jay looked a little shamefaced. 'I asked around. Learned there was a young girl missin' from a big house called Wychwood. But you was in such a state, lass, there was no way on earth I was takin' you back. It's twenty or so miles from here, Oxford way; I thought you knew, I thought to myself that was why you'd come here!'

Perhaps, deep in her heart, she *had* known. She closed her eyes briefly, hearing those harsh voices: *Some day the brat's going to find out the truth, and what then? What then?*

It was as if she'd been drawn here. Georgie Jay was watching her anxiously. 'We'll ask around if you like, me and the lads, see if we can find out anything,' he promised. 'Seeing as you'll be here for a little while.'

'Yes. For a little while.' She drew a deep breath. 'Thank you, Georgie, so much. And—'tis good to see you all.'

Then Georgie Jay helped her spring up into the cob's saddle; and Tassie turned her horse back, towards the Dower House. But as the wind moaned around the churchyard, and rustled the branches of the bare trees, she quite failed to see the dark-haired man on horseback, who'd been watching and listening in the shadows.

For Marcus had saddled up Dancer, and followed Tassie unseen. He was fifty yards behind her when he saw her pause at the crossroads outside Hockton. When the shadows beneath the graveyard yews moved, and a little band of men, four of them, came out to surround her, his hand had flown to his pistol. But then he saw Tassie gladly sliding off her cob and greeting them all, by name; and he recognised the lanky red-head who'd accompanied her to the Angel; and a different kind of anger burned in his soul, because he realised who they were.

He could hear a few faint words; could see them, gesticulating towards Hockton and then pointing south. He was surprised by the force of his own emotions when he heard her tell them clearly that she was staying. ''Tis a matter of honour, you see, Georgie Jay. I've made a promise, and I will keep it.'

It was enough to tell him she wasn't running away. He needn't fear for his scheme to outwit his vile enemy Sebastian Corbridge. It was a matter of honour, as she'd said. And it was also a matter of keeping his own disturbing desire for a beguiling little beauty under rigorous check.

Chapter Eleven

It was now almost halfway through March, less than two weeks until the time when Marcus had resolved that Sebastian must be challenged; and yet for the little community at the Dower House the days passed uneventfully, almost pleasantly. Marcus was kind, and not too overbearing, as he continued to tutor Tassie in the role she was to play. Just occasionally Tassie showed her old spark of resistance; but Hal was always there to ease any tension between them. Sir Roderick rarely went out, but every afternoon without fail Tassie would go up to his chamber—a spacious room filled with all sorts of treasures from his past—and talk to him, or play a hand or two at cards. Sometimes he asked her to read to him in her clear, sweet voice from his well-worn volume of Shakespeare, or from one of Master Cowper's poems. Sometimes Marcus would enter silently and listen as well.

At other times, Hal and Marcus would go over to the Hall, taking Tassie with them, in order, Marcus said, to familiarise her with the surroundings to which those with whom she was about to mingle were accustomed. Marcus would set fires blazing in the hearths at each end of the long gallery, and light all the candles, so that the room was almost restored to its former glory. They never went up to the banqueting hall on the next floor, the room from which Tassie suspected some paintings had gone. And Tassie never mentioned it to Marcus. After all, she might be mistaken. And she knew now that even if her suspicions were true, it could have nothing to do with her friends.

Sometimes, when the weather was too bad for riding or walking, Marcus and Hal would fence in the gallery of the Hall, for exercise; Tassie would raptly watch them gliding to and fro as if they were taking part in some elegant but lethal dance. After one particularly successful parry, Marcus stepping back, grinned at Tassie's absorbed face and said, 'If I were conceited, minx, I'd say that was admiration in your eyes. However, as I'm not, and you detest me, I know it can't be.'

Tassie had clambered to her feet from the sofa beneath the window where she had curled up to watch them. Ignoring his taunt, she held out her hand. 'I want a go, Marcus. Please, teach me!'

He nodded and passed her a foil; and she thought how much easier everything would be if she *did* detest him.

Since the first, almost disastrous, day of his stay here, she'd managed to conceal the disturbing unease with which his presence filled her. But just occasionally, something about the way he looked, the way he moved, would shake her so badly that she felt her heart thump and her senses quicken warningly; though she learnt to smother it with action or a jest before he should guess at it.

He gave her some basic lessons in the art of fencing; and, as in everything, she was a quick learner. But Marcus pointed out, gently, that it was imperative that he did not neglect to teach her the more womanly arts. He would watch as she practised gliding gently up and down the wide staircase, growing used to the feel of the way her grandest gown, a hooped polonaise with a low-cut neckline, swayed and rustled as she moved. She grew accustomed as well to the look of open admiration on Hal's face, and the reluctant approval on Marcus's.

One rainy afternoon as they all sat in Sir Roderick's room playing cards, Marcus produced a lace-edged fan for her, and she practised peeping over it demurely until Roderick was chuckling and Hal was in stitches. A few evenings later Marcus persuaded Peg to lay on an elaborate meal with several covers, using the services of some hired local girls to carry the plentiful dishes to and fro; and Tassie handled the variety of silver cutlery with surprising delicacy, sipping at her wine as if she was born to such things. Afterwards, when the men had spent a brief time over their port, they went to join Tassie in the cosy sitting room, where she poured tea for them. Marcus found himself sitting beside her, and he silently wondered at the ease with which she handled the fragile china.

'If I didn't know better, Tassie,' he said at last, 'I would swear you were well used to this kind of life. I've asked you before, and I know you don't like to talk of it. But surely, you've not always been part of a lowly band of travellers?'

He saw how her slender fingers tensed suddenly around the little teacup she was holding. 'I lived somewhere else, long ago,' she said in a low voice. 'But it was never, ever my home.'

Marcus suddenly remembered something he'd strained to hear on that night she'd met her friends as random phrases were carried to him on the breeze. *Tassie, didn't you realise how close the old place is?* He'd seen her shaking her head; he'd heard no more, but the expression of shock on her face had disturbed him. Now, taking the cup from her hand, he said, 'I've no wish to trouble you with unhappy memories.'

He smiled suddenly. 'And besides, I can see that my godfather is itching for you to partner him at whist.'

If Tassie didn't like talking about herself, then neither did Marcus, but as the days went by he told her a good deal about his cousin Sebastian: how he was shallow, vain, boastful; how he had all but frittered away his own substantial fortune before the idea had come to him of relieving Sir Roderick of his.

'So you knew each other as boys, then, Marcus?' asked Tassie curiously.

Marcus smiled. 'We came across each other from time to time. I always thought Sebastian a lying toad, and no doubt he had his own, equally strong opinion about me.'

'Fie, he was probably scared to death of you,' she responded crisply. 'I should think most people are.'

They were sitting in the library of the Hall one night, just the two of them, and they'd been playing cards. Marcus had lit a fire, and candles glowed brightly in the ancient gilt sconces on the walls. Tassie had just beaten Marcus easily at piquet, and he had to confess that he hadn't been able to catch her out once; in fact, he was delighted with her prowess.

'Were you scared of me?' he asked her now. 'When you saw me at the Angel?'

She grinned. 'Scared? Why, Marcus, when you came up to my table, and I recognised you as the very man whose pocket I'd picked earlier that evening, my teeth were chattering so loudly I thought everybody must hear.'

'Didn't you recognise Hal?'

'I didn't, no. He's not as unmistakable as you, not as—' She broke off in confusion.

'Not as frightening?' he offered. She said nothing. He smiled, that slow, thoughtful smile that sent her pulse racing wildly. 'You played your part exceptionally well that night,' he said. 'Your demeanour was impeccable. Your appearance, however, let you down.'

'Why? What was wrong with my appearance?' she demanded.

Marcus laughed, leaning back in his comfortable chair. 'Do you really want to know? Your gown was tawdry and cheap, and several sizes too large—obviously borrowed.' *Stolen, actually, from Moll,* mentally corrected Tassie. Marcus went on, 'Your hair was crudely arranged, and you had applied too much rouge.'

'Fie! I thought all ladies of fashion wore too much rouge!'

'Perhaps they do.' He clasped his hands behind his head, studying her in a way that made her blood run hot and cold. 'But then, you see, you don't need to. Your colouring is quite perfect.'

Tassie had never known that she could blush so thoroughly. Rather desperately, she picked up the cards and leafed through them, hardly aware she was sending all the hearts to the bottom, one of her favourite tricks. At last, still conscious of his eyes on her, she said lightly, 'So you think I'll fool Sebastian, then?'

'Ah, yes,' he replied softly. 'Sebastian will be enchanted.'

Tassie was silent for a while longer, letting the cards ripple through her fingers like fine silk. Then she lifted her head to gaze directly at Marcus.

'I heard you and Hal talking the other night,' she said. 'I heard you talking about a woman called Lady Sallis, who runs a gaming house in Mayfair where Sebastian often goes. Are you going to send me there when the time comes to play him?'

'My God, no,' he said with vehemence, thinking of Lady Sallis's wily young female accomplices and the pleasures they offered. 'Never in a thousand years, Tassie. We'll find you a small and private establishment in which you can entice

Sebastian to play on your own terms. A place where Hal and I are able to watch out for your safety. And, Tassie—you shouldn't eavesdrop. I've told you that before.'

'I just needed to make sure,' she said, 'that you weren't putting me in a bawdy house. That's all.'

Her voice was light, but Marcus saw that she looked pale, and her huge emerald eyes were haunted with something very like fear. Putting his hand over hers, he said earnestly, 'Do you think that I would put you in a place where you were at risk? God forgive me if you do, if I haven't given you reason to trust me. I tell you this, Tassie. If my cousin Sebastian so much as lays a finger on you, I will throttle him with my bare hands.'

Tassie was horrified, and delighted. 'But what if he does not *wish* to play with me, Marcus? What if he has no taste for my kind of looks?'

Marcus was silent a moment, considering. Then he said, 'My dear girl. Have you seen yourself lately?'

Tassie stammered, 'Nay. I am not used to looking glasses, you see. Well, I glance in the little mirror in my bedroom briefly now and then, to check that my face is not dirty from the stables or the kitchen-range, but that is all.'

'You did not look in your mirror as you put on that gown you are wearing?'

'No. Why should I? Peg kindly helped me into it, for I could never manage all the stupid hooks and buttons on my own.'

'Then come over here with me. Now.' And he took her hand in his.

Rows and rows of leather-clad books lined the walls of the old library. Cobwebs hung in the corners of the oriel windows, and the little mahogany tables were covered with dust. There was a long mirror set in a panel at the far end of the room giving the illusion of a further library adjoining this one; and it was to this that Marcus led her and said, 'Look at yourself, Tassie.'

She looked. She saw a stranger, an elegant and slender female in a blue-striped polonaise, with a tiny waist, and full looped skirts. The bodice of her gown was low and tight-fitting, and the rounded curve of her small but full breasts was clearly visible. Her fingers flew to her throat, as if to cover herself, but Marcus caught at her hand and said, 'Tassie, you are exquisite. I'm telling you this, not to make you conceited, but to give you confidence in yourself, so you know that you can hold your head high in the company of any of society's beauties.'

She gazed at herself, at her wide green eyes and creamy skin that Marcus said had no need of cosmetics. She saw how her thick golden curls, neatened with such surprising skill by old Peg, clustered round her forehead, and tapered gently to the nape of her neck. And, in the mirror, she saw the way Marcus was looking at her.

She forced herself into calmness. That look in his steel-grey eyes, that burning gaze that thrilled her soul, it meant nothing, she told herself shakily; he was simply flattering her to boost her confidence, so necessary to the success of his scheme. *That was all...*

'Fie,' she laughed, 'are you trying to turn my head with your flattery, Marcus? It will not work, I tell you. Take away the finery and I'm just Tassie, companion to wandering players, varlets and tricksters. I am no lady of quality.'

'No!' said Marcus, almost fiercely. 'No, there is more to you than that. I know there is. If only you would *tell* me about your past! Do you really trust me so little?'

She turned slowly to face him. 'There is little to tell, Marcus. Do not be making some fairy-tale mystery out of me. I was an orphan, brought up in some cold place out in the wilds by people who detested me. I was locked in my room, often, as punishment, and I was beaten.'

Marcus closed his eyes briefly. 'Why?' he grated out. 'Why were you punished so?'

She smiled a little shakily. 'Doubtless I was as obstinate then as I am now.'

'You were only a child! Who did that to you?'

'The man who owned the house. At the bidding of his sister, a miserable skinflint of a woman, who taught me my lessons. When I did not learn fast enough, or was rebellious, she told me I was wicked, and fetched him to beat me.' She shivered. 'In the end I ran, and Georgie Jay found me.'

'How old were you then?'

'I was nine. Old enough to know I wanted no more of it.'

Marcus's face was tense. 'This man beat you. And yet his sister gave you lessons and kept you in a room of your own, as if you were of gentle birth... Why? Who were your parents? And—where was this place?'

She shrugged, but he could see that the pain was still there. 'I really don't know; I never thought much about it.'

He guessed that she was lying, that she *did* think about it, often. He wanted so much to reach out and comfort her, and persuade her to confide in him; but knew that there was danger in that as well, for both of them.

'I won't pry any more,' he said at last, 'since it's so obviously distressing to you. But I say this to you again; I would not willingly cause you any further unhappiness. You may back out of our arrangement at any time you wish, and return to your friends.'

'Fie, Marcus,' she said lightly, 'and say goodbye to all that money you promised me?'

Their eyes met in the mirror. He said, quietly, 'You want that money very badly, don't you?'

'But of course I do! Why else am I here?'

'Tassie,' said Marcus, 'Tassie, I will give you the money anyway. For the time you have spent here. For the pleasure you have given my godfather. You can leave here—*tomorrow* if you wish.'

She said rather wildly, 'But, Marcus, I can't, not now! Your godfather will be quite finished if he loses Lornings in the autumn to that rogue Sebastian! I'm your only hope—you *need* me—I've heard you and Hal talking…'

Her voice trailed away as Marcus pulled her closer and cupped her face with one hand. 'Dear God, Tassie. Don't take all of this upon yourself. I will find some other way to settle the business of Roderick's debts, I swear I will.'

'No,' she breathed, her heart thudding at his touch. 'You've tried, haven't you? Visiting those lawyers and everything! I will do it. I promised I would, and I will!'

Her voice was brimful of defiance, but as Marcus instinctively put both hands on her shoulders he felt her trembling. And he acknowledged silently that he would have been devastated had she accepted his offer to leave.

Ever since he'd arrived at Lornings, and seen her slide off the back of that farm lad's pony and come running joyfully towards him in the rain, he'd been aware of the sharp ache of wanting her physically. Day and night he was obsessed by the need to possess her slender body, and to kiss her sweet face into an oblivion of pleasure. Day and night he held himself back grimly, restrained himself with all the strength he could muster, because he knew that if he touched her again he was lost. Hal had actually asked him one evening if he was ailing in some way, not to respond more warmly to such a lovely girl as Tassie. But devil take it, if he was kind to her, he knew he'd end up burning to hold her, just as he was doing now, burning to kiss her, and carry her in a frenzy of desire to the nearest bed. He longed to make her realise what love could be like.

He was too close to her now. He wanted to taste those delicate, teasing lips, to breathe in the sweet perfume of her soft clean skin, her golden curls. She was driving him to madness. Summoning all his control, he said at last, 'If you are sure you can go through with this, Tassie, then I will be there for you, all the time. I swear it.'

She smiled up at him, rather faintly. 'Are you sure that is such a good idea, Marcus, you being with me all the time? Perhaps you had better let go of me now. You are hurting me.'

He let his hands fall instantly. 'Ah, little minx,' he said softly. 'You are wiser than you first appear.'

'I am a fool,' she said bitterly. 'Let me go. Please.'

He drew away almost brusquely. Another dangerous moment averted—no thanks to him. 'We had better get back to the Dower House,' he said. 'It will be cold outside now that night has fallen. Philippa and her mother used to say that the wind from the Gloucestershire hills in March was the bitterest of the year.'

Tassie watched him almost blindly as he set off towards the stairs. As well, to be reminded of Philippa. Wasn't it because of Philippa that Marcus was going through with all this? No wonder he took such trouble to flatter Tassie. If she were to back out, his scheme to secure Lornings as his inheritance would be ruined. She brushed her hands agitatedly down her crumpled gown where he had pressed her briefly against him. Her body still burned where he had touched her.

He was waiting for her at the foot of the stairs. She hurried down after him, pulling on her cloak, and he held open the door for her. Then he locked it, and strode off along the windswept drive, almost cheerfully.

Tassie followed. *You are a fool,* she scolded herself in acute despair as she battled her way through the gusts of hostile wind a few paces behind Marcus's distinctive figure.

'Fie on you, Marcus,' she called out at last as her little boots crunched on the uneven gravel. 'How can I be expected to play the part of a lady, when you go striding off at such a pace that I need to go at the gallop in this stupid dress just to keep up with you?'

He turned to her, laughing, his dark hair ruffled in the breeze, and held out his arm. 'My sincere apologies, my lady,' he said, bowing his head to her; and Tassie, as she laid her fingers on his sleeve and felt the warm strength of him seeping through her fingertips to her whole body, wished she'd held her silence and trailed along after him at a distance. Far, far safer.

Soon, all this would be over. When she said goodbye to Marcus, she would use her purseful of guineas, and her fine clothes and her fancy manners, to find out the truth about her past. And if her search came to naught, why, she could be a governess, or a lady's maid, as Caro had suggested…at which thought her heart quailed within her.

Suddenly she remembered something old Matt had said to her once: *Sometimes it takes courage to face your past. But it's often in the past that your future lies.*

She drew a deep breath. In truth, facing the present also took courage; for she knew she could no longer pretend now that Marcus's money was her sole reason for her continuing with this wild plan.

He had offered to give her fifty guineas, this very night, but she had refused. And why? Because if she took his money, and agreed that their bargain was indeed concluded—she would never see Marcus again.

They played whist with Hal and Sir Roderick when they got back to the Dower House; Tassie was subdued, though no one seemed to notice. She and Roderick won as usual, and when Roderick had gone up to bed, beaming with delight, Hal poured them each a small glass of brandy.

'Let us drink a toast,' Hal said gravely. 'To the success of Marcus's plan.'

The men stood, and Marcus raised his glass. 'To Sir Roderick, and Lornings.'

'And to the lovely Tassie,' added Hal gallantly.

'To Tassie,' agreed Marcus. 'And to the downfall of my cousin Sebastian.'

Tassie reached for her glass. 'Fie, Marcus, you have high expectations of me. I only hope you're not sorely disappointed.'

'I have every confidence in you,' Marcus said lightly, lifting his glass to drink. 'To our success. I think we are almost ready.'

You might be, but I am not. Oh, I am not, thought Tassie rather wildly to herself as she took an over-large sip of brandy and felt it burning its way down her throat. To have him standing so near to her, so tall and imposing in his long black riding coat and cream shirt, with his dark, vividly handsome face that haunted her dreams smiling down at her, did not help her to sort out her stupidly seething brain at all.

She lifted her glass defiantly, and gazed at her two companions.

'To my fifty guineas—and to the luck of the cards,' she proposed, and Marcus laughed.

Over the next few days, the weather changed. The spring-like sunshine that had just begun to warm the valley was swept away by big leaden clouds rolling in ominously on a stiff north-easterly breeze. The air was raw, and chill.

'My sakes, looks like snow,' said Peg dourly as she thumped at her bread dough in the warm kitchen of the Dower House. 'Snow, this late in March—can you believe it? My brother Dick at the farm and his boy, Will, they'll be worrying themselves silly about the lambing ewes up on the hillside!'

Tassie, who was helping Peg to shape the yeasty dough into loaves and buns, was only half-listening. She had her eye on the partly open door that led into the breakfast parlour, and she was watching Marcus pacing up and down with growing trepidation.

Less than half an hour ago, a messenger on horseback had arrived with a letter for Hal. Hal read it swiftly, then spoke in anxious tones to Marcus, who also looked worried. Then Hal had taken the letter up to his room. Now Tassie, unable to bear the suspense any longer, popped the last batch of bread into the oven, tore off the big white apron that covered her dove-grey morning dress, and hurried into the parlour.

'Marcus,' she said anxiously, 'something's wrong, isn't it?'

He turned swiftly to face her, and she realised that though he looked anxious and abstracted, he wasn't angry, not with her. The relief flooded through her.

'Well, minx,' he said slowly, his face softening, 'you're still being a paragon of virtue in the kitchen are you? Yes, Hal has received some worrying news. Caro isn't well.'

'Oh, I'm so sorry. Is she back in London now?'

'Yes, but she must have caught a chill on her journey home. She makes light of it in her letter, but she's been in bed with an inflammation of the throat. Hal is reproaching himself, of course, for leaving her for so long. He's returning to London immediately.'

'I hope she recovers swiftly,' said Tassie quietly. 'And I shall miss Hal.'

'So shall I,' said Marcus. He smiled down at her. 'You will have to put up with my bad-tempered company alone from now on, I am afraid.'

Tassie's heart did a strange lurch. 'I do not mind,' she said in a tight little voice. 'I do not mind at all.'

He touched her cheek in a gesture of affection. 'We shall do well enough together, you and I,' he said softly. 'Get back to the kitchen now, before old Peg starts screaming at me that I am distracting you from your duties.'

Tassie felt a smile tugging at her mouth. 'Really? I cannot imagine anyone screaming at you and getting away with it, Marcus.'

'She knows she'll get away with anything when her fresh-baked bread's on offer.'

Hal had lunch with them: a cold roast of mutton left over from the previous night together with the warm loaves Tassie had helped make, spread thickly with butter from the farm. Sir Roderick had stayed in his chamber, and Tassie was worried about him as she took up his tray. She was sorry, too, that Hal was going. She knew she would feel even more vulnerable, all alone with Marcus.

After lunch, Hal went to pack. Tassie helped Peg tidy the kitchen, feeling a strange sense of foreboding as dark as the clouds that gathered above the distant line of hills. Then Jacob arrived at the kitchen door, letting in a blast of icy air, stamping the half-frozen mud from his boots before entering.

'Look at the man,' exclaimed Peg, her face red and her arms covered with suds from washing the pots. 'He'd leave that door wide open if we were all freezin' to death, I swear! Shut it, do! And don't you come in wearin' those filthy boots!'

Jacob slammed the heavy door shut before pulling off his boots. Then, taking no further notice of Peg, he clumped across the well-scrubbed flags of the kitchen, muttering, 'I always guessed this would happen! Always warnin' Sir Roderick, I was, blast it!' And he went into the parlour where

Marcus was sitting, pulling off his old, battered hat as he did so.

Tassie knew Jacob had been to make his weekly check of the Hall. Because the building was so vast, he inspected a part of it only, each time; he often grumbled that the place was too much for one old man to look after on his own.

She realised Jacob had left the door to the parlour slightly open. She heard Marcus's voice. 'Is something wrong, Jacob?'

Tassie's spine tingled in warning. She edged closer to the door, the dish she was drying clutched tightly in her hand.

'Indeed it is, sir! I've just bin checkin' the banqueting hall where all those great big old paintings are...'

Tassie's heart suddenly began to thump very loudly. She felt slightly sick, and her fingers were almost nerveless around the plate she held. Peg had gone down the long passageway to the storeroom to put some pans away; Tassie hurriedly put down the dish and edged closer to the half-open door, every word driving like a spear into her stricken senses.

'Of course I know the banqueting hall,' Marcus was saying. 'Go on, Jacob.'

'Well, sir,' said the old man heavily, 'some of them paintings 'ave gone! Must be real recent, I reckon, 'cos I checked that part of the 'ouse only a while ago, and they was all there then! You can see the places, 'cos the hooks are still there, and the panellin' looks all bare. 'Tis terrible—some of them's been there since the first master of Lornings had the place built, and I don't know how on earth I'm goin' to tell Sir Roderick...'

Tassie leaned back faintly against the wall. With terrible, mind-numbing premonition, she knew exactly what was going to happen next.

Frozen to the spot, she heard Marcus walking heavily

towards the door behind which she lurked. He opened it abruptly, so that she almost fell into the breakfast parlour.

'Ah, Tassie,' he said in a chilling voice, his hands on his hips. 'I was going to invite you to come in, but I see that you have anticipated my request. I wonder why?' He turned to old Jacob and said, levelly, 'Thank you for that useful information, Jacob. Would you leave us alone now, please? I have something I wish to discuss with Tassie.'

He shut the door firmly after the old retainer. Then he turned to Tassie. They were alone. She faced him bravely, though her spirits had sunk to the darkest depths. Oh, why, why hadn't she *told* him about the paintings, straight away? Yet—he couldn't accuse her, Tassie, of stealing them, surely? And he didn't even know that Georgie Jay and her friends had been staying close by. Did he?

She should have known him better by now.

He was angry, and, more than that, clearly dismayed. He said, 'Oh, Tassie. I had hoped—nay, I *believed*—that you and I were starting to trust one another. But I was wrong. I must admit that I find it most difficult to know how to proceed *at all* in such circumstances.'

She faced up to him with clenched hands held tightly at her sides. Bright spots of colour burned on her cheeks. She said, in a shaking voice, 'God's teeth, so you accuse me of stealing paintings now, do you, Marcus? Well, that is novel at least! Much good would they do me. And where would I hide them, pray? Under my bed? Inside Edward's cage?'

His expression did not change. 'A good try, Tassie. But perhaps I should warn you, before you make yet more of a spectacle of yourself, that I am aware of the little rendezvous you had a while ago with your vagabond friends.'

The colour drained abruptly from her face. 'You—you knew that Georgie Jay and the others were here?' she faltered, aghast.

'Indeed.' His voice was quite cold now. 'Having been suspicious of your urgent desire, all that particular day, to leave the house on your own, I kept watch on you. I observed your—rather unorthodox—exit from your chamber and decided to follow you, in case you were getting yourself into trouble.' His grey eyes suddenly hardened almost to black. 'If I'd known what you really planned, Tassie, I'd have pulled you from your horse's back before you even left the stable yard.'

'I planned nothing!' cried Tassie desperately. 'Nothing, I tell you! Georgie Jay and the others—they were worried about me—they'd followed me, all the way from London, to see that I was all right! That was all!'

'That was all? Can you really swear to me that they weren't asking you about the Hall and its treasures?'

Tassie's shoulders slumped. Billy. He had made a stupid jest about stealing from the Hall... Tilting her chin up to face him, her face white with misery, she breathed, 'All right, so the valuables at the Hall might have been mentioned—just in passing! But my friends would never steal like that, especially when I told them not to!'

Marcus's expression grew harder. 'Perhaps your influence isn't as great as you think. After all, the pictures are missing, aren't they?'

Marcus was, in fact, bitterly disappointed at this latest turn of events. He'd known that Tassie was a rogue when it suited her, but he'd thought that she and he had a special kind of trust. Even now, he wanted desperately to believe that she knew nothing of the theft, that she had given her rapscallion friends no secret advice on how to enter the Hall.

Then she confounded him yet again by declaring vehemently, 'But the pictures were already missing, Marcus! I used to wander round by myself, and I noticed it days before my friends arrived at Hockton. It's true, I swear!'

The disbelief was etched clearly now on every feature of his face. 'God's blood, girl, but you wriggle like an eel in a trap. Why, then, in heaven's name, did you not tell me so, straight away? Can you not see that it is of less than any use to tell me this *now*?'

'I meant to tell you,' she faltered. 'Truly, Marcus! Only— while you were locking up that night, and I was waiting for you in the darkness, Lemuel came creeping up to me, with a message; and I was so surprised to hear that my friends were nearby that I quite forgot about the pictures...'

Her voice trailed away as Marcus walked over to the fireplace. He whipped round to face her, his arm resting on the mantel, his long fingers drumming impatiently on the stone shelf. 'Oh, I see,' he said. 'And when your friends talked about the rich pickings to be had at the Hall, you *still* didn't think to tell me about the pictures you'd noticed were missing?'

'I—I saw that it was probably too late to tell you anyway. And it wasn't them who stole from Lornings, I would swear to you on my honour!'

'Honour among thieves,' Marcus declared flatly. 'Please spare me your romantic clichés. I hope for your sake as well as theirs, Tassie, that your friends have gone a long way away. Dear God, and there was I beginning to think that I could trust you.'

'I think you've forgotten where we've started from, Marcus!' Tassie threw back. 'I thought you picked me off the streets because you had *already* decided that I was a—liar, and a cheat, and a rogue!'

The chill wind blew threateningly against the casement, sending smatterings of sleet against the glass.

'I didn't expect you to cheat *me*,' said Marcus, and Tassie stepped back as if he'd struck her.

Just then Hal came in, looking distracted. He said, 'I'm all ready to leave, Marcus. Perhaps you'll arrange for my bags to be sent on after me?'

Marcus said tersely, 'Hold awhile, Hal. I rather think I might be coming with you.'

Hal looked puzzled, and his eyes flickered over to Tassie, whom he'd only just noticed standing in the corner. 'But—shouldn't you stay with Tassie? After all, there's so little time now until your plan is to be set in motion...'

'That's exactly it. You see, I'm not at all sure now that our plan should proceed.'

Tassie stepped forward. 'In truth, neither am I,' she said, white-lipped. 'If you don't trust me, Marcus, then say so, and I, too, will leave this house—for good!'

And, as Hal watched in astonishment, she marched, head held high, from the room.

Chapter Twelve

Marcus departed for London with Hal, later that very afternoon. From her room, Tassie watched them go riding down the wide drive between the trees with their collars turned up against the bitter north-east wind. At least Marcus had listened again, with a little more patience, to her continued insistence that her friends would not, *could* not have stolen the pictures; though whether he believed her or not she could not tell. 'I'll take up the matter with the Gloucestershire constables, and in London, too,' he said curtly. 'It's likely that whoever stole them will try to pass them on at one of the city auction houses. And I'll arrange for a couple of local men to keep watch on the Hall from now on.'

'So you're not setting up a hue and cry for my friends?'

He hesitated. 'I would need to have evidence first. Fortunately all the truly valuable works were locked away when Roderick moved out of the Hall; the stolen paintings were not of great worth.'

That, at any rate, was something she should be grateful for. But there was nothing for her to be grateful about in the way he had then told her, curtly and coldly, that while he was in London he would meet his lawyers to see if there was any other way to stop Lornings going to Sebastian in September. Tassie said in a low voice, 'I will still play my part in your scheme, Marcus.'

He lifted his shoulders in a shrug, and his eyes were bleak. 'No one is fool enough to gamble with a letter promising him an estate the value of Lornings. Not even Sebastian.'

Tassie was desperate. 'But we discussed it. I'll let him think he can *win*! I can do it, Marcus, I *know* I can!'

'For Sir Roderick, Tassie?'

'For Sir Roderick, yes!' Her words were steady, but her heart was in wretched turmoil.

'I need time to reconsider it all,' he said flatly. He was already dressed in his long riding coat, ready for the first stage of his journey on horseback with Hal. 'But I trust you with this much, Tassie: to say nothing of our bargain to Sir Roderick, to keep him company, and to continue to treat him with the true kindness—I say this in all honesty—that I've always seen you display towards him. Will you promise?'

She'd gazed up at him. 'I promise, Marcus,' she said, her cheeks very pale. 'Though what value you can place on my word, I cannot imagine, since you do not believe me about the paintings.'

'I trust you, but not your friends.'

'Then,' she breathed, 'you are making a bad mistake, since *I* would trust them with my life!'

The two men left shortly afterwards. Marcus did not once turn to look back at the house. Tassie watched him go with a desperately aching heart. 'Fie,' she scolded herself softly, 'are you mad, girl? You knew you could never have his love.'

She thought about Georgie Jay and the others. She was tempted to leave this place for good, and besides, they needed warning, about the pictures, but soon night would be falling. And she'd given her word to Marcus that she would stay with

Sir Roderick, who was fretting openly about Marcus's abrupt departure.

'What took him away so suddenly?' he said again and again as they played piquet while the wind howled outside. 'When will he be back?'

Tassie tried to sound reassuring, even though her heart ached so sorely at Marcus's name. 'He'll be back soon,' she soothed. 'Dear Sir Roderick, do not let me see your hand, pray! I shall wipe you out within minutes!'

Sir Roderick chuckled, temporarily diverted. 'That, my sweet girl, is inevitable anyway. I am a poor hand at cards compared to you.' His elderly face crumpled suddenly. 'What possessed me, to play so deeply, to lose so much at the gambling tables? Oh, what a fool I am. A half-witted old fool.'

Tassie touched his hand quickly. 'No, you're not, Sir Roderick! You are too kind, too honest, that is all!'

'Admittedly I am not the first, nor the last, to lose a fortune in such a stupid way,' he said heavily. 'But the worst of it is that my stupidity has cost my godson both Lornings and Philippa; it was always his dream to marry her, but of course her parents will not allow her to marry a man with no prospects.'

Tassie shivered, in spite of the fire blazing in the hearth. 'Philippa should stand up for what she wants,' she breathed. 'If she loves him only for his inheritance, then her love is not worth much. Is it?'

But Sir Roderick did not hear her, for her words were drowned out by the rattling of sleet at the window panes. Tassie, pulling herself together, said in an effort at calmness, 'These people you played with in London, Sir Roderick. If they were known swindlers, as Marcus suspects, then surely your debts to them cannot be enforced?'

'That is what Marcus wondered—but how can we prove they were sharpers? Sebastian Corbridge has my signature on that letter acknowledging my terrible debts; there is no going against that.'

Tassie's heart went out to the elderly man in his distress. 'Marcus will think of something,' she said with an effort. 'Truly he will. You must trust him.'

Sir Roderick's face softened. 'Aye. Marcus will save Lornings for me if anyone can.'

For himself, you mean, thought Tassie sadly as she shuffled the pack. *His inheritance is all he's interested in.*

'Such an honourable and devoted godson,' went on Sir Roderick, his faded blue eyes alight with pride and love. 'He will go to any trouble. Why, only a few nights ago he was telling me of a discussion he had in town with a rich London banker, Sir Thomas Fortescue. There was some possibility of a plan for Sir Thomas to buy Lornings from me, thus giving me enough money to pay off my debt to Sebastian, yet with the proviso that I should be allowed to live in Lornings until my death...'

That was when the cards began slipping unnoticed from Tassie's hands. She leaned forwards slowly. 'But—that means that after your death, Lornings and everything in it would not go to Marcus, but to this Sir Thomas.'

'Exactly, my dear,' said Sir Roderick, nodding. 'I told Marcus that on no account must he go ahead with such a scheme and lose all chance of his inheritance. But he said he doesn't care about himself, and that anything is better than seeing me turned out of Lornings.'

Tassie was speechless. Had she really been so wrong in her judgement of Marcus? Was it possible that he was, after all, doing this for his godfather and not for himself?

She gathered the cards up and re-dealt them with unaccustomed slowness. It scarcely mattered now anyway. If she had misjudged his motives, then he had made an even worse error by accusing her and her friends of stealing. And it was too late, far too late, to do anything about it.

Over the next few days, the weather grew ugly, with a steady wind driving in from the north-east, and brief snow squalls that hinted at worse to come. Every morning, the fields and hedgerows were rimed with unseasonable frost, and the water in the troughs and pails of the courtyard was black with ice. Waiting for Marcus's return with a sense of doom in her heart, Tassie, in breeches and boots and a long coat that Will the farmer's son had lent her, helped Jacob every morning to carry the sacks of oats out to the horses, her breath steaming in the bitter air. Will was busy with the lambing ewes, trying to bring them down to the farmstead before they gave birth. In the distance Lornings Hall looked, if anything, lovelier than ever, with its multitude of windows glittering like diamonds in the setting sun, and its crenellated towers encrusted with sparkling frost. Tassie gazed at it from her bedroom window, but felt no desire to visit Lornings now. After all, she thought bitterly, in spite of the watch he'd had set on the place, Marcus might still accuse her and her friends of stealing.

She tried to turn her mind to her future, but for the moment she could not see the path ahead. How could she possibly have imagined that uncovering her past, and the mystery of the place called Wychwood, could be her way forward? No—those dark memories were better left buried.

Could she be a governess, as Caro suggested, or a lady's maid? That thought, at least, was almost enough to make her smile. Resolutely she picked up a pack of cards. 'I will run a gaming salon instead,' she declared, 'and make my fortune, like the Lady Sallis Marcus is always talking about!'

'Darling Marcus! Darling Marcus!' Edward suddenly

squawked, and her smile was gone. She let the cards fall, and covered her face with her hands.

In London, the chill winds raked the streets, keeping people either indoors or wrapped warmly in furs inside their carriages. During the last few days Marcus had trodden the icy pavements with increasing despair. Sir Thomas Fortescue, the banker who had ventured an interest in purchasing Lornings, was having second thoughts about Marcus's request that his godfather must be allowed to live freely on the estate for the rest of his lifetime.

'Not sure about that, my boy,' drawled Sir Thomas as Marcus sat with him in his club in St James's. 'Know I'm a youngster compared to Sir Roderick—forty-nine, you know—but my own health's been none too good this last year. I've no fancy to pay over the odds for a place that I won't have the chance to enjoy. No, no, Marcus. Sorry, but it's just not on.'

Marcus was staying with Hal and Caro in Portman Square. To leave London, he was informed, was impossible at the moment; the snow was moving in from the west country, and what with that and the half-frozen mud, even the mail coaches were unable to get through to the rural districts. Caro had recovered well from her illness, and Marcus suggested they attend the theatre, but that proved to be a mistake, because he found himself reminded vividly of the last time he'd seen a play, in Tassie's vibrant company. He could not forget the look of rapt enchantment on her wide-eyed face as she gazed at the brightly lit stage, and the plot was lost to him as his thoughts were engulfed by memories.

Damn, but he'd been bewitched by the minx, he told himself angrily. She'd grown up in the company of swindlers and thieves, and was a trickster herself—that, after all, was why he had hired her. And yet she had begun to tug at his heartstrings in a way he couldn't ignore. He wanted to watch over her, to protect her...

Protect her? he chided himself. *You want to bed her, that is all, and mayhap it would have been better if you had done so at the very beginning, to get rid of this damnable itch.* But would that have worked? he asked himself silently. More likely he would have got even more deeply involved with the girl—impossibly deep...

In spite of everything, he trusted her implicitly to stay with Sir Roderick, and to look after him. He hoped, how he hoped, that he had not been mistaken in *that.* And Philippa? Philippa, he'd learned, was out of town; but there was a note for him, delivered to Caro's house. *Dear Marcus. I will be staying with my parents in Caytham for the next four weeks, so I will be close to your godfather's property. Please come to visit me...*

He folded it up in a harsh gesture. So she was in Gloucestershire. Why did she want him to visit? To make some rich new suitor jealous?

Their box at the theatre received the attentions of several visitors during the interval. Amongst the more conspicuous of them was Lady Amanda Sallis, looking ravishing in a low-cut gown of apricot-and-cream striped silk.

Marcus rose quickly to take her hand, aware of speculative eyes turning towards them. 'Lady Sallis,' he said. 'What can I do for you?'

Her blue eyes sparkled mischievously as she eyed Marcus's attractive physique; but then she sighed a little and said, 'Well. It is, on this occasion, more a matter of what I can do for *you*, Major Forrester. I need a word with you about Lord Sebastian Corbridge.'

Marcus's strong face tightened, and he drew Lady Sallis a little way from Hal and Caro, and their circle of visitors. 'Does he still visit your salon, Lady Sallis?'

'Oh, yes. None more regularly. And he is playing heavily, Marcus, getting deeper and deeper into debt.' She lowered her voice. 'I have heard that he is talking, rather rashly, of how much your godfather owes him, and is boasting of acquiring further credit from his moneylenders on the expectation of getting his hands on vast sums from the sale of Lornings in September.'

Marcus had gone very still. 'Why are you telling me this?'

'I cannot afford to offend Sebastian and his clique. But— he has insulted me from time to time, and this is my quiet way of getting my revenge.'

'For which I thank you. But Sebastian should take care,' said Marcus grimly. 'The matter is by no means settled.'

Lady Sallis shrugged her exquisite shoulders. 'Sebastian thinks it is. For he has, I hear, been negotiating the sale of certain objects from the hall—a half-dozen or so paintings, I believe—with a shady Bow Street art dealer. Rumour has it that they are already in his possession.'

Marcus had gone very still. 'Paintings. *Paintings*... Are you quite certain?'

She shrugged lightly. 'I only report what I have heard. But that is, perhaps, only the start. Where will he stop? Will he gamble, perhaps, with your godfather's letter of promise to him? All in all, Marcus, if you want to save the Lornings estate, then you must, I think, proceed rather swiftly, my friend.' She leaned a little closer. 'Now, I know you aren't a gambling man, my dear. But there are other entertainments on offer, you know, at my salon. To you—without charge.' Those dimples again, a clear and personal invitation; and then she was gone, as quickly as she had come, leaving only the lingering trace of her perfume behind. The curtain was starting to rise again, and people wandered casually back to their seats, with much rustling of silks and satins, and the murmur of their gossiping voices faded at last as the play resumed.

Of the rest of the play, Marcus heard not one word. Lady Sallis's news had driven all else from his mind. Sebastian Corbridge, the cowardly, scheming villain, was trying to sell some works of art—reputedly from Lornings—here, in London. It must have been Sebastian, or men hired by him, who had stolen those paintings.

He remembered Tassie's stricken face as he confronted her. Her desperate defence of her friends. *'But the pictures were already missing, Marcus! And it wasn't my friends who stole them from Lornings, I swear to you on my honour!'*

He rested his face in his hands, protected by the darkness around him. Tassie had always, always told him she never let down friends who trusted her. And she'd counted him, Marcus, as a friend. More fool her, seeing as he'd bullied her, forced her by foul means as well as fair into a risky venture, come close to seducing her, and finally accused her and her friends of an ugly theft.

He needed her forgiveness. And if Sebastian, stupidly, criminally reckless as ever in his gambling fever, was on the verge of promising to back up his gaming debts with the entire Lornings estate, as Lady Sallis had just hinted, then quite probably Marcus's only chance to save Lornings for Roderick now lay with Tassie, and his original scheme. Indeed, it was a wild gamble, but it was all that was left.

By rights the girl should tell him to go to the devil, and thrust his bargain back in his face. But out of sheer, stubborn pride, Marcus believed Tassie *would* challenge Sebastian, and lure him into a deep, private game, and play him with her delicate yet lethal finesse for the letter that held the threat of ruin over his godfather's head.

Yet could he use her as he had planned, when she had grown to mean so much more to him than she should?

He left the theatre before the play was over, murmuring apologies to Hal and Caro. Sleet was falling from heavy black

skies as he tramped through the streets. Marcus's thoughts
sped to Gloucestershire, where he guessed that the sleet
would be coming down as snow on the rolling Cotswold
hills. Thank God Tassie would be safe and warm with Sir
Roderick in the Dower House.

There was a message waiting for him in Portman Square
from his latest lawyer, a stoop-backed, dishevelled man with
dusty clothes and an ancient wig; his name was Erasmus
Digby, and he spoke as slowly and as interminably as a deaf
country parson. Marcus tore it open. *Concerning the matter
in hand, I think that we might be making certain progress
with reference to the case I mentioned to you, of Smithson
versus Southcott, which occurred five years ago, and of
which certain clauses might provide a useful precedent...*

Marcus was weary of false hopes and promises, weary of
the endless disputations of the law.

His lawyer could wait. So could Sebastian—for a short
while. Because first he had to see Tassie, and make an apology.

It was two in the afternoon, and Tassie came from a game
of All Fours with Sir Roderick to find Will Daniels with
Jacob in the stone-flagged kitchen. Will was clapping his
chapped hands together, and his cheeks were red with cold.
More snow had fallen overnight, and though the morning
skies had briefly brightened, fresh flurries were now whirling down from the leaden afternoon sky.

Tassie heard Will say anxiously, 'There's at least three of
our ewes stuck up in the snow just beyond Oaker's Ridge,
Uncle Jacob! I'll do my best to get to them, be sure of it, but
if the ewes drop their lambs up there alone, they'll die for
certain in this cold.'

Tassie stepped forward anxiously. 'Aren't there any shel-
ters for them up there, Will?'

'Aye, mistress Tassie. There be a ring wall up in the lee of the ridge, and a shepherd's hut a mile further. But, don't you see, 'tis getting the creatures there that's nigh impossible!'

Jacob said, 'Can't your father help?'

'He's nursin' a stiff leg from where he slipped yesterday on the ice in the yard. And you ain't no use, either, Uncle Jacob; it needs someone young and fit.' Will sighed. 'I'll set off up there again to try it, but there's only two or three hours of daylight left at most…'

Tassie frowned. There'd been several young lambs brought down to the barn in the last few days, and she loved their long, wobbly legs and their helpless, bleating cries. She couldn't bear to think of the new lambs lost in the snow.

'Well, nephew,' Jacob was saying heavily to Will, 'you could ride over to Hockton for help, but the farmers there will all be a-strugglin' with their own flocks. There ain't much more we can do.'

But there is, thought Tassie desperately. *There is.*

During her travels with Georgie Jay and his friends, she'd often helped with the lambing. Old Matt, who'd been a sheep farmer before the enclosures took away his livelihood, had taught Tassie everything: how to spot a ewe about to birth, how to cut the cord, and rub the feeble infant briskly, and push it towards its mother to feed.

Quickly, not saying anything to either Jacob or Peg because she knew they'd disapprove, she followed Will out into the bitter cold of the yard. 'Will,' she called, clutching at his arm. 'Wait a few moments, Will. I know all about lambing! I'll come and help you!'

'You, Miss Tassie?' His jaw dropped open. 'But—'

'Don't I know how to ride, and milk cows as well as any country girl?'

'Aye, you do! But—'

'I'm coming with you, Will. And that's final.'

He grinned and touched his curly forelock. 'I wouldn't dare argue, Miss Tassie.'

The snow was falling steadily by the time they'd mounted their ponies and headed up towards the exposed slopes of Oaker's Ridge. There they found several heavily pregnant ewes taking cover behind a stunted thorn thicket that was little more than a windbreak. The animals needed proper shelter out of the cold, especially as one of them was distressed. Tassie feared that her lamb was on its way. She tried to remember, rather desperately, what old Matt had told her.

'Keep them calm, Tass. Mother Nature will take her course, long as they're not panicking. It's if they struggle the little lamb gets hurt.'

They must get the ewes into shelter. They must.

Will was crouched over the birthing ewe, ready to help her. But, above the ominous moan of the strong easterly wind as it drove the snow across the hills, Tassie could hear another, far-off sheep crying out, bleating piteously. 'Will,' she cried, 'there's another one up there. Can you hear it?'

'Aye, that I can,' replied Will grimly. 'But it will have to wait, Miss Tassie. This little 'un's on its way. Can't leave it now.'

He was right. The ewe strained, her eyes rolling in distress. Again, Tassie heard the distant sheep calling: a forlorn, chill sound, up on the heights above the tree line. Tassie made up her mind. 'I'll go to that one, Will. On foot—the pony won't make it, not in this snow.'

Will looked anxious, but he was fully occupied with the straining ewe. 'Could be you're too late anyway to save her, Miss Tassie.'

'I hope not. Oh, Will, I hope not.'

'I'll follow you up when this one's sorted. Don't risk yourself too much, now, will you, girl? Looks like some real heavy snow comin' in.'

It was a long, hard struggle to the top of the ridge, and the cold wind took Tassie's breath away. The afternoon light was starting to fail, and the snow was clinging thickly to her coat and boots by the time she found the ewe, lying terrified in a drift. When it saw her it struggled to get up. 'It's all right,' breathed Tassie quickly, kneeling down beside it. 'It's all right, my lovely lass. Stay where you are. I'll see you come to no harm…'

She was a long, long way now from Will. Looking back down the hillside, she saw that the driving storm had obliterated her view of the entire valley. Fighting down a little surge of panic, Tassie inspected the ewe. Her lamb was on its way. Tassie sheltered them from the howling demon wind with her body, while willing the mother on. Nearly there. Oh, nearly there…

The tiny lamb slipped out, and its mother's strainings eased. Tassie drew the sharp knife from her boot, using it and some twine Will had given her to separate and bind the cord, then pushed the damp, quivering bundle towards the ewe. 'Here you are, mother,' she whispered. ''Tis up to you now. I can do no more.'

And slowly Tassie, forgetting her weariness, forgetting her cold, began to smile with pure delight as the weary ewe nudged at her new-born lamb, licking it and caressing it into life, until at last it lifted its head and bleated before latching on to feed.

Tassie knew she could allow herself little time to sit and gaze at it. This was different indeed to the spring lambings she was used to, amidst gentle green meadows, with skilled people around to help. This was a matter of life and death. Snow whirled around, thicker and thicker, and she knew that dusk was only an hour or so away. The wind was wailing like the devil himself around the white wastes of the snowbound hills. And yet here, just before her eyes, was warmth and life and hope, as the tiny creature staggered to its feet.

Life, yes—but how much longer would the lamb be able to cling on to life in this chilly wilderness? They all needed shelter, badly. Tassie looked round with straining eyes, trying to pierce the white storm of snow. There was no way she could get them both down into the shelter of the barn. She might just make it to the home farm with the lamb tucked inside her coat, but that would mean leaving the ewe, weak and chilled and full of milk for her lamb, out here alone in the snow. That she could not contemplate.

Perhaps Will would reach her soon. She crouched over ewe and lamb, trying to shelter them from the worst of the vicious, snow-laden wind; but as the flakes began to settle thickly on her head and her shoulders, she knew she had set herself an almost hopeless task.

And she had a dreadful feeling, as the snowstorm closed in around her, that Will would never be able to find her now.

Marcus arrived at Lornings in the late afternoon, just as the snow was taking the countryside in its fierce grip. By changing horses frequently he'd completed the journey from London with just one overnight stop. He was apprehensive, as well as saddle-weary, by the time the snow-encrusted chimneys of the Dower House came into view against the darkening sky.

How best to explain to Tassie that he had made a terrible mistake about those paintings? A mere apology would not be enough, he knew. Oh, she'd accept it, no doubt, with formal composure. But would he ever again see that look of bright, humorous regard in her expressive eyes? Would she ever again look on him as her friend? He found himself longing for her trust, almost more than anything. He feared, very much, that he had lost it for good. The business of Lornings, he realised suddenly, was no longer occupying the whole of his mind, as it had done for so long.

He rode his horse into the snow-covered courtyard of the Dower House with a feeling of relief, for the going had been hard, and the roads were, as he'd been warned, impassable for all but the hardiest traveller. As he dismounted, the kitchen door flew open, and Peg came running out to fling her arms round him as Jacob hurried to take his horse's bridle. Marcus steadied Peg, laughing at the warmth of her embrace.

'You've missed me, Peg, haven't you? And I've missed you. Anything good in that oven of yours? I feel as if I haven't eaten for days.'

'Oh, Master Marcus,' sobbed Peg. 'I swear, you won't want a thing to eat when you hear the news. You see, Miss Tassie's gone a-missing, sir!'

Marcus hadn't realised how utterly weary he was, until that moment. His spirits sank like lead. 'Gone missing?' he repeated. 'You mean that she's *out*, in this?'

Jacob spoke up grimly. 'She went up after new-born lambs with young Will this afternoon, just as the snow was a-settin' in. We didn't know, sir, or we'd have stopped her for sure. Will came back down from the hills just a few moments ago, frozen to the bone. Miss Tassie went on up over the ridge, he said, after a ewe she could hear crying out. He went a-lookin', calling out for her, but the snow was real bad, and he was carrying two new-born lambs he had to get back to shelter. He hoped she might have found her way back down here.'

Marcus ran his hand distractedly through his hair. 'And she hasn't.'

He was answered by their silence.

Peg said tearfully, 'Will and Jacob, they was all for goin' up into the hills after her, sir, but Lawd's sake, how will they find her in *this*? The snow'll be two foot thick up on Oaker's

Ridge, and it'll soon be dark. 'Tis the worst spring weather we've seen in years.'

Marcus said swiftly, 'Where is my godfather? Does he know Tassie is missing?'

'Poor Sir Roderick's bin in his bed these last few days—his joints are real stiff with the cold—and we thought it best not to worry 'im... Oh, sir, what can we do? That poor lass, out there in all this by herself!'

Marcus felt desperate with anxiety, yet he knew it was not their fault. He said quickly, 'She's plucky and resourceful. She'll have found somewhere to shelter, never fear. But on no account must she be left to stay out all night. I'm going after her.'

Peg began to wail again. Jacob said resolutely, 'Then I'm comin' with you, Master Marcus! The lad'll come, too. Real upset about Tassie, he is. He's just gone to tend to the new-born lambs in the barn, then he'll be with you.'

Marcus gently touched the older man's shoulder. 'My thanks, Jacob, but this bitter cold will have you frozen up in no time. And Will must be exhausted if he's already spent all day up on that hillside. No, I shall go alone. I'll just see my godfather, to tell him I'm back, and in the meantime, Peg, would you get me a small bundle of food together? Bread, cheese, anything.'

His godfather had been nodding off before the fire, but was sleepily glad to see him. 'Send Tassie to me later, will you, Marcus?' he murmured. 'I've a fancy for cards, as well as the sight of her bright smile. She's a fine lass, that one.'

'I know,' responded Marcus quietly. He went then to change into a heavy coat, stout leather boots and warm gloves. He pushed a tinderbox into his pocket, and a little silver flask filled with brandy. He worked with swift intensity, trying not to waste time thinking. *How long would anyone survive out there on the bleak hillside in this kind of storm? How many hours?*

Of one thing he was certain. Unless he found her swiftly, her life hung in the balance.

Chapter Thirteen

Tassie had managed to carry the lamb a few yards upwind, with the mother ewe stumbling along behind, to the shelter of a nearby wall; but truth to tell, the piled-up stones offered little shelter now, so deep were the snowdrifts, so bitter the whirling wind. She knelt over the animals, trying to shelter them with her body; but her teeth were chattering, and her fingers were growing painfully numb in their damp woollen gloves.

Darkness was setting in. She had never known snow like this before, and still it came, spinning around her in myriad whirling flakes, until there seemed to be nothing else in the whole world.

Tassie was frightened now. Even if they had come out looking for her, how would they find her in this? She hardly had the energy to shout, and anyway, the wind would whip her words away.

The little lamb bleated piteously. She hugged it to her, and began to whistle.

Marcus was on the verge of giving up when he heard that familiar sound. He was so glad, he wanted to shout for joy.

For nigh on two hours he'd been searching the snowbound hillside as darkness set in; he was trying not to admit it, but he knew full well that every minute that passed gave him less chance of finding her. Then he heard an almost miraculous sound in the distance—someone was whistling 'The Bold Ploughboy'. Calling out, 'Tassie. Tassie, I'm on my way,' he struggled on knee deep through the drifting snow.

He found her at last, crouched in the darkness in the lee of a snowbound wall, hugging a tiny lamb in her arms, while a weak, exhausted ewe lay in a snowdrift beside her. Tassie clambered to her feet, still holding the lamb, her wide green eyes wary, her mouth lifting in a tentative, hopeful smile.

'Oh, Marcus,' she said simply. 'Marcus, please don't be angry with me for wearing breeches, or for whistling. I'm so *glad* to see you.'

He wanted to pull her into his arms, to warm her with his own body, to cover her precious face with kisses. Instead he touched her cheek with his gloved hand. 'Hello, minx,' he said softly. 'So what, in the name of Methuselah, have you been up to now?'

She flinched a little, uncertain of him. 'The ewe was so weak,' she said quickly. 'And the lamb—oh, Marcus, how could I leave the lamb?' As if rejecting the very thought, the tiny animal bleated protestingly.

Marcus said gently, 'You couldn't. I understand. No recriminations, Tassie.'

In fact, Tassie had been overwhelmed to see him. Her heart had given a great, painful jolt as she recognised his distinctive figure striding unevenly but purposefully towards her through the deep snow in the fast-fading light.

Marcus was assessing the situation swiftly. 'We'll never get back down to Lornings tonight,' he said practically. 'Not unless we abandon the ewe and her lamb.'

'We can't do that!' cried Tassie, aghast, hugging the lamb to her again. 'Oh, Marcus, we can't!'

'I know,' he said softly. 'We can't stay here either, Tassie— your nose is almost blue with cold already. But we can, I think, make it to the shepherd's hut just along the ridge. Do you know it?'

The lamb was bleating piteously; Tassie tried to soothe it. 'I know it, Marcus,' she replied earnestly. 'I thought of trying to get there earlier, but the ewe wouldn't make it, and I can't carry her...'

'I can,' he replied gently. 'Follow me. If you walk in my footsteps, it should make the journey a little easier.'

With sure strength he swung the ewe up across his shoulders, in the way the shepherds did, and set off through the blinding snow. Tassie hurried after him, clutching the little lamb to her heart, scrambling in and out of the deep footprints left by his boots. She was too exhausted to think properly of anything now except staying on her feet, but she was conscious of an overwhelming feeling of gladness that Marcus was here.

She'd been so afraid that he hated her, because he suspected her and her friends of stealing from Lornings. Perhaps he *was* still angry with her, but there was something new in his steely-grey eyes, a kind of peculiar, burning intensity of gladness as he'd greeted her, that made her hope, so much, that he didn't hate her after all.

The stone shepherd's hut was looming up out of the snowstorm just a little way ahead. Marcus reached it first, and pushed open the door. Putting the ewe carefully down on the beaten earth floor, he drew the tinderbox from his pocket and lit the stump of old candle that sat on a shelf. There was a bale of ragged hay in here too, and a small heap of firewood left in the hearth by the hill-shepherds for any of their number who might find themselves benighted here.

Marcus looked over at Tassie. Her face was white with weariness; but she was gently setting the lamb down, pulling out hay for it, rubbing its woolly fleece and laying out a soft bed beside its dam, so it could reach her full teats. It began to guzzle greedily, little tail wagging. Tassie knelt on the floor, gazing in delight. 'Look, Marcus. Isn't he a darling? Look how well he feeds! He will be all right, won't he?'

Marcus smiled. 'The little fellow looks as though he will, thanks to you. Were you there at the birthing, Tassie?'

She looked up at him apprehensively, and he realised she was wondering if he was going to shout at her. God help me, but I must seem an ogre to her, he reproached himself silently.

'Yes,' she said almost defiantly. 'I heard the ewe bleating in distress, far away from where I was with Will. I couldn't ignore her, Marcus! She was almost too weak to give birth—I had to help her.'

He unwrapped the parcel of bread and cheese Peg had given him and broke off a portion for her. 'I take it you've helped with lambing before?' He was past registering surprise; Tassie, it seemed, could turn her hand to anything. He tried to picture, with a certain wry amusement, any of the society ladies of his London acquaintance assisting at such an emergency. He tried to picture Philippa. He couldn't.

'Yes,' she asserted earnestly as she took the food, 'of course I have. But never, Marcus, in a snowstorm such as this! We often worked on upland farms in the spring and early summer, helping with the lambing and the shearing, me and—me and...'

She was going to say, he knew, 'me and Georgie Jay and Lemuel and the others.' But she didn't, because, he guessed, she was frightened of rekindling his anger. He caught his breath at the look of uncertainty in her lovely, wistful face. Dear God, what a fool he was. He had driven her to this fear of him, with his arrogant ways, and his condescension towards the lowly but vital life she had led with her companions, his bullying refusal to listen to her, to trust her.

He realised now that he had always wanted her physically. From that first kiss outside the gaming hell, his desire had been aroused—though what man's wouldn't be? She was breathtakingly lovely, with her sweet face and her slender yet wholly womanly figure.

Yet it was more than simply a desire to bed her. He'd always been aware that Tassie was someone special. She'd touched his heart, in a way no one else had ever done. And yet he'd made her frightened of him, as frightened as she'd been of the guardians who had scarred her lonely childhood.

Feeling a despairing sense of anger at his own stupidity, he began automatically to arrange the firewood that lay in the little brazier in the chimney-place, and struck a spark amidst the kindling. The flickering firelight blended with the glow from the candle, casting soft shadows across Tassie's hesitant, vulnerable face. God's blood, he had been a fool in his dealings with her.

She saw him watching her, and quailed inwardly. She had been so glad to see him! Her heart had blazed with happiness, just like the bright flames in the hearth. But the expression in his iron-grey eyes was smouldering, dark; she guessed he was still impatient with her, still angry. And with reason. He could have died, coming up here into the wintry wilderness, looking for her. And it was all her fault. Oh, why had she been so stupid as to think that he could care for her? When would she ever accept that she could never belong in his world?

There was a wide stone ledge running along one side of the hut. She finished off her mouthful of bread, and sat on it with her hands folded on her lap, feeling cold. 'Marcus,' she said hesitantly, 'I'm sorry about all of this. I always seem to be getting into scrapes, and you're always getting me out of them. And I'm sorry, too, that I didn't tell you earlier about those paintings. I know they must mean an awful lot to you, for you to get so angry about them.' She started to chew at her forefinger, then pulled it away and tilted her chin defiantly. 'But—I *know* that Georgie Jay and his friends didn't take them. I would swear it on my life…'

She was pale with tiredness and cold, but even so she gazed at him with a frankness and honesty in those clear green eyes that moved him more than he could say. He knelt down quickly before her and put his hand on hers.

'Listen to me, Tassie. I know it wasn't you or your friends. In London, I learned that it's my cousin Sebastian who's been secretly stealing from Lornings, to fuel his passion for gambling.'

A mixture of emotions crossed Tassie's expressive face. Relief, gladness, then anger. 'Why,' she breathed, 'the scheming, low-down thief! So he couldn't wait till September to get his hands on it all! Marcus, you must take me to London, *now*. You must give me the chance to get even with him.'

Marcus smiled. 'Tassie, I know you'd run my fencing sword through him if you could. But—hear me out—I'm not at all sure that I want to go on with this. It was a mad, foolish scheme I concocted, because I was so crazy with anger against Sebastian—but it's too much of a risk, Tassie. I'll think of something else.'

He was wishing, even as he spoke, that he'd been to see his London attorney Digby about the new information the man had hinted at in his latest long-winded note; but Tassie distracted him by jumping to her feet, her emerald eyes blazing with anger. 'Marcus, you can't possibly back out now! Why, when I think of your grasping cousin robbing poor Sir Roderick's treasures from under his very nose—I vow, if I caught him at it, I'd deal with him myself! Fie on it, what are a few card games to me, where's the danger? I'll wipe the floor with him, you see if I don't!'

She was pacing angrily to and fro, her big coat swirling around her booted legs. Marcus, too, leapt to his feet, grabbed her and swung her round to face him. 'Tassie, we're not talking here about a card game between tinkers round a camp fire! We're talking about fortunes, lost and won. Men will do anything for such stakes, will kill, even... You know nothing of such a world, nothing. And I was a fool to think of introducing you to it.'

She seemed to crumple at that. 'I understand,' she whispered. 'I know I'm foolish, and know nothing about being a lady. I'm not surprised you wish you'd never, ever set eyes on me and Edward. I'm not surprised you get so angry with me. Oh, Marcus.' She forced her expression into a rueful smile, but he saw the hint of bright tears trembling behind her lashes. 'I only ever wanted to please you.'

'Oh, my dear,' he said. 'Oh, Tassie, don't look at me like that. Please don't ever look at me like that. I'm not angry with you, Tassie. Even when I roar and bellow at you like a wounded bull, I'm not angry with you.'

She sniffed, and rubbed quickly at her eyes with the back of her hand. 'Then you should be,' she pronounced sharply. 'I picked your blasted pocket, did I not? And since that day, I have been nothing but trouble to you from start to finish. That is why you shout at me so much, isn't it? Because I exasperate you beyond bearing.' She broke off, fumbling desperately in her pocket. 'And now, I haven't even got a dratted handkerchief!'

Marcus's heart ached at her distress. 'Here, have mine. Please, Tassie, don't cry.'

'It's all right,' she said woodenly, accepting his large kerchief and scrubbing furiously at her cheeks. 'I quite understand. You must have beautiful ladies after you by the score, and of course there is Philippa, and...and—'

'Philippa is nothing to me,' he interrupted. 'Anything I felt for her has long since vanished from my life.' He realised, even as he uttered the words, that it was quite true. All he could think of was Tassie, who was gazing at him, speechless, wide-eyed. He met her gaze steadily. 'Do you think Philippa could help with lambing, or ride astride to round up lost heifers?'

'But—she is a fine lady. And everyone says how much you loved each other. And Emilia said—'

'Ah, people spout all kinds of nonsense. Yes, she is a fine lady. But...' He turned from her almost fiercely to pace the room, then whirled back to face her. 'Oh, Tassie. Don't you know, my darling girl, why I am such an ill-tempered oaf with you? Don't you realise it?'

She blinked back her tears. 'Because I drive you beyond the limits of patience,' she said flatly. 'You told me that yourself earlier.'

His face was hard with restrained emotion, his hands clenched at his sides. He said in a low, burning voice, 'You drive me beyond the limits of patience because I want you more than anyone I have ever known. Every time you lift your face to mine, in argument or defiance, I want to kiss the words from your sweet lips. Every time you confront me, in your ridiculously enticing clothes and your shorn curls, which you cut off because of *my* stupidity, I want to take you in my arms and never, ever let you go.'

'Oh, Marcus,' she said, quite awed, crumpling her kerchief in her hand. 'I wish you would. Take me in your arms, I mean...' And then, as the full force of what he was actually saying hit her, she stared at him in wonderment. 'Do you really mean it? Do you?'

A groan tore from deep within him. He reached out, to draw her to him, and the longing surged, hard and relentless, through his entire body. Ah God, but she was so exquisite, so vulnerable, lifting her sweet face to his with her eyes still disbelieving, yet her mouth softly parted for his kiss. She could not be a virgin, he groaned inwardly, not leading the life she had led—and yet everything about her proclaimed her utter innocence.

There was still time. Still, just, time for him to move back. For him to save them both from folly.

Then she seemed to shrink back from him, and she lowered her eyes, saying in a voice that tore at his heart, 'Of course. I quite understand if you do not wish to kiss me. After all, I am not exactly the kind of female you are used to, am I?'

He gathered her even closer, crushing her against him. 'No. You are a thousand, thousand times better,' he breathed. He kissed her cold cheeks, her tearstained eyes, her little tip-tilted nose, her lips, feeling her warm and soften beneath him like an unfolding flower. He wanted her, so badly. The desire burned at his loins. She was pressing herself instinctively against him, curving her sweet body into his, reaching to twine her fingers in his dark hair and pulling his face down to meet hers as the intensity of their kiss deepened and grew. Her coat, her foolish man's coat that all but drowned her, was wide open; her firm breasts were pushing at her thin shirt so he could feel the pressure of them against the hard wall of his own chest, could feel the tautening crests of her nipples as she nestled in his arms, responding thrillingly to his kiss, to the silky pleasure of his tongue's deep penetration.

She was offering herself. And there was no way on God's earth that he could refuse. The moment was as sweet as he'd dreamed. He drew back just for a moment to shrug off his own long coat and drop it to the floor; then, splaying his warm hands round her back, he tenderly drew her down with him on to the outspread garment, and clasped her close once more. She clung to him as if to let go would cost her her life, her breath. He kissed her again, feeling her slim legs in their ridiculous breeches twining urgently against his own strong thighs. With ardent fingers he ripped open the buttons of her shirt, cradling and cupping her small breasts with his hands. She cried out as her nipples hardened against his palms, and gripped his wide shoulders; his lips moved down her cheek, her throat, to the softness of her bosom. As his mouth caressed those rosy crests, he felt her trembling, and knew it was not with cold. Her body burned, as did his. He lifted his head to gaze at her, his eyes dark and molten with desire.

'Tassie,' he breathed. 'I do not want to hurt you. But I am a man, Tassie, with a man's passions. You must say, now, if you want me to stop.' *Though God help me if you do,* he groaned to himself, *for it will take all of my strength to pull back now.*

She gazed up at him, her eyes soft with love, her cheeks flushed from his kisses. 'And I am a woman. You will not hurt me, Marcus,' she whispered. 'I know you will not. You see, I need you.'

He was lost. As gently as he could, he parted her garments, pulling her breeches down from her slender hips. He cupped her flesh, held her tight against his own still-clothed figure. And Tassie, feeling his desire, his iron strength, let out a little cry of longing. There was a sweet pull at her loins so intense it was almost a pain. As his strong shapely hands skimmed her breasts and belly, and slipped between her thighs to caress her there, she moaned aloud, rubbing herself against his firm touch, arching her melting core towards him. She was beyond any thought but her love, her need for this man.

Marcus tried his best to restrain himself. But she clung to him instinctively, lifting herself to meet him, thrusting her tender breasts to his mouth until he was wild with desire and his manhood was pulsing hard within the confinement of his garments. Moving now to kiss the lovely, wanton mouth that pleaded for his touch, he freed his garments with one hand, and arched himself over her, his face taut with longing.

He parted her trembling thighs with the utmost gentleness, and positioned himself against her. He felt the shock ripple through her as she became aware of the rigid heat of his arousal, and he saw the sudden fear in her eyes. He was angry, that the act of love should frighten her. He could not bear the thought of some lout deflowering her in the past, taking his own harsh pleasure and leaving her with nothing but the memory of male lust, and pain.

That in itself was enough to make him strong. To help him hold back. He kissed her again. 'Tassie,' he said gently. 'Take your pleasure from me, my darling. Use me. Take all the time you want.' He continued to murmur endearments against her softened mouth as gradually he let her feel the strength of him, let her feel what it was like to be loved, as he gently, oh so gently stroked her melting secret place.

She cried out, her eyes wide, as his manhood slipped at last between her silken folds. He bent to kiss her face again, then moved downwards to caress the hard pink nubs of her nipples with gentle teeth, swirling his tongue round the rosebud tips. Ah, but she was lovely. Tender, yet wild and passionate...

She was moving her loins instinctively against him now, wanting more, her breath fluttering on his cheek. Marcus, agonised with the need for restraint, cupped her hips and held back awhile; then, his face dark with longing, he rocked slowly forwards and deliberately began to sheath his ardent length in her silken softness. As he further penetrated her, she went very still, her body arched against him to receive him, her eyes wide and yearning, her lips murmuring his name...

And then, Marcus encountered resistance. So brief, so slight he scarcely noticed it; but at the same time he heard her gasp of wonder, saw the flash of wide surprise in her emerald eyes, and he suddenly realised—this was her first time.

He should have known. Yes, she had lived wild for years with a band of travelling rogues; but they had their own kind of honour, these folk, and he should have known, from that first entrancing kiss outside the Angel in the pouring London rain, that everything about her was proof of her innocence. But now it was too late even to think of stopping, far too late, because she was holding him tighter now, pleading with him, needing him. He responded, driving harder into her welcoming softness, feeling himself at one with her, and he was lost. She clung to him as if she were drowning, her face wide-eyed, dazed with pleasure as her fingers clutched at the rippling muscles of his back beneath his shirt. He stroked slowly, deeply at her very heart, seeing the pleasure build up in her flushed face, his body arching strongly over her as she began, at last, to utter little, breathless cries; and as she shuddered almost violently against him, clinging to him as the extremity of her pleasure overwhelmed her, he heard her whisper, in a soft yet passionate voice, *'Oh, darling, darling Marcus...'*

With that, he felt his own formidable restraint breaking at last. He plunged hard into her, again and again, feeling his own convulsive release shuddering through him, until at last he lay quite still in her arms.

Tassie, too, was motionless in the flickering light of the solitary candle as his heavy warmth pressed against her. The dark pleasure of his intimate caresses still pulsed through her; it had been like fire consuming her body, a heat building up with each delicious stroke, each tantalising caress; she'd hovered briefly on the edge of oblivion, before soaring into unimagined bliss.

And now, Marcus's head lay on his outstretched arm. His

eyes were closed, his dark hair curled loosely around his dear familiar face, and his lips were still softened with pleasure. This man had touched her soul. Tassie felt her love for him tugging so painfully at her heart that there was a huge lump in her throat.

He opened his eyes slowly, as if aware of the intensity of her gaze.

'Oh, Tassie.' He drew himself quickly up on one elbow and gazed down at her. 'Why did you not tell me? You have not lain with a man before, have you?'

She bit her lip, and her eyes were very bright. He was angry with her, of course. Had she not heard on her travels how men despised young women who tried to trap them with their innocence? 'And so, does it matter?' she said airily.

Marcus almost groaned aloud. What had he done, in taking advantage of one as innocent as she? Yet the pleasure had been as sweetly intense as he'd ever known. And if she kept looking at him like that, with her wide, over-bright eyes and tremulous lips, then it would not be long before his virility was renewed, and he would be kissing her soft mouth and rosy-tipped breasts with fresh passion, and driving himself into her lovely, responsive woman's body again...

He had let his male instincts run riot. He had taken complete advantage of their isolation, out in the snowbound countryside. He fought down the overpowering urge to take her again in his arms and kiss the doubt, the uncertainty from her lovely eyes. Instead he said, 'We must talk, Tassie. We must think about what is to be done.'

Tassie felt herself shrivelling inside. Did Marcus regret what had happened? Had she disappointed him? Had she done something wrong? 'The fire is dying,' she said in a small voice, turning her back to him and getting to her feet. 'We need more firewood to keep the ewe and her babe from freezing. There's a copse down just below this field—I will go and fetch some.'

But Marcus too was on his feet, pulling up his heavy coat from the floor and shrugging himself into it. 'I'll go,' he said tersely. 'You stay and tend the animals. I'll be back as soon as I can.'

Just then the lamb let out a piteous bleat of hunger. Tassie went quickly towards it and kneeled, helping it to find the slumbering ewe's teat. Her heart wrenching within her, she heard him leave.

Shivering, she revived the dying fire in the brazier, then walked to and fro to keep herself warm, her head bowed. She loved him, almost more than she could bear. And she had thought, earlier tonight, that he loved her. But somehow that, too, had gone wrong. *Why did you not tell me, Tassie?* he'd said. *We must talk...* What about? He must think her either a fool, or a scheming temptress. She dashed the tears from her eyes. Then she spied something on the floor, half-hidden by straw. A sheet of notepaper, folded up tightly.

She picked it up, and something about it—some lingering scent, perhaps?—reminded her of another time, another place. Her little room, in the attic of the Blue Bell. Marcus's wallet, that she'd stolen from him as he tried to help her. The lock of hair. The scent. The note...

This was a different note, but from the same person.

Dear Marcus, I will be staying with my parents in Caytham for the next four weeks, so I will be close to your godfather's estate. Please come to visit me, as you promised. I have an answer for you at last. Ever yours, Philippa.

The words thudded through her head. A promise. An answer. But what was the question?

Emilia's taunt came back to her. *'Of course it's been clear since they were childhood sweethearts that they'd marry one another.'* Tassie wanted to tear the scented letter into a thousand pieces, and hurl the shreds into the dying fire.

So Philippa was in Gloucestershire. That was why Marcus had returned from London so swiftly, in the teeth of the snowstorm! That was why he'd been so horrified to discover that Tassie was a virgin! It would make her less easy to discard.

Shivering badly now, she pulled her old coat tightly around herself and lay huddled before the fire, her head pillowed on her hands, her heart aching with despair.

At long last, when it seemed to be the very dead of night, and all she could hear was the menacing whistle of the wind across the hills, she heard the firm, uneven footsteps crunching across the deep snow, and heard the door begin to open. Quickly she squeezed her eyes shut, and pretended to be asleep. Marcus stood over her a long time, no doubt inwardly cursing her for the trouble she had brought into his life. She wished he would go, before a stupid, traitorous tear rolled out from under her closed eyelids. She heard him moving at last, piling wood into the brazier, and the next thing she knew, he was laying his big, warm coat as extra covering over her curled-up body. 'Sleep well, Tassie,' he said quietly. 'We will talk properly in the morning about our agreement.'

That was all she ever was to him. Part of—*an agreement.* Her tears really started to flow then. Still trying to keep up her pretence of sleep, she squeezed her eyelids together so hard she thought they'd burst. The ache in her throat almost choked her. She heard him putting more wood on the fire, tending it into a low, banked-up core of heat that would keep away the bitter cold till morning, though not from her heart.

Chapter Fourteen

Lady Amanda Sallis was on the point of retiring to her bed-chamber when her maidservant came to tell her there was a girl at the door, asking for her by name. Lady Sallis looked incredulous and declared, 'It's near three in the morning. What business can this person—this *girl*—possibly have with me?'

'I don't know, m'lady, truly I don't! But she does say it's really important...'

Sighing, because she was looking forward to a restorative night's sleep made all the more enticing by the prospect of a tryst with a handsome young guards officer the next after-noon, Lady Sallis drew her fringed silk shawl more closely around the shoulders of her low-cut polonaise and made her way down through the discreetly luxurious house in Albe-marle Street, past the supper hall where her wealthy clients refreshed themselves with iced champagne and dainty mor-sels of poached salmon, past the big, empty gaming rooms that had been so satisfyingly full earlier. She smiled as she remembered the gentle clink of money, the enticing rattle of the dice box. It had been a successful evening, with the high-rolling Lord Sebastian Corbridge and his fashionable set at the core of the gambling as usual. She despised Corbridge, but he brought money in—for the moment.

She moved on down the wide staircase to the candlelit entrance hall, where James, her footman, stood staring with a certain amount of unaccustomed helplessness at the young woman who hovered just inside the door. A hooded cloak all but covered her slender figure, and a wicker box draped with a cloth stood on the floor by her feet.

'Yes?' said Lady Sallis sharply. 'What business do you have with me at this hour, pray? Your reasons, I warn you, had better be good.'

The girl lifted her head almost proudly and pushed back her hood. Lady Sallis smothered a quick gasp of surprise, because she was beautiful. Even in that drab attire—and her state of near-exhaustion judging by the dark shadows under her emerald-green eyes—she had a lovely heart-shaped face. Her hair, golden as a bright new guinea, clustered in silken curls round the crown of her head, and trailed in soft tendrils down the slender column of her neck. Lady Sallis felt a brief pang of envy, and interest.

'I have come looking for work, Lady Sallis,' the girl said in a clear, well-modulated voice. 'You see, I play cards.'

'Do you, indeed? And what is your game, pray?'

The girl shrugged. 'Piquet, whist, faro—I am expert at them all. Hazard, too, if your clients have a fancy for dice. I would look after your interests well, my lady.'

Lady Sallis frowned, intrigued in spite of herself. 'Where have you run from? Not from doting parents, or some angry husband, I hope?'

'Oh, no,' said the girl quietly. For a moment there was a look of haunting sadness in her lovely green eyes. 'No one at all will be looking for me, I assure you.'

'Come through into the parlour, so we can talk. James—see that the fire is rekindled there, will you?'

And Tassie, picking up Edward's wicker cage, followed in the wake of her ladyship's rustling skirts.

Marcus. Oh, Marcus.

It was a little over a week since the night she'd spent with Marcus in the shepherd's hut. They'd been found at dawn by a search party up from Hockton village; Tassie was just stirring from sleep as they arrived, but Marcus was wide awake and waiting for them outside as their rescuers scrambled up the hillside through the deep snow.

There'd been no time to talk in private. Tassie, though reeling from her discovery of Philippa's letter, had been aware that Marcus was treating her with care, with tenderness even, watching over her as the kindly village men helped her down the hillside. As the sun rose over the hills, warming the air and melting the snow, Tassie felt her hopes rise tentatively with it. After all, it was only a letter—perhaps some very *old* letter, that Marcus had quite forgotten about.

But at the Dower House, Philippa was waiting for him.

A big coach, with a proud coat of arms emblazoned on its doors, was drawn up in the courtyard; and Philippa, with Peg and Jacob hovering anxiously in the background, was pacing to and fro in the mixture of mud and snow, heedless of her expensive kidskin boots, looking quite beautiful in a rich chestnut riding habit and feathered hat, watching as the little party of villagers drew near with Marcus and Tassie in their midst.

She rushed towards Marcus as if there was no one else there. Tassie, numb with dismay, heard her murmur, 'Marcus. Oh, my love. I heard that you were lost, up in the hills! I came over here from Caytham at first light, the roads are just passable… *Thank God* you are safe. Marcus, please get rid of these—people, and then we can talk properly…'

Then she was reaching up to kiss his cheek. Tassie felt the pain slice through her. It was as well that old Peg was already fussing over her, drawing her inside into the big warm kitchen. 'Tassie, Tassie,' she was scolding. 'What were you thinkin' of, to go out up there, into the darkness with that snow a-coming down?' Tassie sat heavily in the chair to which Peg guided her; allowed Peg to rub her frozen fingers into warmth. 'Now, you must change into something decent and dry! And there's some of my good hot broth simmering on the stove…'

Strangely enough, Tassie was shivering wildly now that she was safe in the warm kitchen. And she felt tired, so tired. 'Philippa,' she muttered between chattering teeth. 'When did Philippa get here?'

'She arrived here an hour ago, with her maidservant and groom, from Caytham—she'd heard that Master Marcus was out lost in the snow, and she couldn't rest, poor girl, for worryin' about him.' She bustled to the stove to stir the savoury broth. 'Now, this is almost ready, my pet. Will you have a bowl of it? It'll warm you up…'

Tassie hardly heard her. She was hearing Marcus's voice instead. *Philippa is nothing to me,* he'd said last night. *Anything I felt for her has long since vanished…*

'It'll be a summer wedding,' Peg prattled on happily. 'It's what her parents always wanted for her. Maybe they've had certain disagreements lately, but everyone can see that they're made for each other.'

By then she was talking to herself, because Tassie had gone up to her room, to change into dry clothes—breeches, of course, and a thick jacket and sturdy boots. Then, though exhaustion still numbed her, she slipped out through the back of the house, and through the melting snow to the crossroads just outside Hockton, to leave her mark for Georgie Jay and his friends: three straight twigs, set one upon the other in a star shape, between the big roots of the forked oak. She prayed they would still be nearby.

Once back at the Dower House she kept to her room for the rest of the day, pretending to be asleep. Early that evening, when the purple dusk had fallen over the snow-clad hills, she took Edward in his covered travelling cage, and a little bag of clothes, and crept from the house in secret, though it grieved her not to say goodbye to Sir Roderick. In the shadows by the crossroads, Georgie Jay and the others were waiting for her.

'Thank goodness you came,' she whispered as Georgie Jay put his arm round her and the others clustered around.

'Aren't we always here for you?' soothed Georgie.

'Take me back to London with you. I have business there.'

'Of course. But—' and he drew her to one side '—there's the matter of the big house, girl...'

Wychwood. She shivered. She had almost forgotten—because there was so much she wanted to forget. 'Did you—did you find anything out?'

He pushed his cap back from his head. 'Tass, girl, the house is all shut up. The folk who lived there are dead. No one lives there now.'

So it was a house of ghosts. A place that held no answers, opened no doors. *Some day the brat's going to find out the truth...* Planning to use the riddle of the past to solve her future was another illusion; just as, for a short while, she'd thought that her future lay with Marcus.

Georgie Jay was saying to her, 'We'll set off this very night—there's a carrier's cart going our way—and there'll be no more talk of you bein' sent off to Moll's brother. Your place is with us! Isn't that right, lads?'

She nodded, but she knew that there was no going back

to her old life; her way ahead was once more an open book. Except that first, there was something she must do. A promise to keep.

Now she followed Lady Sallis into a candlelit parlour, with the haughty footman James scowling at her as he went to add coals to the fire. She prayed Edward would remain silent in his cage. But just as Lady Sallis was spreading out her skirts to sit down, and pointing to another chair for Tassie, the parrot let out a piercing squawk.

'What, in God's name,' breathed Lady Sallis, jumping to her feet, 'is that?'

Tassie said quickly, 'He's my parrot—I swear he'll be no trouble! He's just upset, that's all, at being somewhere new.' She bent to lift the cloth and whispered, 'It's all right, Edward. It's all right.'

James the footman looked as if he'd gladly strangle the bird, and Lady Sallis sat again, rather slowly. She had a feeling she was going to regret this. But she also had a practised eye for the type of female who would appeal to her wealthy male punters, and this young woman, with her stunning looks and quietly determined manner, might well cause something of a sensation. Even the parrot could be an asset.

'James, bring me a fresh pack,' instructed Lady Sallis curtly. 'And *you*, girl—show me how you deal the pack for faro.'

Tassie quickly discarded her cloak and took the pack James coldly offered her. Lady Sallis watched fascinated as Tassie rippled the cards with sure, swift fingers, then gathered and dealt them with a competence that was staggering.

'You are almost too good,' Lady Sallis said flatly. 'My clients will be suspicious that you are cheating them. Do you cheat?'

'Me? Oh, no, my lady,' protested Tassie, with such wide-eyed innocence that Lady Sallis wanted to chuckle aloud.

Instead, she said briskly, 'Well, just make sure you don't cheat me, my girl. And use your tricks carefully with the punters. I want no accusation of cheating or other knavery in this place, do you hear me?'

Tassie gazed at her. 'Does this mean you are offering me a post here?'

'It does. One of my girls has just left unexpectedly—shall we say that a better offer came her way? So I am a little short-staffed. But I warn you, you are on trial.' She eyed Tassie's drab clothes with some distaste. 'You have, I take it, some more appropriate clothes for an establishment such as this?'

Tassie felt herself colour. 'No. I fear I've mislaid them…'

Lady Sallis pondered this. 'So. You've run from somewhere, in a hurry. Well, you're clearly no fool, and neither am I. I'll ask no more questions, as long as you don't bring any trouble here.'

'I won't, my lady. That I swear.'

Lady Sallis nodded. 'We'll find you some new attire,' she promised. 'Something that will flatter your delicate colouring. As you are no doubt aware, my customers, who are all male and naturally of the highest classes, come here not only for the gaming, but also for pleasant companionship and conversation. You do understand that, don't you? That, at times, my gentlemen find their appetites a little—jaded with the cards, and wish to seek alternate pleasures, which are available in my private rooms upstairs?'

Tassie lifted her head and said, 'I understand, my lady. But perhaps I can prove myself at cards first? I assure you, my skill at play will be my greatest asset to you.'

Lady Sallis took leave to doubt that. The girl was lovely, and her air of well-bred innocence, feigned or real, would hold strong appeal for some of the more jaded *roués* amongst her clientele. But she would move gently, at first.

'Then play you shall,' she pronounced. 'Tomorrow night you can just observe the tables. The night after, you may, perhaps, try your hand at piquet with some of our less important clients. All winnings return to the house—and remember, I will be watching you.'

'Thank you, my lady.'

''Tis my pleasure,' said Lady Sallis, and found she meant it. The girl was intriguing. 'What is your name?'

'Sarah,' said Tassie, after a brief hesitation that told its own tale to the shrewd Lady Sallis. But she chose to let it go.

'Very well—Sarah. I'll get a maid to show you to your room. Breakfast is at ten.' She rang the bell, and the maid-servant came quickly to guide Tassie through the big house, past more gaming rooms, and up more stairs into a region of secretive, silk-curtained boudoirs that made Tassie's heart beat rather fast.

'See in there?' The maid twitched back a curtain as they passed by. 'Those are the rooms for private games, and it's my guess you'll be soon as busy up here as in them rooms below.'

Tassie said, 'Lady Sallis has offered me a job at her card tables. That is all.'

The maid laughed again as she led her up the stairs to another floor. 'Saints alive,' she said, 'you're an innocent and no mistake! Where have you come from?'

'The country,' said Tassie quickly.

'Well, the best of luck to you,' chuckled the maid as she pushed open a door to a small bedchamber and put down the candlestick she was carrying. She cast a wary eye at Edward's cage as the bird started to squawk. 'Dratted creature. He'd best not keep *that* up all night. Sleep well, Sarah. You'll need to learn fast, I think, if you're to last long here.'

She turned to go. 'Wait—please!' called Tassie, putting Edward's cage down carefully on the floor by the little bed. 'Would you just tell me—does a man by the name of Lord Sebastian Corbridge play here?'

'Corbridge? Oh, aye, he's here most nights with his cronies. Plays deep, too. What on earth d'you want with him? Don't waste too much time on trying to rook him, for remember, all winnings go straight into Lady Sallis's fat purse.' She turned to go again, saying over her shoulder, 'Sweet dreams—*Sarah*.'

As soon as she'd gone, Tassie undressed slowly down to her shift, blew out the candle, and climbed into the small bed. She wanted to confront Sebastian Corbridge, and entice him into the deepest game he'd ever known. It was the one thing she was determined to do, before she turned her back on this disastrous episode in her life for good. She was going to gamble with him for the highest stake of all—the letter that was proof of Sir Roderick's crushing debt.

Afterwards, she would go back to Marcus with the precious document, and present it to him with cold formality, and tell him that their bargain was now truly fulfilled.

''Tis a matter of honour, you see,' she would tell him defiantly. 'This is for Sir Roderick, who has been a true friend to me.'

She hoped Marcus would be ashamed. She hoped Philippa would not be there with him, for there were some things she could not bear.

At the Blue Bell, Moll was busy filling big earthenware jugs with creamy ale from a barrel when the gentleman came in. She spotted him straight away, even though the taproom was crowded; firstly because he had a slight limp, and secondly because, in spite of that limp, he was a tall, well-made specimen of manhood, around twenty-five or so, with wide shoulders, and powerful legs, and a face handsome enough to please any woman's eye. Moll patted her dark curls beneath her lace cap and moved towards him.

'Anythin' I can get you now, sir? Ale, brandy, what's yer fancy?'

'I'll have a pint of your best ale.' He was looking round the room as he spoke; Moll was mighty disappointed, because he didn't even seem to notice her bright smile, or her low-cut new gown. 'And there's something else. I want to speak to a man called Georgie Jay.'

She was instantly wary then. Was he after the lads for some mischief? 'No one of that name here,' she snapped, filling a foaming tankard and pushing it in front of him. 'Two pence, if you please.'

The dark-haired gent put the coins down. But then suddenly, instead of picking up the ale, he went striding off towards the back parlour. 'Stop,' called Moll. 'That's private in there, that is! Stop!'

But she was too late. He was already shoving open the door to the little room where Georgie Jay and his cronies sat over their pipes and their drinks, playing whist; he must have glimpsed them through the half-open door. She bustled quickly after him, muttering to herself, and was just in time to see Georgie Jay getting quickly to his feet, as the dark-haired gentleman said flatly, 'You're Georgie Jay, aren't you?'

'Maybe I am, maybe I'm not,' declared Georgie Jay, while old Matt and Lemuel and the others got to their feet on either side of him, and Billy clenched his brawny fists.

'Let's cut the riddles,' said Marcus. 'I saw you one night, at the crossroads outside Hockton, talking to Tassie. Do you know where she is?'

Georgie Jay folded his arms across his chest. 'Well, now. It strikes me that if she wanted you to find her, she'd have told you herself where she was going. Wouldn't she?'

Marcus reached into his pockets and slammed some coins down on the table, but he immediately realised his mistake as Georgie Jay shoved them back towards him, saying, 'Oh, no, my fine friend. We are not for sale.'

Marcus quickly took the coins up again. 'I apologise. I only want to know that the girl is safe.'

'Really? Now, unless I'm mistaken, you're the fancy gent who took her to that place called Lornings, on account of some crazy bargain. Well, you can keep your money, mister; maybe our Tass is best kept away from the likes of you.' He gestured to his companions to sit down again, and began, impassively, to deal the battered cards for a fresh game.

Marcus put his hand over the cards to stop him. 'You needn't even tell me where she is. Just tell me that she's all right, and I'll leave.'

Georgie Jay frowned, his knowing dark eyes assessing Marcus anew. 'Where have you been looking for her so far, mister?'

Where? Everywhere, it seemed. Marcus had scarcely slept since that night on the snowy hillside, since the day she had disappeared. He'd scoured the countryside all around Lornings, riding to every village, every farmstead, asking every carrier and packhorseman he met if they'd seen the girl.

He knew it was all because of Philippa that she'd gone. He found it hard to forgive Philippa for the clinging possessiveness with which she'd greeted him that morning when he got back down from the shepherd's hut with Tassie.

'I made a mistake, Marcus,' Philippa had pleaded. 'I miss you, so badly. There's never been anyone else but you.'

He'd been surprised, wondering briefly as he took in her fine carriage, her beautiful clothes, how she could possibly have persuaded herself that she could ever be happy married to a man without money. But he didn't spend too much time thinking about it. 'You're too late, Philippa,' he'd told her curtly, leaving her side almost instantly because he'd realised Tassie had disappeared. He'd gone then to find her, but she was asleep, Peg said, and mustn't be disturbed. By the time he'd pushed his way into her room later that evening, she'd gone.

If only he'd told her how very much she'd come to mean to him. If only he'd told her he loved her.

Now, in reply to Georgie Jay's question, he said, 'I searched everywhere around Lornings. Then I learnt that a party of travellers had recently left Hockton, heading for London. I came here at once, guessing Tassie was with you.'

Yes, he'd come to London, to Hal and Caro's house; and there had been another message waiting for him there from his lawyer, Erasmus Digby; a note that for once couldn't have been clearer. *Major Forrester: You failed to reply to my last note, so I write again. A witness has emerged, to say that Corbridge deliberately set up the circle of gamesters who stripped Sir Roderick bare; they are all of them well-known swindlers. A threat of investigation may be enough to make Corbridge renounce his hold on your godfather's estate. Come and see me at once.*

Marcus had wondered, suddenly, if Philippa had already heard it whispered amongst her father's banking circles that Lornings would one day be his after all. It really didn't matter. What mattered now, urgently, here in this dingy tavern room, was that he got these men, Tassie's friends, to trust him.

'How did you know to find us, here?' old Matt was asking him suspiciously.

'Tassie once mentioned a place called the Blue Bell. My God, there must be a score of taverns in London of that name, and I think I've tried them all.'

'And why do you want to find her?' asked Georgie Jay

flatly. 'Why do you expect us to help you, when you've unsettled her so badly? Our Tass is too good for you.'

The others murmured agreement, and Marcus bowed his head in acknowledgement. 'I think you are right,' he said. 'Just tell me, will you, if she's safe?'

Georgie Jay glanced at the others. He said at last, 'Now I'd tell you if I could, mister. But the truth is, we don't even know where she is ourselves. To be sure, she travelled with us to London. All upset and quiet, she was, not our Tassie at all, so we guessed something was wrong.' He frowned. 'Then in London she seemed to perk up for a day or two, but it was only to fool us, we reckon. She was up to something—in fact, asked if we knew anyone who'd draw up fake documents.'

'Fake documents?'

'Aye. Old Matt gave her a name or two, but when he asked her why, she shrugged and said it didn't matter. Then a few mornings ago, we found her bed empty, and that bird of hers gone with her. We've searched high and low, but to no avail.'

So she was in London, but alone. And—fake documents? He got abruptly to his feet. 'I must find her,' he said. 'She could be in danger.'

Georgie Jay, too, had risen. 'You think we don't fear that? You think we're not still looking, and got all our London friends also out searching for her, every hour of the day and night? But why didn't she trust us, like she's always done?'

'She must be planning something, and she didn't want even you to know about it.' Marcus looked haggard. 'If you hear anything at all, will you let me know?'

Georgie Jay was looking at him with those dark, steadfast eyes. 'That depends. Are you sure you don't mean the girl any harm?'

Marcus met his gaze. 'I want to marry her,' he said.

'Even though she's a poor orphan, who's lived in our low company for years?'

'I know that you treated her with absolute honour. And the fact that she's a penniless orphan matters nothing to me.'

'In that case,' said Georgie Jay, looking round at the others, 'there's something you should know about the lass. About her past. About the big house she ran from when she was a child…'

Because Lord Sebastian Corbridge's coachman was several minutes late in bringing his carriage round to the front of his big town house just off Brook Street, Sebastian had to wait by the steps in the dusty heat of the early evening. April had brought unexpected warmth to the city, driving away all memories of the bitter spring chill; but the sunshine did not improve Sebastian's temper.

'It will be a beating for you, my man, if you are late again,' he warned.

'My humblest apologies, my lord! One of the buckles broke, and I had to change the harness—'

Sebastian cut in contemptuously, 'Spare me your excuses. Take me to Albemarle Street.'

He sat back in the velvet cushions of his new carriage, carefully adjusting the expensive Mechlin lace at his wrists, smoothing the dove-grey satin of his close-fitting breeches. And, as the carriage took him steadily through the mellow dusk towards Lady Sallis's, he assessed his situation with a gathering frown.

He was short of money. Those damned paintings from Lornings had proved scarcely worth the trouble of stealing them, so the recent quarter day had seen Sebastian unable to pay the rent owing on his London house. It was still five months before the Lornings estate would be his, and the trouble his cousin Marcus had stirred up about the whole matter of Sir Roderick's debt had raised dangerous doubts in his creditors' minds. Sebastian stroked his ivory-tipped walking cane thoughtfully. How he hated Marcus Forrester. And yet, in one respect at least, Sebastian's luck had changed rather dramatically in these last few days.

For three nights on the run, he'd been winning, rather spectacularly, in Lady Sallis's rooms in Albemarle Street. And, what was more, he was winning off an interesting newcomer there; a shy but winsome blonde, who smiled at him and fluttered her thick eyelashes at him in the most delightful way, even when he was beating her hollow.

'Why should it matter to me that I'm losing, my lord?' she'd dimpled at him sweetly last night. 'After all, it's Lady Sallis's money.' She leaned closer and added under her breath, 'The old witch.'

Sebastian felt the time was right to thank the girl properly. His lips curling into a cold smile, he pictured the delectable, teasing little wench melting into his arms. Oh, she feigned innocence all right—last night she'd even pretended to be shocked by his suggestion that they take supper somewhere, privately. 'My lord!' Her eyes had widened. 'Surely you don't think I'm *that* kind of girl?' No doubt she'd played the same game with many a fine gentleman. Her slender body and tantalising mouth would be a pleasant distraction from Marcus and his damnable meddling.

The carriage rumbled to a halt, and a black page with a lantern ran to open the door as the coachman called out, 'Lady Sallis's, my lord.'

'Watch it, there's that Lord Corbridge arriving just now, Sarah,' warned Bella, one of Lady Sallis's girls, pointing to a group of newcomers. There was a mid-evening lull in play, and Tassie—here known as Sarah—and some others were providing company for the guests in the supper room.

'My thanks, Bella.' Tassie calmly moved towards the hall. But Bella, who'd been here almost two years, followed her and said quickly, so no one else could hear, 'Look, my girl. You're a fool to dally with Corbridge. He's all over you now because he's winning, but he can turn nasty if the cards fall the other way. And if you're hoping to continue your game with him somewhere away from here, then forget it! Last of our girls he took out for the evening said he cut up really rough with her. She came back black and blue, poor creature, and then of course Lady Sallis sent her packing.'

Tassie listened with a sinking heart. She didn't need Bella's warning. She hated Lord Corbridge, with his cruel mouth and his mean, pale eyes.

She'd let him win for three nights in a row at piquet, so much so that Lady Sallis was beginning to watch her rather suspiciously. Night after night Tassie had upped the stakes, and slipped him the highest cards, and made weak, stupid discards, though not stupid enough to make him suspect her of anything other than mild incompetence at the game.

Last night, he'd pocketed over a hundred guineas. Tassie knew she must persuade him to meet with her somewhere away from here, or Lady Sallis would be refusing to let her play with him any more. 'It's about time you got some of Corbridge's money back, Sarah,' Lady Sallis had said pointedly earlier that evening. 'He knows there are rooms upstairs, and he would pay you handsomely.'

Tassie felt nothing but repugnance for those rooms, and what went on behind the silk curtains. She had to go past them often on her way to and from her attic bedroom. They were supposed to offer privacy, for supper and cards, but there were no tables, only cushioned *chaises;* and often Tassie heard murmurings and sighs that made the blood rush to her cheeks.

Lord Sebastian Corbridge was coming into the room now, distinctive in his suit of pale grey satin with his carefully powdered hair, and his eyes were already searching the room for her.

'Don't worry. I can look after myself,' she whispered quickly to Bella, and moved gracefully towards him, thinking, under her breath, *I only hope 'tis true...*

She'd dressed with special care, in a polonaise of pink striped satin belonging to a girl who had recently left. It had elbow-length sleeves that ended in rich flounces of cream Brussels lace; and a tight, boned bodice that pushed Tassie's small breasts into a prominence that made her blush all over when she saw herself in the looking glass. She saw Sebastian's pale eyes devouring her as he took her hand and bowed over it, and she steeled herself against her repugnance. Marcus had said she was a born actress. How right he was, in that at least. She gazed up brightly at Sebastian, hating his thin smile, his smoothly powdered complexion. He wore a little velvet patch at the corner of his sharp cheekbone, and his eyes glittered.

'My Lord Corbridge,' she breathed. 'How pleased I am to see you again.'

'And I you, Sarah,' he responded coolly, his glance resting for a moment on the bared curve of her bosom. 'I trust you will play with me again this evening?'

She gazed up at him with beguiling green eyes. 'Whatever you wish, my lord. I am yours to command.'

They played piquet again, for five-guinea stakes; only this time Tassie began to win. She saw Sebastian Corbridge accept this at first with easy resignation; but then, as his pile of tokens grew smaller, his expression began to tighten. Tassie, aware as ever of everything that went on around her, realised that James the footman, who kept watch on all their tables to make sure that none of the girls pocketed a single guinea of their winnings, had gone to have a quick word with

Lady Sallis; and Tassie saw Lady Sallis throw a quick look of approval in her direction.

Sebastian ordered more wine. He was drinking heavily, though he did not show it. He had gone down almost two hundred guineas in the last game, in which Tassie had quite rubiconed him; a light sheen of perspiration was breaking through the powder on his thin face.

'Another game, my lord?' said Tassie lightly, gathering up the cards.

'I am afraid I have not enough tokens,' he answered, 'and the house will not allow me more credit.'

Tassie refilled his glass. 'No more credit? Fie, then Lady Sallis is a fool! You are a rich man, are you not? Tell me, what would you place on the turn of a card, Lord Corbridge? What would be your limit?'

He shrugged. 'A hundred, a thousand guineas? What is it to me, when I have the expectation of a great estate within months?'

'Ah, yes, Lornings,' breathed Tassie, looking impressed. 'I have heard about Lornings. And yet Lady Sallis will not allow you more credit! I vow I find her household most tedious.' She lowered her voice. 'Now, I find my mind dwelling on the notion of a comfortable, private place where we could play really deep, Lord Corbridge. Just you and me...' She fluttered her fan and dimpled coyly.

He was watching her from beneath hooded lids. 'Have you somewhere in mind?'

She looked around and leaned closer. 'I have at present the use of a boudoir in Clarges Street, my lord, which I think you would find to your liking. Might I dare to hope that you would join me there, say—tomorrow night?'

How she hated the nearness of his satin-clad body, the smell of his expensive scent. She thought suddenly of Marcus—of his warm, clean skin and simple outdoor clothes—and she shut her eyes briefly as the pain swept through her. One last night, one last throw of the dice; then it would all be over, for good.

He was stroking the signet ring on his little finger, but his cold eyes never left her face. 'Are you talking of card play, Sarah?'

'Why, yes. Piquet, preferably. It is my favourite, as you know. But after that, why, I am open to—*interesting* suggestions, Lord Corbridge.'

His eyes flickered like a reptile's. 'You spoke of playing deep. What, I wonder, have you got by way of a stake?'

She frowned prettily. 'I have a purseful of ten-guinea rouleaux I have smuggled out from under Lady Sallis's eyes!'

'You are a teasing jade,' he drawled. 'What if I say that is nowhere near enough?'

She knitted her brows. Then, pretending to toy with the lace at her neck, she mused, 'If I become *truly* down on my luck, why, then, I think you will have to name the forfeit, won't you, my lord?' She met his eyes steadily. 'After all, I shall be quite in your power.'

He licked his lips. His hand moved suddenly to cover hers, and Tassie fought to conceal the shudder of revulsion that swept through her. She pulled her fingers away and went on lightly, 'So, I think we understand one another, do we not? You will visit me in Clarges Street tomorrow night—say, at ten—and the play is to be deep. What will *you* stake on our game, Lord Corbridge?'

'What would you suggest?' He was still gazing at her.

She fingered the cards on the table thoughtfully. 'Why,' she said, 'I do declare that I have a fancy to play for something truly—original!'

'Such as, Sarah?'

'Could you show me, for instance, the letter that promises you Lornings? The thought of all that wealth in one single piece of paper excites me more than any gold! What say you to playing for that, my lord?'

'You surely jest.'

'Perhaps I do,' she pouted. 'And perhaps my luck will desert me. But, my lord—I promise you it will be an evening you will always remember.'

'You are full of surprises,' he said. 'I shall look forward to tomorrow night.'

And I will rook you so soundly, you will curse the day you ever thought to cheat poor Sir Roderick, thought Tassie fervently. Smiling in agreement, she reached out to pour him more wine.

But inwardly, she was shaking, because the thought of being alone with Lord Sebastian Corbridge filled her with trepidation.

Fie, she told herself defiantly, she would be finished with him long before the slimy rogue had time to lay a finger on her! During her travels with Georgie Jay's band she'd learnt tricks that would see her through anything; once she'd achieved her purpose, she would slip through his slimy fingers and run like the very wind. Her spirits rose.

And then, across the crowded room, Tassie saw a footman open the big doors ceremoniously to yet another group of visitors; as she scanned their bored, foppish faces, she felt her heart quail within her breast.

Viscount Lindsay was there. 'Piggy' Lindsay, the one whose face she had slapped at the theatre. Would he recognise her? It was unlikely—she had been wearing a veil that night—but Marcus had said he was a close friend of Sebastian's.

She couldn't afford any risks. Time for drastic action.

The portly Viscount Lindsay was already pushing his way between the packed card tables towards the little alcove where she sat with Sebastian. He stopped to talk here and there to people he knew. She had perhaps a minute, no more.

She sprang up quickly, her pink-striped skirts rustling, and Sebastian arched his thin brows in a look of enquiry. 'I have an idea! Let us go now,' Tassie breathed. 'Take me from here, please, Lord Corbridge. I will plead a headache, and pretend to retire to my room. Is your carriage round the back?'

If he was surprised, he hid it well. 'It is,' he said slowly. 'I can be down there within minutes. Are you suggesting we go to Clarges Street?'

Damnation. Tassie had booked the room—in a down-at-heel gaming house that she had inspected with care—for tomorrow night only. 'Not tonight,' she said quickly, 'we cannot go there tonight.'

His lip curled. 'Is, perhaps, one of your fellow-professionals using it? Well, there is always one place we can go, at any hour. And that is—my house.'

Tassie caught her breath. *No.* But she could see Viscount Lindsay getting closer. She had no choice. 'Then I will go down the back stairs, my lord, and meet you outside—'

She broke away just as Lindsay reached them. She saw the fat viscount watch her with interest, heard him say, 'A pretty wench, that one, Corbridge...'

And then she was hurrying away from them, searching desperately for Bella. She found her presiding over the vingt-et-un table in the other room.

'Bella,' she whispered quickly, 'if Lady Sallis should ask, would you tell her I've gone to my room with a headache?'

Bella's hands froze over the cards. 'You're never going off with that Lord Corbridge!' she said under her breath. 'Faith, didn't I warn you, Sarah? He's a nasty, vicious piece of work, that one—you're making a bad mistake, my girl.'

Tassie didn't want to hear any more. 'Don't worry, Bella,

please. I know what I'm doing.' And she sped off to the back stairs, to fetch her cloak.

But Tassie wasn't so confident when she was alone with Sebastian in his fine carriage, and he edged so close to her that his body touched hers from shoulder to thigh, and he slowly turned towards her so that his thin face was close to hers. She could smell the wine on his breath, and the strong perfume he used, and her body curled in revulsion.

'Well, Sarah,' he drawled, 'you've been promising me much all evening. And we will be so much more comfortable at my house…'

He was going to kiss her. She edged frantically away and saw the sudden leaping suspicion in his eyes; then she smiled her sweetest smile, even though her heart was hammering. 'Remember now, Lord Corbridge,' she pouted, 'you promised to play cards with me for the letter that is worth a whole estate, in return for my favours, including each kiss—that was our bargain, was it not?' *And once I have the letter, I will be running as fast as I can…*

Lord Corbridge's thin lips curled. 'You torment me,' he said. 'But it shall be as you say. And then, my sweet, I shall be the one to call the order of play, I think.'

Tassie was afraid of Sebastian, afraid of being alone with him in his house. Then she had a sudden fleeting vision of Marcus smiling down at her, teasing her. *'You, Tassie, scared? I didn't think you were scared of anyone.'*

The anguish of the bittersweet memory shafted through her. She bore it till it was over, and shrugged. Marcus had used her and betrayed her; and once she'd discharged her obligation to him, why, her whole life lay ahead of her, and she never wanted to see him again.

She bit her lip. Gazing silently out of the window at the lamplit London streets, filled with expensive carriages and people in their finery, she fought against the sudden hot tears, because that was a lie, too.

From his seat at the other side of the carriage, Sebastian watched her. This one needed teaching a lesson. Oh, he would play piquet with her as he'd promised. But then, regardless of who won or lost the charade, he would take his prize. She might struggle and protest a little, but that was all part of the game, wasn't it?

And even if it wasn't a game, even if her cries were in earnest, her pleas for help would get her nowhere, for once she was inside his house the doors would be securely locked, and his brutal manservant Jessop would dutifully turn deaf ears on any protests she cared to utter. Jessop was used to Sebastian's ways, and indeed was often invited to take Sebastian's leavings himself.

The girl, Sebastian guessed, was spirited and passionate. So much the better. A little resistance always added piquancy to Sebastian's enjoyment. What a fool she was to put herself in his hands. He fondled the head of his walking cane, amused to discover that his pulse was racing at the thought of the dark pleasures in store—pleasures that would be enhanced throughout by what he'd only just learnt tonight from his friend 'Piggy' Lindsay about the girl who called herself Sarah.

Chapter Fifteen

Hal came hurrying round to the stables at the back of the house in Portman Square as soon as he heard the hooves of Marcus's big horse clattering on the cobbles. 'No news?' he frowned, holding the horse's head as Marcus dismounted. It was warm this evening, almost oppressively so; tiny beads of perspiration glistened on Marcus's brow.

'No news,' confirmed Marcus, running his hand tiredly through his hair. 'I met Georgie Jay again, earlier this evening. He and his friends are looking for her, too. Between them they must have covered every lodging house, every low-life den in London these last few days—and if they cannot find her, what chance have I?'

A groom had appeared, to light the lanterns and take the big gelding into the hay-scented warmth of his stall. Hal rested one hand quickly on his friend's coat sleeve and drew him to one side.

'Perhaps you have been looking in the wrong places, Marcus. Listen. This might be nothing, a false trail, a blind. But I have been hopping about like a cat on hot coals waiting for you to return, because earlier this evening, at my club,

I overheard Lord Freddie Wyatt—you know him? A rich, pleasant enough simpleton—telling someone that there is a new girl at Lady Sallis's place. She has caused something of a sensation, I believe. She is young and beautiful, with curling golden hair and a very direct manner of speaking. Her current favoured partner is none other than Lord Sebastian Corbridge.'

He saw that Marcus's strong face had gone quite pale in the flickering shadows of the glowing lantern. 'Corbridge? Oh, God, it must be her. I must go there now, and stop whatever idiotic trickery she's up to.'

'Hold hard, man,' Hal said warningly. 'This girl's name, apparently, is Sarah. It might not be her...'

'It has to be her, Hal.' Marcus looked at him in despair. 'But why is she tangling with Corbridge, of all people? And while she's under Lady Sallis's roof, Sebastian will assume she's for sale... I must go and get her out of there, before she's in too deep.'

Hal said quietly, 'Have you thought that she might be trying to get Lornings back for your godfather?'

'There is no need,' replied Marcus in a bleak voice. 'I've been to see my lawyer, today. It can be proved that Roderick was duped into debt by a known gang of sharpers, deliberately hired by Sebastian; one of this gang, arrested for another offence, has talked. Sebastian will have no choice but to back down. Tassie is risking herself for nothing.'

Hal swore softly. 'And she's playing into Corbridge's hands... I will come with you to Albemarle Street.'

But Marcus stopped him. 'No. Best if I confront Sebastian on my own. I will send for you when I need you.'

'I'll be ready,' promised Hal. 'But what of the other matter concerning Tassie, Marcus, the business from her past?'

'There, I have made progress. But none of it is of the slightest significance, unless I find her in time.'

And the stakes, he knew, were as high as could be. Earlier this afternoon Tassie's red-haired friend, young Lemuel, had confessed to Marcus that on their first day back in London Tassie had cajoled him into buying a lady's pistol for her.

Tassie's heart was thudding warningly as she dealt the last hand. They were playing piquet, and on the polished mahogany table between them lay Sir Roderick's letter. Tassie had let Sebastian win, to begin with; but slowly, surely, she had caught up. And now everything rested on the last game.

Sebastian had led her into his spacious first-floor drawing room, which was extravagantly furnished with velvet drapes at the windows, and an Aubusson carpet on the floor. Branched candelabra on the little satinwood tables cast their soft glow on the silk-hung walls and striped damask couches. Sebastian had ordered a second bottle of white wine to be brought; he was drinking steadily, but his pale eyes were full of calculation as he watched her deal the cards.

It was hot, suffocatingly hot. Although darkness had fallen, the April night seemed warmer than the day, and Tassie longed for a fresh country breeze to cool her skin. Her stiff satin gown with its stays and lacings tormented her. She longed for this to be over. So far Sebastian had not tried to touch her again. But, win or lose, she had a pretty good idea what game he had in mind for afterwards.

Yet Tassie's fingers were steady as she examined her hand. No need to cheat in this *partie;* Sebastian was a poor player and a fool. She glanced swiftly at the door. Sebastian had told her meaningfully that he had sent his servants to bed; and she could see for herself that Sebastian would soon be quite fuddled with wine. She was confident she could be out of here within minutes. Meanwhile she continued to play clearly and decisively, putting a charming little frown on her face as she pretended to puzzle over her discards.

At last she laid down her cards and smiled up at him beguilingly. 'I hold *capot*—all twelve tricks,' she breathed. 'I think I have you at last, my lord. The game is mine.'

The rich lace at her wrists brushed the table as she reached out nonchalantly to pick up the rolled letter with its seal and pink ribbon. 'A pretty prize,' she breathed, caressing it with her fingertips. 'I have a fancy to study my winnings. I'll just take it over here, where the candles are brighter—'

Untying the pink ribbon as she spoke, she got up from the table and moved over towards the light of a candelabra, near the door. Sebastian eyed her silently from where he sat, and poured himself yet more wine. Why, thought Tassie, he must be as steeped in liquor as a pickling barrel...but he showed no signs of it. Her skin prickled in the heat, and her every sense was on the alert as she held the letter up to the candlelight. 'By my faith, Lord Corbridge,' she said merrily, 'no wonder these lawyers charge such fancy prices. Listen to this. *On the day of...heretofore...by my hand...* What rigmarole!'

'That rigmarole's good enough for me,' drawled Sebastian, watching her from under hooded lids. 'It entitles me to take possession of a fine estate in four months' time.'

Tassie spun round. 'Entitles *you* to the estate? Fie, Lord Corbridge! I played you for this letter, and won!'

'A pretty jest, sweetheart.' He grinned unpleasantly and rose slowly to his feet. 'And your little game is over now, I fear.'

Tassie stood very still, clutching the letter. 'I think not,' she said steadily. 'But *yours* is, Lord Corbridge.' Whipping the door open, she ran outside—straight into the arms of Sebastian's burly manservant, standing guard. He must have been there all the time. He carried her, kicking and struggling, back into the sitting room. The letter fell to the floor. Sebastian was watching her, his arms folded.

'Let us have an end to this charade, shall we?' he said softly.

The manservant was pinning Tassie's arms behind her back, hurting her. Tassie struggled vainly. 'By my faith, Lord Corbridge,' she said angrily, 'tell this great ape to let go of me, will you? I vow, Lady Sallis will not be at all pleased to see me later this evening with my wrists all black and blue!'

He walked slowly to her. 'Have no fear on that account, my dear. Lady Sallis will not, I think, be enjoying the pleasure of your company for some time. You have, you see, rather a lot of explaining to do. To me.'

'You're mad,' declared Tassie, still trying to shake herself free of Jessop's grip. 'You'd better let go of me, or I'll report you to the law!'

'Will you? And what name will you use? Will you call yourself Sarah? Or have you some other name up your sleeve? You seem to juggle with names as easily as cards.'

'I have not the slightest idea what you are talking about.'

He moved closer and gripped her chin, turning her face up to meet his. Tassie squirmed in revulsion; from behind, the manservant gripped her more tightly. She could feel his hot breath on the nape of her neck. 'Haven't you?' said Sebastian coldly. 'You're surely not going to deny that you're Marcus Forrester's little lightskirt, sent by him deliberately to trick me, and make me look a fool?'

Tassie's heart stopped. Then she tilted her chin in defiance. 'Marcus? Who is Marcus?' she responded airily. 'I tell you, I am new to London. I know no one except those whom I have met at Lady Sallis's!'

Sebastian's grip tightened. 'You were in London in February,' he said softly. 'You were with my cousin Marcus at the theatre. Viscount Lindsay told me so.'

This time Tassie felt her knees sagging, and her blood ran cold. So just in that short space of time this evening, Viscount

Lindsay had recognised her and had betrayed her. Sebastian had known of her association with Marcus all through this game they'd just played... 'Oh, *that* Marcus,' she answered scornfully. 'I declare, I had almost forgotten the man!'

'You are his mistress, I take it?'

She laughed. 'Me? Waste myself on a limping soldier with no money?'

Sebastian nodded slowly. 'So you say he's nothing to you, nor you to him. I think you are lying. In fact, I think it was Marcus Forrester who put you up to this charade of playing for his foolish old godfather's letter.'

'*No.* No, I swear...'

'My cousin,' went on Corbridge relentlessly, 'is known to have good taste in women, and I'm sure he'll have taught you some pretty tricks. I've a fancy to get you to show them to me—or maybe I'll let Jessop try you out first. I've enjoyed watching him breaking a girl's spirit many a time.'

His cruel eyes glittered. Tassie struggled wildly in the burly manservant's arms, her heart thumping. Oh, no. This was getting worse and worse... She used her heel to kick back, hard, at the leg of the man who held her captive. He howled with agony, but still hung on to her, and Sebastian slapped her hard across the cheek, once, twice. Tassie felt blackness, then searing pain.

'Damn you,' she whispered, 'damn you, let me go. I've got friends who'll be looking for me.'

'You have indeed. Marcus Forrester, no less.'

Tassie froze. 'No! Not Marcus!'

There was a moment's silence. 'So it's true. You and he *are* in this together. You *do* care for him. How very interesting this is going to be.'

'No,' Tassie breathed, 'you wouldn't dare—'

'Shut up.' Suddenly Sebastian gestured to his manservant. 'Leave us, Jessop. On no account are we to be disturbed.'

The servant reluctantly let Tassie go and left the room. Lord Sebastian Corbridge locked the door after him, then turned back to Tassie.

'My God, I hate my cousin Marcus, do you know that? In everything I have ever done, he has done his best to shame me, to ridicule me. Depriving him of Lornings is sweet vengeance indeed. And now, it seems, I have yet more revenge in store, for he has sent his enticing little mistress straight into my hands.' Sebastian smiled, a slow, unpleasant smile, and walked towards Tassie, who was pressing herself, horrified, against the wall, her cheek still throbbing painfully from where he had struck her.

He put his hands on her shoulders, letting his thumbs circle her bare skin. 'By the time you see Marcus again,' he went on in the same languid, repellent voice, 'what a great deal you will have to tell him. And your reunion should not be far away; because, you see, it's absolutely true that he is looking for you.'

Tassie cried out. She could not help herself. 'No! He does not know where I am. He does not care...'

'But he is hot on your trail, my dear, such is his passion for you. And when we arrived here Jessop gave me some interesting news, news that quite confirms your story that Marcus, surprisingly, knew nothing about your ridiculous plan to win Sir Roderick's letter. Marcus has, apparently, been making enquiries all over London for you, in quite the wrong places; but he is homing in, at last, on Lady Sallis's establishment. Once he gets there to find you have gone, and with whom, he will doubtless make his way here, with all speed.'

The desperate hope flared in Tassie's eyes, but Sebastian quickly quelled it. 'Yes,' he continued, 'he will arrive here, and to such a welcome! The street outside is unlit, and there is, most conveniently, a narrow alley a few yards from my door—an obvious place for footpads to lurk. Just as my cousin approaches, a band of ruffians, led by my man Jessop, will emerge from that alley with cudgels, and make Major Marcus Forrester sorry that he ever dared to cross my path. It will look like a chance robbery, and no one will ever be able to prove otherwise. I've told the fellows, by the way, to pay special attention to his left leg. It was our hero's left leg, wasn't it, that was injured in the war?'

'No,' breathed Tassie, 'oh, please God, no…'

'And as for you, my dear,' he went on, his pale eyes devouring her anguished face, 'I think I can ensure that your handsome Marcus will never even want to look at you again, let alone touch you. Oh, I do hope Marcus doesn't arrive too early.' Then he gripped her with a surprising strength and tried to kiss her, forcing his tongue roughly between her lips. For a moment Tassie feigned surrender, then pulled out a small, deadly pistol from her pocket.

Corbridge gasped in disbelief, and let her go. Tassie, pointing the gun at his heart, backed towards the door. 'Touch me again if you dare, Lord Corbridge!' she warned.

Sebastian was right. It had not taken Marcus long to find out that Tassie had left Lady Sallis's gaming house at the same time as Corbridge. 'I warned her, sir,' Bella cried. 'I told her he was no good, that Lord Corbridge! But she wouldn't listen!'

Marcus was set-faced. 'Don't rebuke yourself too much,' he said. 'She never listened to me either.' He turned swiftly towards Lady Sallis, who had heard all this with some unease. 'Lady Sallis, the girl you know as Sarah should never, ever have been exposed to a man like Corbridge.'

Lady Sallis, on the defensive, said flatly, 'She came to me of her own free will, I assure you, Major Forrester!'

Marcus ran his hand tiredly across his brow. 'I'm not disputing that. But she has no understanding of what that man will sink to...' He swung round one last time on Bella. 'Have you any idea where he's taken her?'

'To his house, sir,' Bella faltered. 'I heard him giving orders to his coachman.'

Marcus was already on his way.

Tassie had the letter in one hand; in the other was the little pistol Lemuel had obtained for her, aimed at Sebastian. Sebastian's face was ashen, his hands raised.

'You will unlock this door,' Tassie said steadily, 'and tell your servants to let me go, or I will shoot. You will say *nothing* about tonight; you will abandon your claim to Lornings, or I will tell everyone how you threatened me with rape, and worse.'

Sebastian's lip curled then. 'My God, you gaming-house slut, who would take your word against mine?'

'Many people, I think, Lord Corbridge! Because all of town knows you as a liar and a cheat! Open this door, or...'

But then her words died on her lips, because she heard a sound outside, the sound of a horse's hooves coming rapidly down the street towards Sebastian's house. And then the sound stopped, only to be replaced by the noise of someone banging at the front door, someone strong and impatient— someone like Marcus...

'Dear me,' said Sebastian softly. 'It seems your hero has arrived. Too late, unfortunately. Give me the letter, my dear, and the gun; neither are any use to you now.'

'Never!' She gripped them all the tighter.

'If you are stupid enough to try to shoot me,' drawled Sebastian, 'then Jessop has orders to ensure your hero Marcus is quite unrecognisable by the time my men have finished with him. I have told him to put his eyes out. *Give me the gun and the letter.*'

Oh, no. Nearly every part of her plan had gone horribly wrong. Slowly she handed them to him. Then, before he could stop her, she flew over to the window and flung it open. 'Marcus!' she cried out into the darkness below. 'There are men waiting for you, to attack you! It's a trap—please, please get away while you can!'

But she knew it was too late. Her fingers gripping the window ledge, she gazed out into the street below, uncaring of the tears that streamed down her cheeks. Sebastian dragged her away, and she let him push her into a chair while he went to lock the letter in a bureau.

This had been a final, desperate gamble to win back Marcus's approval, his love. Instead, all she'd done was draw him into terrible danger. Marcus would hate her now. Would Sebastian's ruffians harm him badly? Would they beat him to death on the pavement outside, then vanish into the night, leaving him as yet another victim of the faceless criminals who haunted London's streets? Every sense stretched to breaking point, she heard fresh sounds in the house below, muffled, but terrible to her ears. She could hear the noise of men fighting, interspersed with groans and curses. The sound of several crude villains with cudgels, who would be laying with bloodthirsty ferocity into one brave man, who would fight them for as long as he was conscious. Sebastian's terrible words hammered in her brain: *I have told him to put his eyes out...*

Now that the letter was safely locked away, Sebastian was listening too, and the avid gleam in his eyes as he fingered her pistol quite sickened her. 'I think my soldier cousin is getting his just reward at last,' he said softly. 'Shall we go and see?'

He pulled her up from the chair. Though his touch revolted her, Tassie let him grip her slender arm as he unlocked the door and led her to the top of the darkened stairwell. Sebastian thought she had given up. But even now, there must be *something* she could do, to save the man she loved so much. It was dark in the big hallway below, and there were men moving around there. The big front door was ajar, and someone was lying, moaning softly, against it. Was it—*Marcus?*

Sebastian, still gripping her wrist to pull her downstairs, rapped impatiently, 'Damn it all, Jessop! Light the candles, will you? I cannot see a thing!'

'Right away, my lord,' said a man's voice quickly, almost cheerfully, and Tassie jumped, because that voice wasn't Jessop's at all! And then the candle flared, and she saw that the person with the taper was black-haired Georgie Jay, with a wide grin on his face; and as the sparse light flickered round the big hall, she saw Lemuel, too, and Billy, rubbing his brawny fists together with relish. Lying against the door was the man Jessop, with his eyes closed, and a livid bruise welling up on his forehead; while near his feet lay another oaf, presumably one of Corbridge's thugs, also unconscious, with a heavy cudgel lying by his limp hand.

And old Matt was there, too, but he had his back to Tassie, and he was crouched over someone who was slumped against the wall, someone painfully familiar, whose long dark hair curtained his face, and whose loose white shirt was splashed with crimson…

Tassie raced towards him, stumbling in her haste, her sobs catching in her throat. 'Marcus. Don't die. Oh, please don't die, when I love you so much. I—I'd almost rather you married Philippa than died…'

And then old Matt was stepping back with a big grin on his face, and Marcus was getting slowly but surely to his feet, resting one hand on the wall for support, and turning to smile at her in a way that made her heart stand still. 'I'd prefer neither, minx,' he said in that warm and tender voice that she knew so well. 'I'm going to live a long, healthy life,

and I'm going to marry you, as soon as possible. I keep trying
to tell you, but you won't listen.'

Tassie gazed up at his familiar, wide-shouldered figure
and her heart was overfull. 'But—I thought you were hurt,'
she stammered. 'You lay so still. And—and the blood...'

He put his strong hands on her shoulders, steadying her,
warming her. 'My leg let me down, that is all,' he said. 'One
of Corbridge's villains struck at it with his cudgel before
your friend Billy there felled him with a single blow. There's
no damage done, I'm sure. As for the blood, why, one of
Sebastian's friends had a nasty broken nose, thanks, I think,
to Lemuel—the blood got everywhere.'

He turned, then, to Georgie Jay and the others. 'Our friend
Lord Corbridge seems to have slunk off upstairs. Go and find
him, will you? And hold him until I have time for him.'

They hurried up the stairway, leaving the two of them
alone. Marcus turned back to Tassie, smoothing her tousled
curls from her cheek with gentle fingers. She shivered, and
touched his hand. 'Oh, Marcus. I hadn't guessed he could be
so—vile.'

His face was suddenly dark, and he drew her close. 'I was
in time, wasn't I, Tassie? If that devil has hurt you...' His
eyes roved tensely over her tumbled curls, her torn gown.

'Hurt me? God's teeth, no.' Tassie laughed weakly. 'I could
have held him off for ever, never fear. I had a pistol, you see!'

'So I heard. I hope you didn't use it.'

'No, actually. But oh, Marcus. I'm so glad to see you. How
did you guess I was here? How did Georgie Jay know I was
here?'

'He was waiting to hear from me at the Blue Bell,' he said.
'As soon as I learned, at Lady Sallis's, that you had gone off
with Sebastian, I knew you would be in trouble, so I summoned your friends. Between us, we gave those ruffians an
unpleasant surprise.'

She gazed seriously up at his dear, familiar face. 'I've missed you, Marcus,' she whispered. 'Oh, I've missed you.'

'And I you, minx,' he murmured, drawing her into his arms and holding her there. And Tassie felt the gladness flooding through her, melting away all the unhappiness, all the fear of these past few weeks, just as surely as the sun had melted the spring snow on the hillside, on the morning after the night when he'd made her his.

Then she saw that Georgie Jay was coming down the stairs again, grinning widely. 'Begging your pardon, Major, we have his lordship upstairs. Billy's got him trussed like a porker, but he's still struggling and cussing fit to bust, and swearing he'll never let you have some letter or other. Would you come up and speak to him, or should we just knock him cold, which would certainly be easier?'

'You can leave that pleasure to me, if necessary,' Marcus replied grimly. 'But first we have certain matters to discuss, my cousin and I.'

He started to put Tassie gently from him; she hated to be parted from him for even one moment, but knew that he had to see this business through.

'Marcus,' she said quickly. 'The letter that Sir Roderick signed, promising Lornings to Sebastian—I've got it safe. Here.' She pulled it out from the pocket of her skirt. 'I won it off him fair and square, Marcus, but of course I knew he'd never let me get away with it; so in the midst of the game as he went for more wine I replaced it with a fake I'd had made and pushed the *real* one in my pocket!'

'You planned all this rather thoroughly, didn't you?' said Marcus, his eyes sparkling.

Her face fell slightly. 'Well, my plan actually went a little wrong, for I could not hold Sebastian off with my pistol once he told me his men were going to beat you to a pulp. But seeing as we have Sir Roderick's letter, we can really spoil Sebastian's game now, can't we?'

He drew her once more into his arms, and gave her a long, lingering kiss that left Tassie quite dazed with happiness. 'Sebastian didn't realise what he was taking on when he tangled with you,' he said. 'And neither, my darling, did I.'

Then Marcus went upstairs, to deal with Lord Sebastian Corbridge, and Tassie was able to talk to Georgie Jay and her friends; to question them avidly, to exclaim with them over what had happened; to find out from them, in detail, how Marcus had enlisted their aid.

Lemuel had managed, with some effort, to get over the jealousy he'd felt as he witnessed the reunion of Marcus and Tassie. 'He's a prime 'un with his fives, he is, Tass! You should have seen him laying about them when those ruffians set on us!'

Tassie laughed, but she still felt a shiver of fear when she thought of the danger Marcus had put himself in, for her.

'Georgie,' she said suddenly, 'you told me once that if I got myself into trouble, I was on my own.'

Georgie Jay put his arm round her. 'You didn't really believe that, lass, did you?' he said affectionately. 'We're on your side, always. But—' and his dark eyes twinkled '—I rather think that a new road is opening out before you now.'

And then, before Tassie could reply, Hal, who was also in on it all, it seemed, turned up outside with a carriage; and Tassie, with fond farewells to her friends and promises to call on them at the Blue Bell very soon, allowed herself to be taken back to Portman Square. She hated leaving Marcus; but Hal told her gently that Marcus had business with Sebastian that would take him some time. With that, she had to be content.

* * *

Tassie slept heavily in the big bedchamber where Marcus had first brought her after that night at the Angel. It seemed a lifetime ago now.

When she awoke, the sun was high in the sky, and the birds sang in the new-leafed trees that adorned the square. She put on the gown that Caro must have asked Emilia to leave out for her, and hurried downstairs. Emilia greeted her in a positively warm fashion, and even Sansom was respectful as he set out her breakfast. The only thing that clouded her morning was learning that Marcus, who had apparently returned late last night, had already gone out on business, though she was careful not to let her disappointment show.

Hal was out with him, but Caro kept her company, taking the opportunity to ask kind but discreet questions about Tassie's stay in the country. Tassie tried to respond politely, but her nerves were stretched taut, her heart was over-full, and every time a horse went by outside, she jumped as if she were on strings. Last night Marcus had said he loved her. Surely, surely he must be repenting of that now. That was why he was keeping out of her way, hoping, perhaps, that she would realise her folly and leave...

She could hardly eat. Caro left her in the sunny first-floor salon with a novel from the circulating library, which she only pretended to read.

It was late in the afternoon when at last she heard Marcus and Hal's voices in the hall downstairs. She heard them coming swiftly up the stairs, and moments later they had burst into the room; Caro was behind them, a delighted smile on her face. Tassie jumped up, the book falling to the floor, her heart thumping with tension; and then Marcus was striding towards her, catching her up in his arms, swinging her round and round until she was dizzy.

'We've done it!' he exulted. 'Lornings is safe! We've done it, Tassie!'

Hal, too, was beaming. Marcus set her down, but he still held her close to him, and his eyes were so full of warmth, of love, that she felt her heart turn over.

'So Sebastian has abandoned his claim?' she breathed.

Marcus kissed her tenderly, holding her in his arms. 'How could he do otherwise,' he said, 'when you, my darling, had so effectively beaten him at his own game, and won the letter from him?'

She said, still anxious, 'It's true that I won it from him, fair and square! But—he is quite capable of refusing to accept my victory, isn't he?'

Marcus shook his head quickly. 'No. I have advised Sebastian that he will be wise to accept your win with good grace, and leave behind this whole sordid business while he may. A witness has been discovered, you see, to swear that the gaming den into which my godfather was led was set up by Sebastian for the whole purpose of stripping Sir Roderick of his wealth.'

Tassie absorbed this silently, concentrating on every word. Hal said, 'But Sebastian could still dispute the whole business in court if he'd a mind to, surely?'

Caro, too, was listening anxiously. Marcus nodded. 'He could try. But—' and he held Tassie closer '—Tassie's valiant gamble last night brought things to a head. I was able to warn Sebastian that I would lay charges of abduction and assault if he continued to press his case. There was also the matter of the thefts from Lornings. He argued a little, but I—persuaded him.'

'God's teeth,' said Tassie, 'did you hit the blackguard, Marcus? I vow, I would have done.'

'Bloodthirsty wench.' Marcus grinned. 'Only when he was stupid enough to try to draw a sword on me. Then I hit him twice. Once, for my godfather Roderick. And once, my darling, for you.' He drew her close into his arms, and Hal and Caro together slipped quietly from the room.

Tassie shivered in his arms, still unable to forget her fear last night, for Marcus. 'Oh, I am so very *glad* that justice has been done! But what will Sebastian do now?'

Marcus laughed shortly. 'I suggested to him that—after returning the paintings, of course—he considers moving for a while to the country, to lie low and sort out his creditors.'

'The country? I hope you didn't direct him to Gloucestershire,' exclaimed Tassie in horror.

'Not Gloucestershire,' said Marcus tenderly, 'not anywhere near Gloucestershire, because that, my sweet, is where you and I are going to live, as soon as we are married. We will live at Lornings with my godfather, and help him get the place to rights, and you can rove the countryside to your heart's content, galloping across the hills and rescuing lambs and teaching Roderick all your card tricks until he's as unbeatable as you.'

As the look on her face, of surprise, and happiness, and sheer heart-warming love, filled his heart, Marcus drew her with him to sit on the brocade couch before the fireplace and kissed her with a slow, deep tenderness that expressed all his feelings, and more. Tassie pulled herself away at last and gazed at him earnestly. 'I will try to be a lady for you, Marcus,' she vowed. 'I will truly try to behave properly, and speak correctly, and be everything you desire.'

Marcus held her more tightly. 'You already are everything I desire,' he said. 'And that is why I wanted to ask you to marry me, to obtain your consent, before I tell you my final piece of news.'

Something in his voice made her suddenly tense. 'What is it, Marcus? It cannot be bad news, surely?'

'No, no, there is nothing to worry about. But you must be

told, Tassie, for it concerns the place where you spent your unhappy childhood.'

She turned to him, her eyes grave. 'Perhaps the past should be left in peace, Marcus. It was my intention, once our bargain was concluded, to find out the truth, but I have since found out that the house is locked up and empty, which is maybe where I should leave my story.'

'But what if the story is not finished yet?' Marcus took both her hands in his. 'Please, Tassie. Tell me what you remember.'

Tassie drew a deep breath. 'I was brought up in a big, desolate house in Oxfordshire, called—Wychwood. Yes, I know—it is little more than twenty miles from Lornings. My guardians there were a man called William Norris and his spinster sister, who kept house for him. She also gave me my lessons, and locked me in my room if I did not please her.' Marcus was holding her hand, stroking it. 'Marcus, I tried to put that time behind me, but I could not forget their coldness and cruelty to me. Why was I in their care? Who were my parents? I was sure that I was once deeply loved; I wanted to find out the answer. I thought that, once I had your fifty guineas, Marcus, I could visit my old home, and pay clever people to uncover the truth; but it's too late. Georgie Jay made enquiries for me; he found that the Norrises are dead. The old house is locked up. There is no more to discover.'

Marcus held her steadily in his arms. 'Let me tell you a story now, Tassie. Once, there was a young, well-born man— let us call him Stephen—who was spoken of by those who knew him as brave, intelligent and kind. Because his older brother—far less worthy—inherited the family estate, Stephen left England to take up employment as an agent of the East India Company. Out there he prospered, and married a well-bred English girl who bore him a beloved baby daughter, and his happiness must have been complete.

'But then a cruel tropical fever carried off Stephen Norris and his wife, and many of those amongst whom they lived. In the confusion, their baby daughter was carried back to England by a well-meaning missionary. Armed with the scantiest of information, he tracked down the infant girl's nearest relative, her father's brother, and to him he delivered the poor orphan child—whose name was Theresa.'

He felt Tassie tremble. He touched her cheek, and went on, in a quiet voice, 'You, of course, were Theresa. William Norris was your father's brother; and having heard, you see, of the fortune Stephen had made in India, your uncle was determined to claim it for himself. Meanwhile he kept you in isolation, afraid that if your existence was known, Stephen's money might be taken from him. Only William and his sister knew the full truth of your story.'

Tassie was very pale. 'Marcus. I know you have already told me of your love, so I should not really ask this question. But will it not trouble you, to be married to someone with such an unhappy past?'

He kissed her with the utmost tenderness. 'My darling, I would have asked you to marry me even if you turned out to be some starving tinker's brat. My own past was far from orthodox; it was Sir Roderick, who helped me through, just as Georgie Jay was *your* protector. Besides, we know now that your father was honourable and brave, nothing like his brother William, while your mother was of gentle birth, and much loved; we can find out more, if you wish, when you are ready.' He touched her cheek gently, tracing the delicate curve, caressing her soft skin. 'Oh, Tassie. I love you for what you are, and not who you are. In fact, I think I've loved you since the moment I saw you charging up those stairs in Hal's greatcoat, calling out to that screeching parrot.'

She laughed a little shakily, then got to her feet and walked round the room, to steady herself, because there was so much to take in. Marcus watched her coming to terms with it all, the tenderness and concern shining from his eyes.

'There's something else, Tassie,' he said quietly. 'As you know, your uncle is now dead, his sister also. You are the sole heir to the Wychwood estate. No other possible claimants have been traced.'

It is often in the past that your future lies...

She turned round slowly. 'So—it is all mine?'

'Indeed,' he said. 'There is your own father's money, which your uncle appropriated, and then there is the Wychwood estate. The matter rests with you.'

He watched her, anxious that all this might cause her fresh distress. It was with the utmost gladness that at last he saw the familiar mischief return to her eyes. 'Do you know, Marcus,' she breathed, 'it has just occurred to me that you might be nothing but a dratted fortune hunter!'

He pretended to consider this. 'True. Here I am, snatching you away from the delights of London society, when you could have used your charms and your screeching parrot to ensnare the likes of my cousin Sebastian, or Viscount Piggy Lindsay, who, I believe, is also looking for a wealthy bride.'

She made as if to hit him. 'Wretch!' But he caught her arms, and pulled her to him, and kissed her with such passion that Tassie closed her eyes with happiness.

At last he let her go, though he still held her tightly, and Tassie rested her cheek contentedly on his strong shoulder. But then he felt her stir again, and she looked up at him with some agitation. 'Marcus. There is something else, a matter of some importance, that must be settled before I can finally consent to be your wife.'

He looked anxious. 'What?'

She dimpled up at him in the old, familiar way. 'If we are really to be married,' she said, 'then you must know that I cannot be parted from my screeching parrot.'

Marcus laughed. 'What a price to pay! Very well. If I must, I will even put up with Edward. If, that is, he will put up with me.'

Her face shone with relief. 'I will teach him to like you, Marcus! He was only ever hateful to you because he thought you arrogant, and pitiless, and rude.'

'As you did?' he teased.

'Well, as I did, but only for a very, very little while,' admitted Tassie truthfully. 'And then, you see, I began to love you quite desperately. But, of course, you know all about *that*.'

Marcus was holding her close, letting his fingers trail up and down her back in a way that she found quite distractingly delicious. 'No, I don't think I do,' he murmured. 'Tell me about it, will you, minx? Or, better still—*show* me.'

And Tassie, nestling into his strong arms and lifting her face for his kiss, gladly did so.

The September sun stole through the bedroom curtains, warming her, and chiding her for lying in bed so late. Tassie got up quickly, pushing her curls back from her face, seeing instantly the posy of heavily scented crimson roses that her husband had left for her on the little bedside table.

Her husband. Marcus. Tassie held the rose blooms gently against her cheek, letting her eyes roam over the empty bed, the bed where Marcus held her every night, and filled the darkness with such tenderness, such passion, that she felt quite dizzy with love. Smiling secretly to herself, she put the roses down, then slipped on her silk wrap and went to pull back the curtains and gaze out over the sunlit autumn beauty of Lornings.

They'd been married in June, quietly, in the little church at Hockton, with Sir Roderick, Caro and Hal, and Jacob and Peg all there to witness their happiness. With the lifting of the burden of his debts, Sir Roderick was longing to move back into his true home; but only, he said, as he held Marcus and Tassie's hands close in his own, if they would make Lornings Hall their home, too. 'For it will all be yours one day,' he said to them.

And now the beautiful old house was slowly being restored to life. The paintings Sebastian had stolen had been retrieved and put back in their rightful place; and with the sale of her Wychwood inheritance, Tassie felt free to indulge her own passions: horses for the stables, furnishings for the rooms she and Marcus occupied, the replanting of the gardens that surrounded the Hall. Marcus appointed a steward, a good local man, to put the estate to rights; Peg insisted that if she couldn't be Miss Tassie's personal maid there was no justice in this world; Jacob was butler, and more servants were hired to tend the Hall and bring it to life again. There were neighbours to visit, and new friends to entertain, although they did not see anything of the Fawcetts, who stayed in town and busied themselves in finding more rich suitors for Philippa.

Tassie was shy at first of her new role, but with Marcus's constant reassurance, and Caro and Hal's frequent visits to the lovely old house, she felt herself blossoming, and was soon in fact causing something of a stir in upper-class circles. More than one fine lady was heard making enquiries about obtaining a talking parrot, and Tassie's skill at cards was much admired; though in their after-supper rubbers of whist, she refused to partner anyone other than Sir Roderick.

Georgie Jay and his band had called again in the summer, and helped with the haymaking. Marcus had taken Georgie Jay to one side during the outdoor feast that followed the completion of the work, and asked him if he and his men would stay on. Georgie Jay had refused, but his dark eyes lingered on Tassie's happy face as she presided over the table that groaned with food for all the helpers, and he'd said, 'Be sure that we'll be back whenever you should need us, sir. It's good to see the lass looking so content.'

Now Tassie turned quickly from the window as the door opened and her husband came in. Marcus looked well. His leg had all but healed; his face was brown from the country air, his body fit and strong from the outdoor activities associated with getting the big estate running again. He laughed as he saw Tassie standing there still in her nightrobe, and he pulled her to him, letting his lips touch the top of her gleaming hair.

'Well, minx,' he said softly. 'You're taking well to the life of a fine lady. Becoming a slugabed now, are you?'

She held him close, feeling the play of warm, taut muscle beneath his shirt. She let her fingers rove up his back to his shoulders, and lifted her face to his. 'Darling Marcus,' she teased softly. 'If you would allow me to sleep as I should at night, then perhaps I would rise earlier.'

He kissed her, holding her very close. When he let her go, his eyes were warm with passion. 'Complaints, my love?' he murmured. 'So early in our marriage?'

'No,' she breathed, 'oh, no,' and her heart was full as she saw the contentment in his smile.

Just then there was a knock at the door. Peg came bustling in, carrying on a tray a plate heaped with buttered toast and a brimming cup of chocolate; she gave a quick little curtsy and left. Marcus looked at the full plate, a little puzzled, and said, 'Well. There is enough for two there. What is Peg thinking of?'

'Peg is starting to spoil me,' said Tassie quickly. 'I will be down shortly, Marcus.'

He nodded, and made his way towards the door, only to stop again. 'Farmer Daniels has sent over to Hockton for two draught horses for the autumn ploughing, Tassie! They should be arriving later this morning. You'll come and inspect them with me, won't you?'

'Of course I will.' Satisfied, he strode from the room, and she went to sit down at the little table by the window where Peg had left the tray that was laden with food enough for two.

Tassie folded her hands lightly across her lap, smiling to herself. Old Peg, it seemed, had guessed her secret already.

Later this morning, she would tell Marcus her news.

* * * * *